JOSH SAMUELS

Celebrity Mum

Josh Samuels
Creative.Writing.Coaching
& publishing

First published by Josh Samuels 2023

This novel is a work of fiction. Any resemblance to any actual mothers, living or dead, is entirely coincidental.

First edition

ISBN: 978-0-6459761-3-7

Cover art by Merrilee McCoy

This book was professionally typeset on Reedsy.
Find out more at reedsy.com

This book is dedicated to ... who else, my mother.

"I love her, but she drives me crazy."

- EVERY CHILD IN THE WORLD, WHEN
DESCRIBING THEIR MOTHER.

Preface

This project began life as a sitcom and morphed over the years into a book. It is therefore the first instance of literature comedy, or a "lit-com."
Please enjoy responsibly.

Episode 1

Death. That's what my life is surrounded by.

Not just because I write detective fiction, and often a body turns up dead; but also because I do probate law. It's all about death, and what happens after. Not in the spiritual sense, but in the practical sense.

I'm now facing my own death and rebirth and my 'priest', AKA my boss, Alan the affable attorney, sits before me giving me last rites, in the form of droning on about some changes in legislation that are going to affect the law firm in the near future. I love Alan, but his recitation would actually be more interesting if it were delivered in Latin.

"So if the asset was acquired on or before the 20th of September 1985, then the indexation method doesn't apply," Alan says, "Unless you are disposing of the deceased's asset as an individual, but not as a trust or a complying super fund..."

But today is the day that I put death aside and focus on my new life as a full-time writer. I called my Mum a few days ago to tell her the news, that I would also be making a living as a creative, but as always she was running to set and didn't have time for me. I died a little inside.

My mother has also died many times. She's a soap opera actress, so her characters die and then come back to life. She has also been in a lot of B-grade horror films, bodice ripper dramas, and Hallmark TV movies, which also involve her dying. But no matter how many times she dies, she always comes back. I'm not sure when I'll see her next though, I haven't seen her in five years because she's been off in New York starring in another soap opera, *Destiny's Hope*, and she's too busy to come home to Melbourne and visit. Although the five year break has done my mental health some good. In fact it's probably best if I don't see her until I finish my next book.

Alan keeps on talking.

I nod my head politely and attentively give *Mm-hmms* when there's a pause. I love Alan, but I don't really understand why he feels the need to explain this stuff to me. I also don't have the heart to tell him that his monologue is like a medically-induced coma. But in a strange way I don't want this exit interview to end. In a matter of hours, I'm getting released from my life sentence as a lawyer and I feel more freaked out than I have ever been in my entire life. Freedom can be scary.

My debut book, *The Blonde Wore Black*, was heralded as a breakthrough success in literary circles. It was an odd label though. In fact, aside from an article in a probate law journal on how to 'sex-up' estate tax legislation, the last creative writing I published was a poem in my high school yearbook about an unrequited love. I wrote it under the pseudonym, Blaze Hartley, to avoid looking pretentious. And to avoid Trisha Mathers realising it was about her.

She didn't.

The poem wasn't a hit with the intended audience but my first novel was. The book got reviews by several newspapers and the publisher was kind enough to put a few of them on the paperback. Including the one by the *Daily Telegraph* which read: "This promising first novel is *exiting*." This typo (missed by the proof reader) annoyed me to no end, but my editor assured me that nobody reads the back cover.

They also included: "If Agatha Christie, Raymond Chandler and Mel Brooks had a baby, it would be this novel," by *New York Review of Books*. It's strangely satisfying to receive flattery in the form of an orgy. And for good measure they threw in: "David Hawkes is a good book writer!" *The Herald Sun*. Well... what it lacked in imagination it made up for in brevity. A concept completely lost on my boss sitting across the desk.

Alan stops for a second to sip his coffee. As he leans his head towards the mug, his toupée moves off centre. I touch my dusty blond hair, a subtle suggestion to Alan. He misses the gesture because he's cleaning his glasses with his shirt tail.

Dienstag, DiSalvio & Fischer isn't a sexy law firm like those in primetime television dramas. We specialise in probate work. And probate law is death. Literally. It's wills, estates, and trusts for the deceased. Even the person who looks after the estate is called an 'executor'. This area of the law doesn't attract the type of people who drive Ferraris 100 miles an hour with no seat belt. It attracts the type of people who want to make sure those Ferrari types have their assets fairly distributed to their heirs.

The firm is located in the historic Lombard Building in Melbourne, with its Queen Anne Revival façade, the work is dependable, predictable, and, aside from habitually pinching my finger in the collapsible doors of the hydraulic elevator, it's safe. It's exactly what I thought I wanted coming out of law school.

I've achieved exactly what I thought I wanted. No drama.

But it's time to try for some sliver of excitement, I think, as I look across the desk at Alan. If I don't try it now I'll be here until I'm doing my own will, and I'll be just as bald and droning as Alan. I quickly add another *Mmm-hmmm* and nod my head, adjusting my horn-rimmed glasses and sweeping the hair from my forehead. My real hair. For now.

My publisher was so pleased with how my first detective novel sold that they wanted the next instalment in the *Reid McGowan* series quickly. It took me five years to give birth to the first one and they weren't keen on the concept of spacing your children out. They gave me nine months and a check for an advance. So, before a sense of gnawing self-doubt could creep in, I marched into the managing partner's office and announced that I was resigning to become a full-time writer. After hours of ruminating over it, I felt I owed it to myself to make at least one decision in my life without overthinking. If I was going to get out, it was now or never.

The one problem is that the *Reid McGowan* book was never designed to be a series. I have no idea what I am going to write. I've resigned my junior partner status in a law firm and am going to try my hand at being a novelist. Full time.

I look at the clock on my desk: 2:24pm.

Alan catches his second wind, and goes into the farewell portion of our talk.

Alan, like a lot of lawyers, isn't comfortable with his, what do you call them … feelings. So clichés such as "It's been great" and "Won't be the same around here" are peppered throughout his speech. I get stuck with an eerie sense of reverse déjà vu (not sure what you'd call it, "déjà view"?) that this scenario will repeat itself in the future when I have to re-interview for my job after my book gets rejected and I am forced to pay back the advance. Alan will be talking in the same monotonous fashion but the clichés will be "Glad you're back" and "Not much has changed." At least my old friend, failure, would be back. It's comforting, in a not-so-comforting sort of way.

But I can't think that way. This is the opportunity few people who put pen to paper ever get: a publisher is backing me and wants my next novel.

As my father used to tell me, "Remember son, courage is what brave people have." He also used to say "Just because it's redundant doesn't mean it's not true."

For some strange reason this recollection of fatherly advice helps me to feel comfortable with my decision to leave. Maybe it's the warming glow of the afternoon sunlight streaming in the window and brightening the fluoro-lit office, I don't know. But, whatever the reason, I take a deep breath and know that, while I love Alan and the time I've spent at the firm, it's time to move on. Dread is giving way to a certain sense of something. I think it's hope. I can do this. Nothing is going to stop me from achieving—

My cell phone rings, interrupting both Alan, and my train of thought.

I recognise the number and send it to voicemail.

"Sorry about that," I say to Alan.

"Quite alright. Where was I?"

"You were saying, about the, um, the um … thingy"

My cell phone rings again.

Same number.

Straight to voicemail again.

"Do you need to take that?"

"It's a wrong number, I think." I switch the phone to aeroplane mode. "Now, you were saying? About the, the–"

"Yes the, um–"

"The legal thingy–"

The intercom buzzes. It's Rhonda, the receptionist.

"Sorry," I say to Alan. "Yes, Rhonda?"

"You've got a call from a woman. She says she's an old client but I don't have a record. A Susan Wilde?"

I grab the receiver and stick it to my ear like I'm smothering a fire with a flame retardant blanket. Too late.

"Susan Wilde?" Alan says, suddenly interested, "Like, as in the actress, Susan Wilde?"

"Can you take a message?"

"She says it's urgent," Rhonda replies.

"What was the soap opera she was on here," Alan muses aloud. "Doing her will could attract more high profile clients to the firm. These celebrities "

"I don't know if her profile is that high anymore," I tell Alan.

"Start small, grow tall." Alan rattles off his patented words of wisdom.

Rhonda interrupts: "What do you want me to do?"

"Put her though," I sigh. The line clicks over. "David Hawkes," I say, in the most neutral tone I can muster.

"David, my precious darling son, how are you?"

It's my mother, Susan Wilde.

"I'm good…is everything ok?" I ask, knowing the response before it comes.

"I'm wonderful, darling. Just grand."

"What's the urgent issue?"

"I need a lawyer."

Alan begins to lift himself up and gives me the *should I go?* motion. I shake my head and wave at him to sit down.

"What? Why?"

"Because," she sucks in a sharp breath, "I've been fired from my soap in New York City, *Destiny's Hope.* "

"Again?"

"This time they mean it."

"What did they say, exactly?"

"They said: *You're fired. And this time we mean it.*"

"Really? I say, taking off my horn-rimmed glasses and massaging the bridge of my nose. "First off, I don't do employment law. And I don't practise in the United States. Can't your agent help?"

I hear a screech, a bang and then an "Ow!" in my ear.

"What is it? Are you ok?" Mum can be clumsy. I worry about her sometimes. I know she has boyfriends but she doesn't have anyone to look out for her.

"Yes fine, darling, I just pinched my finger."

"Ok," I say, relieved. "Like I was saying: there's not much I can do from Melbourne. I'll see if someone here can get you a referral. I'm sure we can find someone."

"Yes, someone who can rain legal hellfire down upon their heads and smote them with the brimstone of jurisprudence. David I want them to feel my wrath, before they're forced to hire me back."

Alan begins to lift himself up and gives me the *I'm gonna go* motion with his thumb. I shake my head and wave at him to sit down.

"This sounds like a very complex, um, legal situation." I turn to my soon-to-be-former boss. "Alan, we have people in New York don't we?" I cup my hand over the mouthpiece so she can't hear the response.

"You mean New York, in America?" He cracks up. "That's a good one. I'll miss your jokes."

I remove my hand. "I'll have to get back to you on this."

"Wonderful David, just wonderful. My beautiful boy is on the case."

"Well, I'm not taking the case, like I just said— look it doesn't matter— I'm actually in the midst of a meeting. I gotta go."

Alan gets up fully out of his chair and gives me the *I'll come back* motion with his forefinger. I shake my head *no* and gesture at him to sit down.

I put my glasses back on. The world comes into focus and I see it: my mother, Susan Wilde. With a phone to her ear, she strides into frame behind the glass panelling of my office.

She looks in and smiles.

Right as Alan sits down I wave for him frantically to leave. "No, Alan, go!" But it's too late.

She enters.

"Darling!" she says, startling Alan, who does a double take at the woman wearing a black dress, white gloves, black pumps, and white pearls. She carries a massive Louis Vuitton purse.

"Mum!" I say into the phone, "what are you do—" I hang up the phone and talk to her face. "It's great to see you."

"It's lovely to see you too, David."

Alan stands up and smoothes his toupee, "Aren't you going to introduce us?"

I bang my knee as I come from behind my desk, "Mum, this is my boss, well um, former boss, well almost, uh–"

"Alan Dinsdale, QC," he says, holding out his hand to shake.

"Susan Wilde," she purrs, holding her hand out like a princess, "T.P."

"T.P.?"

"Totally parched. It's been a dreadfully long journey. Is there anything to drink around here?"

"Rhonda can get you a cuppa tea," Alan says.

"Anything stronger?"

"Nescafé?"

"I was thinking, gin. This is a law firm after all." She laughs, Alan laughs.

I don't laugh.

"And you're David's mother?" Alan says.

"Among other starring roles," she says while smoothing my hair.

"It's just he never mentioned anything."

"Really...?"

"Oh, I'm sure I mentioned it before," I say, loosening my tie. Which my mother immediately restraightens.

"No, no, no, I would have remembered that. I have an excellent memory."

"He does," I say, "In fact he was just remembering some stuff about the indexation method and superannuation fund compliance in the meeting we were just having. Which we should probably be getting back to."

"Nonsense," Alan waves his hand, "I was just telling David how much we're all gonna miss him here."

"Why are you leaving your job David? And why, pray tell, did you not tell your mother?"

"I did tell you. Remember I called you?"

"Oh the phone?"

"Yes, on the phone, how else do you call someone?"

"I'll be toddling off now," Alan says. "Lovely to meet you, Mrs. Wilde."

"Miss Wilde," she corrects, putting her hand out again.

"By the way," Alan says, taking her hand. "Do you have anyone, legally speaking, making sure your final wishes are

9

honoured?"

She puts her hand over his, and looks deeply into his eyes. "I think I do now, Alan."

"Excellent." He opens the door to leave.

"Alan darling, how about that drink?"

"You were serious? Oh, well... the only thing we have is the wine for David's farewell drinks. Hey you should come–"

"Mum's probably too jet-lagged," I say to Alan, while trying to close the door at a pace that doesn't appear conspicuous.

"Nonsense, if there's a party celebrating my son. I want to be there," she says.

The door shuts.

She mimes a wine glass to Alan through the glass door as he walks away.

"Do you think he got my order?"

"Mem, he's not a waiter, he's my boss. Well, former boss— almost former boss–" I'm getting flustered now. "Mum, what are you even doing here?"

She kisses me on the cheek and sits down in my leather-backed chair, "Do I need a reason to visit my favourite child?"

"Only child, Mum." I feel simultaneous waves of love and exasperation. I haven't seen her in five years and now here she is in all her glory. The woman who gave birth to me, cared for me, professed her undying love and then repeatedly abandoned me for acting jobs, drink, drugs, and men. She's made as many entrances as she has exits in my life over the past 37 years. I've learned her love for me is unconditional, but her relationship to her career has a lot of conditions which must be met before we can get to my unconditional love.

"Mum, I really want to catch up, it's just, I've got my leaving drink in a few hours and–"

"David, you know I would never dream of keeping you from your work."

"I know, Mum."

"It's just that I've been distraught, so very distraught." Her eyes well up with tears. "You have no idea what it's like out there for an actress, like me, in her early/late-40s." She puts her head on my shoulder, and gets out a handkerchief from her purse.

"I get it, Mum, and I want to hear all about it. I can organise a cab to your hotel now, and I'll meet you for dinner. Where are you staying? Crowne Plaza? InterContinental?"

My phone rings before she can answer.

I answer. "Hi babe. How are you?"

"Do you know why 14 suitcases have just been delivered to our home?"

"Sorry what?" I say.

"Fourteen, Louis Vuitton, suitcases have just arrived on our front doorstep," repeats Katharine, my girlfriend, life partner, and best friend.

"Fourteen suitcases, really?" I say, glancing over at my mother who is looking into her compact and retouching the corners of her eyes.

"I meant to tell you David," she says, looking at where her crow's feet should be. That is if her 50th birthday present to herself hadn't been a trip to Beverly Hills finest. "Is that Kath?"

"Yes, it's Katha*rine*," I say, emphasising the final syllable as a reminder that Katharine hates being called Kath, Kathy, Kat or Kate. But I don't think my subtle hint got through. It's hard to compete with a mirror for my mother's attention.

"Hello darling!" she shouts towards the phone.

"Whose suitcases are they?" Katharine asks, "some of them are clinking."

"My Mother's."

"Wait. Your 'mother' mother," Katharine says, in the kind of disbelieving tone you'd hear at an atheist convention.

"Yeah. What other mothers do I have?"

"No it's just…was this a planned visit?"

"No, it's a …" I'm trying to find the right word while chewing on the inside of my cheek. Mum looks up into my eyes expectantly, "… delightful surprise." She smiles and goes back to staring at her tiny reflection.

I take a moment to reflect on how long I've been staring at my mother staring at her own reflection, and in how many different places. We bounced around a lot during my childhood because of mum's work. We're *from* Melbourne, but we've lived in Sydney, London, Manchester, Dublin, Toronto, Los Angeles, and New York. It all depended on what soap opera, movie, or theatre production she was cast in. She went where the work was, and I went along for the ride. It's the reason I have such a weird hybrid accent, use a mishmash of terminology, and still think in inches, miles and pounds (for weight not money). It's one of the things that Katharine found attractive about me in the first place.

Katharine's only met my mother a few times. The first time was when we started going out around eight years ago and Mum thought I had a foot fetish because Katharine's a podiatrist. The second time was on a layover in the Paris airport where my Mother offered Katharine cocaine when they went to the bathroom together. Despite her discreet and proper nature, Katharine never used the phrase "powder my nose" again.

I attribute the longevity of our relationship to the fact that I've successfully kept the two of them apart. Katharine comes from the suburbs and she's not acclimated (or acclimatised as they would say in Australia) to creative types. She comes from a long line of podiatrists. Her uncle, father, grandfather, all podiatrists. Feet run in her family.

Katharine's a stable, organised, rational, nurturing, and fastidious woman who is the love of my life. She supported my initial foray into writing, thinking it was a neat little hobby for me. However she wasn't particularly keen on me quitting my job to write full-time. In her family, people don't quit their careers just because they're unhappy and want fulfilment. However, after much discussion we decided that we could live on her salary for a year while I pursued my dreams. Ever since then she's been super supportive and even brags to her podiatry friends about her boyfriend the writer. I think it feels slightly romantic for her to be living with a novelist.

"I'm gonna have to call you back," I tell Katharine.

"What do you want me to do with this stuff? It's everywhere." When it comes to tidiness Katharine likes things 'just so' and my mother is a bit more 'so what'.

"As soon as I get home, I will deal with my mother's baggage, ok?"

"I love you," she says.

"Love you too," I sigh and hang up. I turn on my heels to face my mother.

"What's going on, Mum, are you broke?"

My Mother clicks her compact closed like a flamenco dancer snapping a castanet. "Of course not, David. Especially now that I don't have to worry about a mortgage."

"You sold your apartment in Manhattan?"

13

"No. I'm just not worrying about it. The interest rate in this country is criminal," she says incredulously.

"*That* country Mum. You're not in the US now."

"Exactly, darling, I'm not there anymore. I'm here, with you. I came back to Melbourne to be with you. "I'm only staying a couple of days, a week at the most...two if need be, but not a moment longer. I couldn't possibly impose on you and Katharine for more than a month–"

"Mum–"

"So it's agreed three months, and then I'm out of your hair."

"You can stay a week. But there's gonna be some rules: no drinking, no smoking, no drugs, and no guests after 5pm."

"Where do you live? A hotel in 1957?"

I ignore that one and adjust my horn-rimmed glasses.

"Anyway a week is plenty of time for us to catch up, David. I feel like we never get a chance to connect, really connect. I want to know everything, literally everything there is to know."

"Well I've just quit my job, I'm going to be a novelist–"

"Oh but first David, I will need that referral," she interrupts. "Those bastards at *Destiny's Hope* have to realise they cannot mess with Susan Wilde."

"Why did they fire you?" I regret asking the question as soon as it's out of my mouth.

"You know how I was dating Stanley Owsley, the executive producer?" she says looking off into the distance.

"Let me guess, his wife found out?"

"No, his mistress." Mum stands up to deliver her monologue, walking around the desk like she's performing a scene. "But that twisted harpy got so enraged that he was cheating on her, that she told his wife, who's the script editor, and the two of them conspired with the network to have me fired and my character killed off so that they could have him all to themselves. So I've got to find a way to get back there, drive a wedge between the three of them and rekindle my love with Stan."

"This soap opera sounds like a real…" I trail off.

"Soap opera?"

"I was in trouble, like, two words into that analogy." I shake my head.

"It matters, not one whit, my darling. We are going to sue the pants off those animals and we are going to win, and I am going to get my job back–"

"You want to go back?" I say standing up. "You said they killed off your character."

"Oh that's meaningless, it's a soap opera."

"This is insane, you can't go back there."

"Just what do you suggest I do, David?

"Find another job!" I say losing my cool. This is exactly what I wanted to avoid in my first interaction with my mother for five years.

People in the office look at us through the glass.

"Easy for you to say, not all of us can quit our job and have the lucrative world of print media to fall back on!" she says, lighting a Dunhill she takes from a silver cigarette case.

"You can't smoke in here Mum," I say.

She takes another long drag and extinguishes her cigarette in my Star Trek mug.

"Look Mum, I'm sorry." I sit down in the guest chair and compose myself.

"I'm sorry too, David. You know me, I'm just not myself when I'm not working.

"Why don't we just talk at home," I say.

"Well if you think that's for the best David," she says, demurring.

"You've had a long flight. You're probably tired …"

"You'd think flying first class wouldn't take it out of you as much, but it's still gruelling. Even with the free champagne," she says in a wistful yet timid tone.

She suddenly appears very vulnerable to me. Frail somehow.

I kiss her on the cheek and walk her to my office door.

"Just go downstairs," I say, digging the keychain out of my trousers and handing her my house key. "I'll have a taxi pick you up and take you to my place. I won't be that late."

"How did I get so lucky to have a son like you," she says, as she strides off in her Prada heels.

I stare at her receding figure, then close the door and go back to my desk to shuffle a few papers in my last hours at the firm. My thoughts wander, hoping this'll be a good visit with Mum. I wish she'd drop the role of Susan Wilde and be my mother. That she'll drop the *role* of mother and just *be* my mother.

I hear someone knocking.

"Come."

Alan enters with a glass of white.

"I've got your wine Miss Wilde."

"I'll take that," I say to Alan. "She left."

"Is she coming back?" he asks.

"Not tonight."

Episode 2

The law firm is gathered. The wine and champagne are being poured into little plastic champagne flutes from Woolworths. I'm standing by the nibbles table and notice the party planners have followed the book of office etiquette to a T and bought the five C's of an office function: cheese, crackers, celery, carrot, and cake. And egg salad, you can't forget the egg salad. Plus my paralegal Jean has specially gone out to buy my absolute favourite, beetroot hummus. I am going to miss her. I am going to miss all of them.

Almost all of them.

"In the interests of time, I'll keep things *brief?*" says Jeremy, my fellow junior partner. "Brief," he repeats his legal punchline, but it isn't funnier the second time around. As the self-proclaimed office funnyman, Jeremy volunteered to roast me as a way of saying goodbye. "We never thought you'd really go, Hawkesy" Jeremy continues, using the nickname only he calls me. "You don't retire from the law, you die from it."

He taps on the microphone. The home karaoke machine that the firm owns is doubling as a PA system for the occasion. The Song Singer 5000 (complete with two gyro ball disco lights and '10 CDs of Music!') was used once back when it was originally purchased eight years ago for the staff Christmas Party. Alan surprised everyone as he belted out an amazing version of Rod Stewart's *Da Ya Think I'm Sexy*. I did Rick Astley's *Never Gonna Give You Up*, despite my utter inability to sing in key or get the words right. Katharine later told me it was the first time she knew she had feelings for me. Apparently being tone deaf is a turn on to some women.

"I said you *die* from it," Jeremy says, hoping that a second attempt at repeating a punchline will be funnier than the first.

It isn't.

I laugh a little bit just so Jeremy doesn't feel so bad. Although I don't know what would make Jeremy feel bad. The thing that I like about Jeremy though is that he radiates a self-confidence which is completely unearned. He's part of a prominent, well connected, family in Melbourne. They donate to all sorts of foundations and charitable causes. He scraped through law school, barely passed the bar on his fourth attempt, and was hired instantly upon gaining his credentials. His legal brain isn't the best, but his family name brings in all of the affluent clientele from Toorak, East St. Kilda and Hawthorn. In ye olden days, aristocrats would send the family dullard into the clergy so that he couldn't get into trouble. Apparently now it's probate law. He has the rare ability to do half the work in double the time and not realise it gives him a poise and swagger that I somewhat envy.

I'm not saying that I'm a great probate lawyer or a writer for that matter. I just wish I didn't feel like a fraud most of the time

Maybe I could learn a thing or two from Jeremy. I shouldn't be so judgmental. He does have amazing hair.

I look at the Roman numeral clock above the kitchenette.

The hands say 5:30.

Jeremy continues: "We never knew Hawkesy had a creative streak. You certainly wouldn't know it from looking at him. Or talking to him. Or reading any of his discovery notes. They are so full of legal jargon that I have no idea what he's on about." I suspect he's joking, but I'm actually not sure. "However I do know from our university days together that Hawkesy was in the Law Revue so maybe he does have a theatrical streak in him."

"No, no…" I shake my head, laugh, and adjust my horn-rimmed glasses.

"No? You sure? I heard a rumour that you were going to perform for us tonight."

"Don't know what he's talking about folks," I say, laughing nervously.

"In conclusion," Jeremy says, "I think I speak for everyone when I say I will really miss David. He taught us all about the value of hard work, because we had to work so much harder to make up for the work he didn't do properly. Jez-Bone out!" Everyone claps as Jeremy drops the microphone like a man who just bested the competition in freestyle rap battle.

Jean, my paralegal, picks the mic up off the ground. "Thanks for that, um, roast, Jeremy. Now I think Alan Fischer wanted to say a few words."

Alan saunters up to the front and takes the mic from Jean. He sneezes, knocking his toupee slightly off centre again. Everyone sees it, no one mentions it.

"I'm not going to go on too long," Alan begins.

I go to my happy place, It's a mental picture of Katharine and myself at the Sacred Monkey Forest Sanctuary in Bali. I have another mental picture of her holding a monkey like a baby and feeding it a nut, but I don't like to imagine that one because every time I do I feel guilty that we haven't discussed marriage and children in a long time. I would rather remember good things in the past than ignite an uncomfortable conversation about the future.

Katharine and I spoke about the future when I called her back this afternoon.

"I get your mother's logic," Katharine said. "Sometimes just making a run for it is the best way to deal with a relationship which has run its course. Plus, maybe it's time we all connected as a family."

"Yeah, maybe. But just so you know, I told her she could only stay for a week."

"A week, two weeks, whatever." I love her nonchalance.

"I hope so," I said.

"We can take her to all our favourite cafes and restaurants. We can take her to The Brunswick West Project and Yong's Green Foods." Katharine has recently started experimenting with eating more vegan food.

"She'll love eating food with no calories," I said.

Katharine ignored that one. "You can show her around, show her how much things have changed. I mean, when's the last time she's even been in Melbourne?"

"God, it's been … years, probably 10 years or so," I thought back. It had been awhile. "It would've been for Uncle Grant's funeral," I said, musing on mum's close friend who died shortly after I graduated law school. Mum was really distraught and kept saying to me how she regretted that she hadn't kept in touch.

"David this is a wonderful opportunity for you two," Katharine told me. "You guys can get reconnected. Work through all the stuff you need to."

"Yeah, but where to start?"

"Yeah, just, take some time with her. Take her on a day trip down the Great Ocean Road. Just you and her."

"Maybe. I do have to work."

"Work? You're a professional writer now, you don't have to work."

I laugh from the belly. Katharine rarely does insult comedy.

"Did you like that? That was just for you," she says, smiling down the telephone.

"That was like a ninja grade 'get out of jail free card' you played there," I say. "Look, I'll figure out something to do with her."

"What about a winery tour around the Yarra Valley?"

"A winery tour with my mother? I'd rather go to a match factory with a pyromaniac. Plus, that might be outside our budget to pay for us both."

"She can afford it. Surely."

"I'm not sure. She's been fired and she's not paying her mortgage because the interest rates are too high."

"What does even that mean?" Katharine asked.

"Who knows."

"Babe, just be the man I fell in love with, who's strong and sincere, and creative and funny, and, and, and…and…be a man, and, and…and…and…

…I drift back into Alan's farewell speech which is flowing like a babbling brook.

"He's humble and modest, and I don't think he even realises it,' Alan says. "If he did know how modest he is he'd probably never mention it. He knows how to keep things quiet."

I start to drift off again…

"Like how his mother is the actress Susan Wilde."

I snap back into attention.

"You kept a pretty tight lid on that little tidbit, didn't you?"

Everyone looks at me. I laugh nervously.

"She came in today and, I don't want to brag on David's behalf, but she agreed to allow this firm to do her estate work. So I guess Jeremy isn't the only one pulling in high-profile clients anymore."

"Good on ya, Hawkesy" Jeremy shouts for inexplicable reason. He's also put on a pair of shutter shades also for some inexplicable reason.

"So thank you for the parting gift," Alan says. "Our first celebrity client. Now I know she hasn't been on Aussie TV for a while but you'd remember her as the pregnant teenager on the soap opera, *Next Door*. But she has been on other soap operas, and in movies and TV, here and in the UK. I haven't seen them, but…"

Alan keeps talking but I just want the laundry list of my mother's career to be over. I look down, breathing deeply and get a whiff of what is either the egg salad or sulphur.

"And here she is! Speak of the devil," Alan exclaims.

My mother sashays in from the senior partners' office area. She is visibly swaying but trying to hold her poise,

"Hello everyone." She continues to walk and wave towards the circle of staff members. "Please don't let my presence interrupt things. I'm not Susan Wilde tonight," she puts her hand on her breast. "Tonight, I'm David's mother."

She's drunk. And not Winston Churchill, humorously-tipsy, drunk. She is *drunk*–drunk. I have no idea how she got back into the office without me seeing. I called down to the front desk to order her a taxi and they said she got in. But now she's here and in grave danger of causing a fireball if she coughs near an open flame.

She grabs a champagne flute off the drinks table and comes toward the front.

"Did you want to say a few words?" Alan asks.

"Oh I couldn't possibly intrude like that," Susan says, taking the microphone off Alan.

"Susan Wilde everyone!" Alan says, stepping aside.

Alan claps.

Everyone claps.

I don't clap.

I'm gripped by the traumatic memories from my childhood when she's done this before. Mum would make my events totally about herself. Actually, she would either come and draw all the attention onto herself, or she would get distracted, or get called to set, or just forget and not show up at all. I'm not sure which is worse. Being absent or being there and not getting the love and support I wanted from her.

She downs the contents of her champagne flute and sits down on the stool next to the karaoke machine. She gets instantly wistful, like she's about to do a torch song at a cabaret night. "I don't know if words can express how I feel right now. So I'm going to sing. But before that let me tell you a little story about my David."

I step in and try to take the microphone off her, but she won't let go.

"Ok, Mum. Jokes over. I think Alan had a few more things he wanted to say, or Jeremy?"

They both shake their heads 'no'.

"David, I want to farewell you," she says.

"You're not saying goodbye to me, Mum. They are."

23

"I want to tell–"

"Actually, Mum I was actually just about to do my speech."

"I thought you hadn't prepared anything," Jerremy interjects.

"Surprise, I do," I say, getting out the piece of paper which is blank.

"I've got some notes too!" Mum says, letting go of the mic and digging through her purse. Lipstick, keyrings, pill bottles, and miscellaneous detritus start falling everywhere.

While she's distracted I start to 'read' my improvised speech: "What is a home? Is it the location, the neighbourhood, the building? I think it's the people. That's what makes it a home. Dienstag, DiSalvio & Fischer has been my home since–"

"Found it!" She holds up a piece of paper like it's Excalibur. "No, wait, that's my Ambien prescription."

"It's, um, been my home since–"

"This is it," Susan holds up a piece of paper that just has a giant love heart drawn on it. "It means speak from the heart."

She shows it to everyone as she strokes my clean shaven face.

There is a collective, "Awww."

"Let her speak, David," Jean says.

"Yeah, let her speak," another lawyer chimes in.

Jeremy starts: "Susan Wilde. Susan Wilde. Susan Wilde!"

The chant grows to a fever pitch.

I have to either hand my mother the microphone or listen to her name repeated endlessly.

I hand her the mic.

"He's a good boy isn't he?" my mum starts. "Give him a round of applause."

Everyone claps.

Susan straightens up, looks down, breathes out, starts in.

"There's a certain feeling a mother has for her first born. It's not that we love our other children any less, but there is something special about that first child." Her gaze roams the faces in front of her making eye contact. "When you take him home from the hospital you realise that the two of you are now on a truly grand adventure … together. You can laugh in the face of life and say 'do your worst' gods of chance, because from here on out, I'm not doing it alone. You have to be courageous for the both of you, and any fears you may have had before the moment of birth are erased by the sound of his precious little lungs breathing, in and out, as he falls asleep on your chest. That's what love can do. That's what this precious child did for me."

Everyone's eating out of the palm of her hand. I'm eating out of the palm of her hand. Every good memory, every tender moment floods back and I know why I put up with so much trauma and drama. Nothing compares to how she can genuinely express her feelings when she's being real. I want to hug her, to tell her I'm sorry for being so sarcastic, for keeping her at arm's length, but I don't want to break the flow.

Mum carries on:

"David's a good son. He's gorgeous, he's smart, and he's been able to maintain his physique after the age of 30 which is no small feat let me tell you."

Why does she have to mention my weight?

"And loyal," she goes on, "He's loyal. He's always been loyal to me, he's never turned his back on his mother in a time of need. And he has been loyal to this firm. He stuck with this firm and never tried to get a better job, even though he could have."

People start eyeing each other.

"Why? Because, loyalty folks," she carries on. "He is better than this. But loyalty and love made him stay. In fact, he is better than all of you. He should have been billed way higher in the credits based on his previous body of work. But you people took him for granted like those bastards on that teeming cesspit of drivel, *Destiny's Hope*–!"

"Ok, thank you, Mum." I try to grab the mic from her. But she holds onto it with a death grip.

"I'm not done talking about you, David!"

"Susan Wilde everyone! Give her a hand."

We play tug of war with the microphone. I'm trying to be casual about it but it's hard wrestling a microphone from a shouty-drunk soap opera star without it looking conspicuous.

"You can't silence me, David. The world needs to know. They need to hear the truth about an industry that just takes all your best years away by tempting you with money and fame and then throws you in the scrap heap of life when you start to age."

"Mum's really jet-lagged everybody," I say with a fake laugh.

I look at her, pleading with my eyes for her to stop, and I notice it: She's welling up. A single tear rolls down the left side of her face.

I'm confused, lost, tangled. I want to throttle her for yet again making one more event about her, yet I want to throttle the people who've driven her into this state even more.

She gets up off the stool and weaves around me, still holding the microphone connected to the karaoke machine.

"Now David, be a good boy and let mummy have the microphone."

She yanks at the microphone, trips over her massive purse, and falls back into the karaoke machine. I fall back into the nibbles table, upsetting the entire contents onto the ground and onto myself.

Rick Astley's *Never Gonna Give You Up* starts playing.

Everyone would notice my face going beetroot red … if it wasn't covered in beetroot hummus.

I hear the sound of one person slow clapping. Then another. Then another. Then the whole room breaks into riotous applause, and whistling.

I realise they think this whole thing has been some sort of performance piece that I engineered.

"I told you he had something planned," Jeremy shouts.

Not missing a beat my mother starts bowing and acknowledging the ovation as if it was closing night on Broadway. She's soaking it up like an attention sponge.

I can either go with it and have everyone think it's a joke, or I can wipe the beetroot hummus off my face and tell everyone the truth. If I tell the truth I'll ruin everyone's enjoyment. It'll end the party, and my time at the firm, on a dismally sour note. Or I can play along with the game, have everyone like me, think I'm creative, and let my mother get away with it. I can save my reputation or suck it up and finally tell the truth about this farce. I wipe the beetroot hummus off my face and stand up tall.

"And for our next trick, ladies and gents," I say. Everyone laughs.

Susan hugs me.

"We're just gonna go 'backstage' to get cleaned up," I tell everyone. "But please keep drinking. And if you want some food there's plenty on the ground."

More laughter.

I take my mother's hand and lead her down the hall to the bathroom.

"Oh, David, you were positively hilarious out there. Did I pass it down to you genetically? Or was it the environment you grew up in? What's that called, nature or nurture?"

More like nature or torture.

We get in the bathroom and I close the door.

"Now what do you want to do next?" Mum gets a paper towel and starts wiping my face.

"I can do it!" I snatch the towel from her.

"Excuse me! God forbid a mother should take care of her boy."

"I'm a man, Mum. A man!" I say in a whiney defensive voice that completely undermines my point.

"Well then, I was going to suggest we sing a famous duet together, but maybe I'll just sing *Just the Two of Us* by myself."

"You're not going back out there. You're going home."

"But they're expecting an encore. The show must go on, David."

"That wasn't a performance, Mum, that was a shambles."

"Stop being so melodramatic. If I stopped going to all the places I could never show my face at again, you know where I'd be? Sitting, locked away in a tower, doing needlepoint, like Eleanor of Aquitaine."

"Yes, yes, just like in *The Lion in Winter*," I say, crossing my arms.

"It's a dream role of mine," Mum says, a light in her eye. "The strong, stoic queen, who loves her oldest son. Pity, I'm just too young to play it."

She turns her head away in mock despondency.

I roll my eyes.

"I saw that."

"No you didn't."

"So you admit it, you did roll your eyes at me."

Damn it. How does she always know?

"It doesn't matter, Mum."

"It does matter, David. You don't take me seriously." She pauses. Then, "You never have."

"That's not true."

"You think my job is just going: 'blaa-blaa-blah'," she says, flicking her hair about and sticking out her tongue. "And you don't respect that."

"I respect you, and I love you, but I just…"

"I love you too, David. And that's why I'm here. To love you…and to get my career back on track."

"I'm not helping you with your career." I say as I start washing my face in the sink.

"Why not? Helping in times of need is what family is about."

"Really Mum, you want to go down this path? Open this can of worms, lift the lid on Pandora's box?"

"Don't mix metaphors, it's unseemly," she says, offering me a paper towel to dry my face.

I snatch it.

"Unseemly?! What was that display out there?"

"You mean when I was speaking about our first moments after coming home from the hospital together?"

"Yes!— well, no— I mean, that stuff was good. Why does everything have to turn into such a circus with you?"

"Shh … shh …" She puts her finger on my lips and gives me a big bear hug.

"I don't know. All I know is that I love you."

29

As my father used to say: she doesn't mean to be a loose cannon, son. She just is.

I breathe deeply and finally put my arms around her.

"I love you too, Mum. I'm just feeling stressed about quitting my job. Katharine is super supportive right now. I'm just afraid that if my next book gets rejected then I'll have to come back here, and she'll be disappointed in me."

"Sweetheart, dentists like her will never understand us creative types."

"Podiatrist, mum, she's a podiatrist."

"Whatever. The point is David, Kathy is supportive now, but what makes you think she'll really be there for you, for us, in the long run?"

"Well, she's stable, well balanced, career minded... nutrition conscious."

"David, be straight with me. Do you make love to her as if the world is ending?"

How has this conversation shifted to my relationship?

"How serious are you about the relationship?" She asks me.

"I'm not having this conversation with you in the toilets!" I tell Mum. "We've been together for eight years, ok?"

"And still not married?"

"Our relationship is fine for today."

"Fine for today, yes, but will she support your dream of being a writer when you're wallowing in the doldrums of black despair trying to open a vein and tweeze out every word onto the page? How will her training as a podiatrist prepare her for that? Maybe you need someone who shares the creative spark like you do? Who understands you, the real you. Do you want to spend your life with someone whose biggest decision is when to drop by Bed, Bath and Beyond to pick up carpet swatches? Maybe that's why you haven't gotten married yet? Or had children, or bought a house? Or made any kind of tangible commitment."

I can't decide which is more wrong, that my Mother has the gall to say any of this or that she's making a coherent argument for ending my relationship with Katharine while still drunk.

"Let's face it, you're not getting any younger. You need to make some major decisions about your life. Time is a majestic river, rushing around you, speeding up as it moves around bends which never look the same looking forward as they do looking backward. You're in this state of flux, with uncertainty about your job, your relationship. You can't wait to get control of your life back, you've got to take it. Be the man you claim to be."

I never thought I'd say these words to myself. But Susan Wilde is 100% right.

Later at home I try to break the news to Katharine gently, but she doesn't take it well.

"What do you mean you kicked your mother out?!" Katharine asks.

Episode 3

I'm in bed. On freshly laundered, Egyptian cotton sheets. Hands behind my head, laying back on my pillow, staring up at the ceiling. My teeth are brushed and I have a smile on my face. I haven't felt this much joy with myself since I bought that two-in-one blender and juice squeezer. I am going to celebrate kicking my mother out tomorrow morning by having a smoothie or a cold pressed juice. Or both! I can make both and only have to clean one kitchen appliance. A wave of contentment crashes over me.

Contentment is a great feeling. Because nothing needs to change.

Nothing.

Almost nothing.

"Did you put any thought into this at all?" Katharine asks me.

"Hmmm—let me think— no."

"Where is she going to go?"

"I don't know."

"Who is she going to stay with?"

"I don't know."

"What is she going to do for money?"

I don't answer

Katharine gives me the nitroglycerin look that serves her so well as a podiatrist. She can practically freeze plantar warts with it.

"It's not that I don't care, I just ... she'll figure something out. She always does. She's Susan Wilde for god sakes.

When Katharine gets upset she switches into her hyper-rational mode.

"Reason would dictate that she'd be emotionally crushed." Katharine says.

"I don't get why you're so upset over this? You barely even know her."

"Exactly. How am I ever going to get to know her?"

"Ugh." This is really cutting into my contentment.

"Don't 'ugh' me. It's normal for people who live together to know each other's parents."

"That's 'regular normal' not 'Susan Wilde normal.'"

"But she's your mother."

"Exactly my point. She's *my* mother. I kicked her out. It doesn't involve you," I say defensively.

"We're supposed to be sharing our lives together. How does it look to people if I know nothing about your family? I know zero about her or any of your family really. It's like you've got a part of your life that I'm not invited to. Like with your dad–"

"Don't talk about my dad, ok?" I blurt out. "It's just, I love her, but she drives me crazy. Do you know what that's like?"

Katharine says nothing for a minute and stares at me. But not the nitro stare. I think it's compassion.

This whole situation is getting away from me. I was hoping for a much different reaction from Katharine. I thought she'd be so impressed with my decisiveness over kicking my mother out that we'd make love. Passionate, end of the world, love. I now realise I was suffering under a syndrome known as DMT (Deluded Male Thinking). Symptoms also include: believing that if you don't hear a fart it also means it can't be smelled either.

There's not gonna be any sex for me tonight. Not with another person.

"What about all that stuff we talked about earlier too?" Katharine asks.

"I was strong and decisive, well, kind of..."

"I meant about you and her, David. You need to talk to her and tell her what you just told me."

"What are you nuts? Tell her that she drives me crazy?"

"*And* that you love her."

"I do love her. I just wish she could be normal like the other kids' mums."

"You need to work past this. Did it ever occur to you why you're blocked creatively?"

"Thanks, but I don't take therapeutic advice from foot doctors."

Katharine gives me a nipple cripple.

"Don't do that!" I say, "You know it turns me on."

Katharine laughs, she lies down on my chest and cuddles up.

The problem with trying to diffuse a highly emotional situation with humour is that it occasionally works. And I think that if it worked once it will work again. Another symptom of DMT. The end result is I use humour to cover my feelings and avoid being vulnerable to the woman I love.

"You know what the strangest thing is though?" I say, "I kicked her out for us. She was saying mean things about you, about us. I didn't want to hear it."

"You defended me?" Katharine says, looking up at me.

"Yeah of course."

"What was she saying?"

"Just dumb stuff about you, about us."

Katharine kisses me sweetly.

I sense that sex is back on the table.

"She was questioning our relationship. Like you weren't the right person for me because we're not married, and don't have kids, or a mortgage, or whatever. And that somehow showed a lack of commitment. And I was like, 'You can't talk about us in that way, lady.'"

I go to kiss Katharine and she pulls back.

"What?" I ask.

"Your mother's right, though."

"About what?"

"That we haven't talked about marriage and kids and a house."

"We live in a house together. What do you call that?"

"I'm saying we haven't talked about it. We never talk about it." Katharine says. "It's the same way that you never talk about your mother or your family."

"Now just isn't a good time. I'm starting my new book."

"We have to have a talk about these things at some point."

"Why?"

"Because that's what people do."

"Ugh, people ... I hate them," I say. I really want this conversation to be over.

Katharine rolls her eyes.

"Do you even want kids?" I ask out of pure frustration. That is the exact wrong question to ask.

Katharine's eyes dart around. Finding no place to land.

I've opened a can of worms that is going to wriggle around all over the bed, ruining the sheets and any chance I have at sex tonight. I've got to claw things back from my self-sabotage. "I know, let's practise making one right now," I say, going in for a kiss.

The joke doesn't land and neither do my lips.

DMT strikes again.

"I want to talk about the possibility of kids with you. David, this is what couples do. There is a logical progression to life. It's like a relationship escalator."

"Well you can get off whenever you want," I say, crossing my arms and turning away from her.

"Acting like a child is not the same as discussing children." Katharine says.

I look over at my alarm clock on the nightstand. 10:01.

"You don't find it odd that we still rent?" Katharine asks.

"So?"

"So, it's temporary."

"So is life."

"Spare me."

I turn back around, arms still crossed in lockdown mode.

"Really though. Who knows how long any of us are here for? Any one of us could be dead tonight. Tonight Katharine."

Katharine ignores me and moves on to more practical things.

"The point is we can afford to buy. I'm a doctor, you're a lawyer–"

"I'm a writer now, thank you," I say.

"Yeah for now," she says.

What is that supposed to mean? I think back to Mum's

insinuation that Katharine would ultimately be unsupportive of my creative process.

Katharine strokes my hair and touches my ear in the way I like. Down across the edge and up along the inside.

"We don't have to talk about all this stuff tonight. It couldn't have been easy kicking her out."

"It's just…I don't appreciate her swanning in here and expecting me to drop everything in my life and pay attention to her and her problems. She's done that my entire life and I am through with it."

Katharine reassures me with a smile. God I love her smile.

"I just can't handle her and a publishing deadline at the same time."

"Hypothetically: if we did get married would you want your mother there?"

"Mum, free booze, plus a microphone and a captive audience?"

Katharine laughs. I laugh. We laugh together. And kiss.

We lay back down together.

"I love you, ok?" I say to her, "And I do want to talk about things. Now's just not the right time."

"It's fine," she responds immediately.

"When things get a little more settled, let's talk this stuff out. I want to."

I don't really want to, but the thought of losing Katharine right now scares the ever-living shit out of me. Marriage, kids, and houses are just solutions to a problem that we don't have. We love each other.

We kiss more. It's the we're-gonna-have-sex style kissing. Katharine gets on top of me and unbuttons her cupcake-themed pyjama top revealing a silk singlet beneath. We continue to kiss, but just as Katharine is about to remove her silk singlet, the phone rings.

"Don't answer it," I say firmly.

"Your mother?"

"It has to be."

I kiss Katharine but she's not paying attention.

"She wouldn't call this late unless it was an emergency."

"You don't know her."

Katharine takes evasive action and answers the phone.

"Hello?"

I cover my eyes with the back of my wrist, as Katharine lies half on me, half on my side of the bed.

"Mm-hmm … yeah … I'm his girlfriend."

I can tell it's not my mother, but I can't make out the voice on the other end.

"Yes…yes absolutely…I can pass the message on…thank you."

Katharine hangs up.

"Um, David…"

"What?"

"Your mother's at the hospital. She tried to commit suicide."

Episode 4

I throw on my big windbreaker, my watch, slip into some sandals and jump into the car. Katharine gets in and we're off before she even has time to close the door.

The thought: 'What have I done' goes through my brain so many times I'm afraid it's going to give my mind repetitive strain injury. If the last thing I ever said to her was, "Get out of my life," I don't think I'll be able to live with myself. What if she dies before we can talk things through. I just need a moment of connection, a moment of her being real with me. And I'll be real with her. Is that too much to ask, Lord?

I'm not even sure which Lord I'm talking to. The Jewish God I grew up with, the Buddha who I studied later (who isn't even a god), or another one. I'd become a polytheist if it meant I had a chance to see my mother again. I try to remember a prayer from synagogue. But the only thing that springs to mind is the Mourner's Kaddish. I'd prefer to hold off on that one.

Katharine goes really quiet. It's part of her middle class upbringing that I admire so much. Keeping it in. However on this occasion her silence has the effect of leaving me with the engine noise of both the car and my mind.

"Talk to me about something."

"What would you like to talk about?" Katharine asks.

"Anything."

"Cricket?"

"Yes please."

Katharine's love of cricket has always been a source of intense fascination for me. She used to play at her school in Adelaide, and her devotion to the sport hasn't diminished over time. Aside from the physical stamina and excessive concentration required to stay awake between moments of excitement on the field, I think she loves the analytical nature of the game.

I remember when Mum first got cast on an American soap opera in Los Angeles and signed me up for baseball. She wanted me to have 'authentic American experiences' like in *The Bad News Bears* movies and thought it was close enough to cricket for me to enjoy. The coach saw me handling the bat and started me … on the bench, where I was put in charge of keeping the stats. It's something Katharine and I bonded over. It's something I want to get lost in now as I rush past parked cars and trams as we scream down Royal Parade towards the Royal Melbourne Hospital.

Anything not to think about death.

"How are the Aussies doing against India right now?" I ask Katharine.

"They're getting killed," she sighs, then realising her faux pas. "I mean, they're um— how about we just listen to the radio?"

Katharine turns on the radio. Gold FM has The Police's *Can't Stand Losing You.*

She quickly switches to Triple M, broadcasting Guns N' Roses' cover of *Knockin' on Heaven's Door.*

Kiss FM has a techno remix of Blue Oyster Cult's *(Don't Fear) the Reaper*.

The omens are coming. The weight of my guilt is pressing into my chest so hard that it's touching my spine.

Katharine snaps the radio off.

"Let's just take a moment to breathe calmly–"

"We're here."

I pull the hand brake and jump out of the car in the waiting area and dash towards the big red sign that reads Emergency and Trauma Services.

Inside the ward, I run past a sea of injured folks. As I get to the front desk I cry: "My mother's here, she's a famous actress and she might be dead. I need to see her right away! Please, please!"

I realise my mistake in running out of the house without dressing properly. I'm wearing a bright red ski parka over my pyjamas. In the rush of adrenaline, I didn't notice how sweaty I've become. The look doesn't say 'concerned son' it says 'escaped mental patient'. The two big security guards in the waiting area begin whispering to each other.

"Sorry," I say. "Let me start again."

I clear my throat.

"My name is David S. Hawkes, I believe my mother, Susan Wilde was admitted to this hospital earlier this fine evening."

The woman at the registration desk, whose name tag reads 'Candice', types into the computer. She stares over her glasses at the screen. Then she stares over her glasses at me.

"We don't have anyone under that name. Are you sure she wasn't taken to The Alfred?"

"No, I'm not sure. My girlfriend took the message." I try to regain my composure. "I'm just looking for my mum. Can you check your computer, or databases, or whatever, again. The name is Susan Wilde."

"The actress?" a voice behind me says.

"Yes." I turn around and see a doctor.

He's handsome with thick, short cut white hair parted on the left. He's got a long forehead, a trimmed moustache, and rimless circular glasses. He's armed with a clipboard, pen, and a stethoscope around his neck. He's got a white coat and is wearing a collared shirt with a silk tie underneath.

"Dr. Hernandez," he says, sticking out his hand to shake mine.

"David Hawkes."

We shake once and then he wipes the moisture from my sweaty palm on his white coat, never breaking eye contact. "I'm your mother's attending consultant," he says.

"So she *is* here?" I feel a wave of relief hit me, "Thank god."

"She's checked in under a pseudonym," he says.

"What is it?"

"It's a fake name, it comes from Greek–"

"No, I meant what name did she check in under?"

"It's her legal name."

"What happened, is she ok?" I ask, starting to calm down.

"She was admitted for a poly substance overdose," he says clinically. "In layman's terms: pills."

"Pills," I repeat.

"Lots of pills."

I swallow hard.

"We think it was deliberate," he adds.

I take his elbow and lead him to a corner of the waiting room, "Are you sure this isn't an accidental overdose," I continue, leaning in and lowering my voice. "I mean how do we know this was a–"

"Suicide attempt?" he exclaims, totally missing my non-verbal cues for discretion. "This might clear things up."

He goes to his clipboard and flips over a few papers, then reads: "Her bloods showed signs of codeine, cocaine, compazine. Vicodin, Percocet, Ambien, Callosembutal, Rhizomarsipan, Phenophantail, Durorizipan, Panphenotan. And about a litre of scotch."

"Sorry, but some of those drug names sound made up."

"They are made up," he replies matter-of-factly. "By the drug companies. But to your earlier point, we suspect it's suicide because you could possibly kill a horse with the amount of medication in her system."

My mind spirals. This is no Oscar party overdose.

"Not a draught horse, mind you, but a mid-size Arabian, or a Quarter Horse perhaps. Definitely a Shetland pony."

I snap back to attention, "Sorry what's that?"

"It's a small horse from the Scottish Isles. Thick coat, short legs–"

"No, I meant– look, it doesn't matter– So you really think this was deliberate?"

"The bottom line, Mr. Hawkes, is that we can be reasonably certain that this was a suicide attempt by the amount of drugs in her system."

I hang my head. This was definitely my fault.

"That and the note she had on her person," Dr. Hernandez adds.

"She left a note? Isn't that the sort of thing you say first?"

"I'll make a note of that." He clicks his pen and jots something down.

"Can I see it?"

"There's a problem with that," he says. "Hospital policy is that we only release suicide notes to the person or persons they are addressed to."

"Don't tell me it's addressed to–"

"Cutie McLove-Pie," the doctor says, enunciating every syllable.

I cringe.

I haven't heard that name for years. It's a pet name my mother gave me…when I was 17. She thought that if I was growing up then it meant she was getting older too. So she started calling me 'Cutie McLove-Pie' on the phone, in front of my friends in order to infantilise me.

Fortunately, I learned to assert my independence from her. I can stand up to her now and have some healthy boundaries and separation in my life. The exact kind of separation that led me to kicking her out earlier today. Lord, what have I done?

You almost drove your mother to kill herself tonight Cutie McLove-Pie.

"Obviously that's me," I tell Dr. Hernandez.

"It's not one of your other siblings?"

"I don't have any."

"Are you sure?"

"Of course I'm sure." I can't believe this guy. What kind of question is that?

"Still, it's hospital policy. I can't let you see the letter."

"Look. There's no one else," I shout. "I'm Cutie McLove-Pie, I'm Cutie McLove-Pie!"

Candice gives me 'the eye'.

All the injured people in the waiting room give me 'the eye.'

Even the guy with the black eye, who has an eye patch, gives me 'the eye'. The two big security guards take a step closer to me.

"Sorry, I'm just a little emotional," I say.

"Well, it's unorthodox, but ok…"

The Doctor hands me an envelope from his inside pocket.

"Thank you," I breathe in relief. "Is it possible— I mean— can I see her now?

"Have a seat. I'll check." The Doctor goes past the two security guards flanking the entrance to the ward and disappears behind the gliding doors.

As I sit down I turn over the letter. I pause a moment before opening it.

Dear Cutie McLove-Pie,

No words can describe the pain and suffering I've endured since you kicked me out of your life and cast me upon the ash heap of disdain. I understand why you did it. I realise what a failure I am now. A bitter pill of disappointment you have to swallow every time you set eyes upon me. I haven't lived up to my potential, I know that's what you think, and I cannot stand to see the shame in your eyes as you look at me.

The blackness in my soul is so dark now that I cannot even look within it to find the truth inside myself. How will I feed myself if I cannot find truth within me? How can I cross the portico into the mansion of imagination if I cannot see the real me. I now understand the plight of the ageing woman throughout the ages. We lose fertility, our youth and become the scrap heap for discarded fantasies. We are looked through as sexless ghosts. We have so much to give but are called upon to sit quietly in rocking chairs and knit.

It all seems so pointless now. A fool's errand.

Life is all memory, except for the one present moment that goes by you so quickly you hardly catch it going. The past is the past now, as it has always been and forever will be. I hope I can find solace in death's cold embrace.

There is a time for departure even when there's no certain place to go. Please tell your father that...

The note ends. I turn it over. The other side is an official form. I recognise it. It's one of the 'Do No Resuscitate' forms Dienstag, DiSalvio & Fischer keep on file. There's nothing filled in and nothing in the margins. "Please tell your father..." what? Where's the rest?

I stand up and look around for Doctor Hernandez.

Katharine enters the waiting area and comes over to me, gives me a big hug and strokes the back of my hair. I hold her tight.

"I've just seen the doctor," I tell her. "He's back there checking up on her," I explain the situation to Katharine.

I show her the suicide note.

I look down at my watch, it stopped at 11:33. I unhook the clasp on the old leather strap, tap on the scratched face, and listen to it. My father gave me his TAG Heuer Monaco as a present one year when he couldn't make it to my 7th birthday. Well, Mum gave it to me ... from him. It's the same one Steve McQueen wore in the movie *Le Mans*.

"Where's the rest?" Katharine asks, turning the letter over, puzzled.

"No clue. She could have lost it, she could have passed out before she finished it, the doctor could—" I get choked up and can't finish the sentence.

We sit down. I hunch forward. If I look in Katharine's

green eyes I'll cry. I've got to be strong right now. For her, for myself, for Mum. I stare into the blue face of my square, silent, chronograph, rubbing the glass with my thumb. Katharine goes silent and rubs my back.

"You know who I blame for this?" I say.

"Don't blame yourself, honey."

"Acting. It's an unstable existence, with lots of ups and downs, and she shouldn't be doing it at her age."

"How old is she?" ask Katharine.

"She's um, look, that's not the point. It's unstable, she's not stable. It's just not safe anymore … for her."

"What else is she going to do?" Katharine responds, with her insightful yet unhelpful logic.

"Lots of things. She's really smart, she could, um … she could …" I trail off. "Look, I don't know right now. But what I do know is that she needs to retire from this whole circus of show business. I'm going to tell her. It's time to take her final curtain bow."

"Ok, if you think that's the right thing to do?" Katharine says inflecting up at the end of her sentence, making her statement seem more like a question.

"I know what that tone means Katharine, why don't you just say what you're really thinking."

"Hey, hey, hey," she says, running her hand through my hair. "I'm sorry, you're right. I just feel that right now isn't the right time to give her an ultimatum."

"You're right," I sigh. I hug Katharine awkwardly over the black plastic armrest on the waiting room chairs. "But I am going to tell her. She's got to retire from acting, for her own good. It's killing her. I couldn't live with myself if I allowed something like this to happen to her again. I won't back down."

She hugs my arm and pulls herself down to cradle her head on my shoulder.

"Mr. Hawkes!" someone shouts.

It's Dr. Hernandez. He's standing in front of the sliding doors which lead back to the ward.

"Yes."

I stand up quickly.

Too quickly in fact.

I knock Katharine's jaw with my head as I rise.

"Oh, sorry baby." I feel terrible.

I go to comfort Katharine, but I am looking in the direction of the doctor.

"Are you ok?" I ask.

"Mr. Hawkes, this way please," The doctor calls.

"Just go." Katharine says, rubbing her mouth.

"Here." I hand Katharine my watch, and go to the doctor.

"What do you want me to do with this?" she asks.

"Just hold onto it for me. And don't lose it."

I trot to the entrance to the ward.

"Is she conscious?" I ask Dr. Hernandez.

"There's been a development," the doctor responds, giving away nothing. What I wouldn't give for his poker face. He indicates to follow him.

The two huge security guards flank the doors. Both are standing silently still, but I can feel their eyes on me. The doctor swipes his security fob and the doors slide open.

The clock above the entrance reads 12:33.

I step into the ward. Not knowing if Mum is dead or alive.

Episode 5

A million things go through my mind. None of them helpful.

I follow Dr. Hernandez down the twisting passages of the emergency ward. There are bleeding people everywhere. There's a guy with blood all over his face, a man who's been bit on the arm by a dog, and a dude double handcuffed to a gurney who's singing to an audience that only he can see. Even in the state he's in he's still a better singer than I am. The macabre part of me wants to slow down and have a sneaky peak. But the doctor is walking so briskly I'll lose him in the corridors.

Nurses and orderlies whizz past me, looking at charts and pushing wheelchair-bound patients.

I instinctively stick my hands into my pockets and hug them close to my body. I feel something weird in the inside breast pocket. It's a *Phantom of the Opera* mask. I remember I threw this jacket over my costume last winter when Katharine and I went to my friend Anthony's Andrew Lloyd Webber theme party. It's a tradition he's had since his days as a musical theatre major. I went as the Phantom and Katharine went as Eva Perón from *Evita*. She looked amazing as the former First Lady of Argentina.

I put the mask in my left side pocket. No time for memories,

I need answers.

"Doctor?" I say.

"Yes, Mr. Hawkes."

"The letter you gave me. Where's the rest of it."

"I don't understand."

"There's part of it missing."

"That's all she had on her when she was admitted."

We continue twisting and turning down halls until we get to an open area full of beds and curtains, and medical personnel crisscrossing the floor, all walking with a purpose.

"I'm going to permit you to talk to her. She's in a stable condition."

"For once." I say.

"The Doctor Hernandez stops abruptly and turns.

"Sorry, it's a reference to earlier," I mumble.

The doctor stares blankly at me for a second. Then he laughs in a way which sends tiny bits of saliva flying onto my glasses.

"Oh I get it. 'Stable condition', like a horse. Because she took enough pills to kill a Shetland pony. Very droll Mr. Hawkes. However I would caution you from using that kind of humour around your mother. They say laughter is the best medicine but, medically speaking, medicine is the best medicine."

"Good to know." I say wiping spit off my glasses. "Medically speaking, what is best thing for me to say to her right now?"

"Comforting things. Reassure her. Your mother's in a dark place. Let her know you're there for her. The worst thing in the world is for her to be on her own at the moment. Tell her you'll be there for her around the clock. Move her in with you if need be."

"Anything else?"

"The best thing for her would be for her to re-engage with the things she loves the most. Does she have any hobbies?"

"Not really." Unless you consider cocaine a "hobby."

"Her work then? Does she derive meaning from it?"

"The acting? Hard to say. I mean, how do you define something like 'meaning'?"

He rattles it off the exact definition like he was Noah Webster: "The experience of being serious, important, and worthwhile."

I walked right into that one.

"I suppose she derives meaning from it … if you consider dedicating your life to something as being 'serious, important and worthwhile' or whatever," I say.

"Then that's the best thing for her right now: get her back into acting."

"But getting fired from her job is what kicked off this whole mess," I protest.

"That's the point. If she doesn't do any acting now, she may never 'do acting' again."

"Really?" I ask.

"Yes. And if you don't encourage her to act she may spiral into another depression and attempt suicide again. She needs to get right back on the horse and start riding."

"I see," I say. Now I'm in a dark place.

"That was a joke," he says, smiling for the first time.

"Really? So she should or shouldn't start acting again?!" I get excited.

"No. I said 'get on the horse and start riding,' you know because we were talking about Shetland ponies before. She definitely needs to keep acting."

51

With that he immediately strides over to a curtained off area and pulls back the sheet to reveal my mother. "How are we doing here?" he says.

She's lying on a hospital bed, propped up, with a nurse on one side feeding her juice through a straw and another nurse dabbing her forehead with a moist terry cloth.

"Mum," I go over to her.

The nurses exit silently.

"David is that you?" she says.

"Yes Mum. I'm the only one who calls you 'Mum', remember?" I say, gently removing the terry cloth.

"Of course. In my weakened state, I forgot."

"That's ok," I say, holding her hand. "Everything's going to be ok, I'm here now."

"I know, Daniel," she says.

"... It's David, Mum."

"Of course. In my weakened state I forgot."

"You just called me David a second ago."

"Did I ..."

"Yes," I say. My mind slips into suspicion, is this an act? Did she set this up? I feel ashamed for kicking her out, now I feel even more ashamed of myself for even thinking that she would try to manipulate me at a time like this. She's just tried to kill herself and I'm making the situation about me. I'm in a snow globe of emotions.

"In my weakened state I ...I ..." she trails off.

I lean in, waiting for her to finish the sentence.

"... Forgot?" I say.

"I can't remember."

"Memory loss is common after a traumatic event," Dr. Hernandez says. He's standing behind us by the curtain. "You may find that she had trouble remembering names, places, or even the event itself."

"I'm just glad to see you, Mum."

"I wasn't sure you'd come," she says meekly, "After you cast me out like a leopard."

"She means 'leper,'" the doctor corrects.

"It's fine." I say. "I'm so sorry for doing what I did to you."

"Don't be, David. Never apologise for speaking your truth. The way you callously kicked me out of your life was a wake up call. I looked in the mirror after you left and the face staring back at me wasn't mine."

"That's probably because of the facelifts," Dr. Hernandez chimes in.

"Don't you have 'rounds' to do or something?" I ask, unable to hide the prickle in my voice.

The doctor exits silently, pulling the curtain shut.

I go back and focus on my mother.

"You were saying?" I prompt.

"Well, I looked at myself and I thought, 'if David doesn't want me in his life, then I don't want me in my life. I'm a failed mother, a failed actress, he's embarrassed of what I've become: an ugly, disfigured clown hiding the meaninglessness of her pathetic, useless existence beneath layers of makeup and lies. I want to be rid of this cruel circus called 'life' and finally answer Hamlet's one great question. The answer is: 'not to be.'"

"Don't say that, Mum. I thought I'd lost you forever."

"You have, David. After I get out of this antiseptic palace of disease I shan't bother you again. I'll let you live your life without my interference. Susan Wilde is taking her final curtain call and retiring from acting forever."

This is the moment I've waited for. No more acting, no more craziness, no more … all of it. She can just be my mother. We can just be parent and child without the looming spectre of her career casting a shadow on everything. We can connect without the mask between us. It's the words I'd never thought I'd hear her say.

"Mum you can't quit acting," I say. My mouth tastes like a mixture of silver and acid. I can't believe I'm encouraging my mother to do the thing which drives us apart. But the thought of losing her forever is equally terrifying.

As my father used to say: "The lesser of two evils is still evil. But at least it's less."

"Be reasonable, David. I'm past it. There is only one role left for me. Corpse."

"Don't say that."

"No. No David. This is the end. I shall find a cabin with a fireplace, a kettle, and a rocking chair and go into seclusion; my memories will keep me company," she sighs, looking off into the distance. "I might even get a little French bulldog, you know, like the kind we had in the UK."

"Misty?"

"Yes, little Misty, who ran away into the harsh London night."

"She didn't run away Mum, you ran over her with the Vespa," I say.

"Did I? In my weakened state I must have forgotten."

She pulls the damp washcloth back over her eyes while I recall why marijuana and motorised scooters are a recipe for childhood trauma. The worst part was that Mum bribed a local dog walker, who was a fan of the English soap she was on, *South Siders*, to loan her a black French bulldog which she never gave back. Then when I was out walking 'Misty' one day the family of the dog saw me and stole what I thought was my dog away from me. The cops got called and Mum had to charm them into letting us off with a warning. Fortunately the cops were fans of *South Siders* too. But we never had a dog, or a moped again.

"I guess it's for the best. I killed your dog, now I've killed my career," she says. She's sinking deeper into a bitter morass. Soon she'll be suffocating on self-pity, drawing it into her lungs and internally choking herself until she's only able to exhale regret and sorrow.

"Mum, you can't talk like this," I tell her, taking the cloth off her eyes and throwing it at the curtain wall. "You owe it to yourself, and you owe it to me to act again."

She looks at me.

"Yes, to me. I want you to keep acting."

"You never respected my career."

"Of course I respected it. I was just in awe of you, that's why I couldn't show it. You're amazing and I see the way that you affect people. It's mesmerising. You're mesmerising. If I had just an iota of your talent I wouldn't be freaking out about how to start my novel."

I'm realising that there is a little more truth to this impassioned plea than I had anticipated when I opened my mouth.

"You have to keep acting. For my sake, for your sake, for the whole world's sake. Don't hide the light of Susan Wilde under a bushel."

I see the glint in her eye. It's the sparkling stubbornness that would cause any sane person to give up while facing insurmountable odds. It's the I'm-Susan-Wilde-And-I'll-Show-You look that's made many a dark night turn to dawn.

It's the thing inside her that says she's going to prove the world is wrong about her.

Her nostrils flare.

That's a good sign.

"You really think I can keep going, David?"

"Yes."

"You think I still have 'it' in me?"

"Yes!"

"You think I can dazzle audiences, bring them to laughter and tears?"

"Definitely tears."

Mum props herself up on her elbows, colour returning on her face.

"You think I can play late 30s?"

I maintain the unblinking gaze but my mouth is dry and I swallow what little moisture is left.

"… Yes."

The split second of hesitation said too much. We stare directly into each other's eyes, both knowing that I just lied to her.

She flops her head on the pillow and closes her eyes. I drop my head and touch my forehead.

I feel like I am in the digestive tract of a dinosaur.

I'd do anything to cheer her up, to alleviate her pain, to break the negative mental spell. I'd rather have my crazy mother than no mother at all.

"I … I don't know … I just want to rest now …" she finally says.

I stand up. "I'll see the doctor about getting you home."

Dazed, I turn around and exit through the curtain. Dr. Hernandez is standing right there and startles me.

"Doctor, when do you think my mother will be ready for release?"

"She's on a 24 hour watch, so how about 11pm tomorrow?"

"Yeah that should be fine."

"We can schedule her for discharge later if you like?"

"No, no, that should be fine," I say.

He slaps me on the shoulder in an avuncular way as he leads me out of the ward. We push our way through the long corridor. It feels more narrow this time, like the walls have contracted by a few feet.

"The main thing is to get some rest," the doctor says.

"Thanks, but I'm too wound up to sleep." I say, adjusting my horn-rimmed glasses.

We stop right before the sliding doors to reception.

"Take this," the doctor says, he scribbles something on a piece of paper on his clipboard, and hands it to me. It's a prescription for sleeping pills. "If you need them."

The automatic doors part with a mechanical whirr and I'm spat back out into the waiting area.

Katharine stands up when I get out. "How is she?"

I explain the situation, and Katharine hugs me.

"The important thing is that she's ok," Katharine says.

"Yeah," I mumble. I feel even more shaken up now explaining the situation to Katharine.

Katharine offers to drive. The night air is chilly as we walk to the car park and my pyjamas don't afford much protection. I zip up my wind breaker and put my hands in my pockets. I feel the Phantom mask in my left hand pocket and the prescription for sleeping pills in my right.

We get off the elevator on the top level of the parking structure. Melbourne is being gently covered with an overnight mist. The glowing brand name signs on top of the skyscrapers illuminate the damp haze. I throw the prescription out into the night air.

I'll sleep when I get my mum back.

Episode 6

It's been weeks since I've seen my mother. I never thought that *not* seeing my mother would drive me nuts. She's been holed up in our spare bedroom for a month. We put her in there with her luggage, booze, Toblerone, and a brand new pair of Egyptian cotton sheets Katharine recently bought as an anniversary for us. The only time she comes out is to go to the bathroom and she does it so infrequently I'm beginning to suspect that she's got a pee jar in her room. Either that or she's going out the window, which is a little too uncouth even for her; even though the fences are high enough that the neighbours would never see. I wonder what they would think if they did see a former star of *Next Door* going to the toilet behind a bush. No one in the neighbourhood knows that Susan Wilde is my mother.

Our house is a red brick, semi-detached, townhouse at the end of a cobblestone driveway. Pushed back from street view, it's a modern, single story abode on a tree lined street in the Brunswick neighbourhood.

The house is decorated by Katharine in a combination of Swedish designed and op-shop furniture in a style I call Scandinavian Shabby Chic. She's combined the hard edges of Nordic design with hipster-like found objects (which are meticulously cleaned before they enter our house). It's not like Katharine's a neat freak, she just prefers the copies of *Modern Podiatry* magazines to be arrayed in a perfect fan on the coffee table in case a parcel delivery person looks through our front window.

The one room I designed in our house is my study. It has an IKEA desk made up of three parts. Two black sawhorses and one white laminated rectangle of chipboard. There's a lamp and a computer and a cup for pens and notebooks. And that's about it. I am very Zen and minimalist when it comes to my space.

Then there's the garage. Inside are my fixed-gear, flat-handle men's bike, and Katharine's purple six-speed women's, the "his" and "hers" of inner-northside Melbourne living.

Also inside the garage is seven years' worth of stuff.

Anybody who's ever lived indoors knows that over time you accumulate 'stuff'. What kind of stuff? Just stuff. Houses are the perfect breeding grounds for stuff. Especially garages. Their empty spaces and flat floors are like soil and sunlight. Just plant people in the house, add a few boxes as fertiliser and given enough time you've got a perfect hothouse for growing 'stuff'.

People have lots of categories for their stuff: "I'm gonna use that again", "I might use that one day", "I should get rid of this but…" and the "I need that for XYZ" (*insert thing you probably won't do again*).

There are two general categories in our garage: Deal-With-It-Now, and Deal-With-It-Later. It's not good to let things pile up in the Deal-With-It-Now category so I designed a system. Basically, if something is in the Deal-With-It-Now pile for too long it gets shifted into the Deal-With-It-Later category.

That way you don't have to walk around knowing that there is a lot of stuff piling up that requires your immediate attention.

Good system. I designed it all by myself.

However there is something that I do need to deal with now.

"Mum?"

I tap on the spare room door.

"… Mum?" I say.

Katharine and I stand outside the closed bedroom door with a breakfast tray.

"Mum, Katharine made some vegan scrambled eggs. They've got no fat, no salt, no cholesterol. They're … um, delicious?"

Katharine gives me a look.

"Well they were," I say, but Katharine's not buying it. It's a myth that all lawyers are good at lying. The truth is they're great at it. I'm just not a lawyer anymore. Plus I was never any good at it to begin with.

"Are we sure she's even in there?" Katharine asks.

"Trust me this is normal."

"This is normal behaviour?"

I realise my mistake in saying that. She isn't used to 'Susan Wilde normal' yet.

When mum got turned down for a big part back in the day she'd hide in her room for a few days, and I'd have to be quiet until the mood lifted and she came out ready to face the world again. One time in England she even pulled me out of boarding school so I could be quiet around the house while she moped in her room after getting rejected for a West

End revival of *Streetcar Named Desire*. When she came out I went back to boarding school and she went back to work. This time is different though, it's been going on longer than 'normal'.

Katharine has been extremely accommodating and supportive since Mum's moved into the house. The other night we shared a vegetable Pad Thai and Katharine said, "This is what family is all about. We've got to think more like a family now David. It's not just you and me anymore, it's all of us. This is going to be a great bonding experience."

However Katharine's patience has only lasted marginally longer than the leftover Pad Thai.

"How long is this going to last?" Katharine asks, indicating towards the door.

"Depends on what she got at duty free–"

"I mean her staying with us," Katharine says, cutting me off. "Being shut off like this. Drinking. Making us be quiet. This can't be healthy … for the family."

Katharine's right though, things between us have been sensitive since Mum went into lockdown. Tensions have been simmering since yesterday when I asked Katharine to keep it down while vacuuming. Even though I did ask very politely.

"We can't play music, we can't watch action movies, we can't have friends over. I'm hosting the annual party for my graduating class and I might have to cancel. Do you know how embarrassing that is?"

"To host a bunch of podiatrists?"

"Hilarious, David," she says. "You know what isn't funny? You haven't written a word since she's been here. What about your big dream of you being a writer?"

"The dream's alive. I'm just hitting the snooze button on it while I get Mum back on her feet. Plus I've written stuff. I just came up with a few titles. How about this one: *The Girl Who ... did the thing ... with the thing.*"

"Inspired," Katharine says dryly. "This is no way to live. You know we haven't-" Katharine switches to a whisper, "haven't made love since, you know." Katharine nods at the door.

"I know."

"With her around I can't ... unclench." Katharine says through clenched teeth.

"And I want you to unclench, for both of our sakes," I say, "I just need to take care of Mum first."

"I can't live like this, babe."

"Katharine, I'm all she has now. She's got no money, no job, no house, no boyfriend or husband at the moment. There's no light at the end of the tunnel. We need to have some compassion. She could be in there slitting her wrists on the bed."

"What? On the new sheets!" Katharine says in a panic. Then, realising, "I mean, Susan, are you ok?!"

Katharine tries the knob and the door opens.

"Well done," I say. My surprise mixes with relief and I instantly forgive Katharine's callous slip.

I go in and shut the door with my foot, leaving Katharine outside.

I enter the darkened room. The place is trashed, clothes everywhere;,LV patterned luggage strewn about. There are empty Absolut and Johnny Walker bottles. Toblerone, Lindt and Godiva chocolate wrappers scattered about. Open, dried up tubs of Jurlique creams, a half full perfume bottle. It smells like a detoxing alcoholic showering with Chanel N° 5 inside

Willy Wonka's factory.

On the bed lies my mother, Susan Wilde. Hair tangled, one arm in the sleeve of a monogrammed silk robe. She's lying spread eagled in the middle of the bed with a pillow over her face.

"Mum …?" I make my way through the terrain. My footsteps clink in the glass laden underbrush.

She removes the pillow.

"Do you mind? I'm trying to suffocate myself."

"Don't joke about that."

I put the tray on the bed and open the blinds. She squints in pain and puts the pillow over her face.

"Who's joking?" she puts the pillow back over her face.

"You need to eat something," I say, tossing the pillow into the surrounding abyss.

"I can't, I feel sick to my stomach, David," Mum says, pulling an engraved silver hip flask out from the sheets and taking a swig. I grab it out of her hand and take a sniff. It smells like paint thinner.

"Come on mum, You'll bounce back, you're Susan Wilde."

"Not this time David. I'm old and typecast. People only see me as Veronica Chasen from *Destiny's Hope*, and she's dead. Like my career."

"I'm sure there's lots of meaty roles for women in their 50s–"

Mum glares at me.

"40s?"

Mum glares at me.

"Mum, *I'm* in my 30s," I say. I can't play this game beyond the point of logic. I'm not Willy Wonka.

"That is the point, David. There's nothing out there for

women my age. They want you to ooze sensuality until they decide you're too old to be vivacious. Then they put you out to pasture to frolic with the other mares who society deems unworthy of being the object of desire."

"Come on Mum, lots of men still find you attractive."

"David, you have no idea what women my age go through. We still have life in us. It gnaws at the soul when you reach a stage in life when men in the street don't bother to look twice at you, or give you a sideways glance. You become a ghost. People just look right through you to the next generation. That's who producers audition and that's who men yearn for."

I hold my Mum's hand, and wish I could take her pain away. I've heard her confessions before but this one seems more heartfelt.

"Oh David, without my art, what do I have to live for?" she sobs into the pillow.

"Well ... you have ... me."

She sits up in bed suddenly. Breathes in sharply. Touches my shoulder.

"Yes of course, David. And you mean everything in the world to me. That's why I came back, so I could be with you." She touches my face gently. "Now, I'd like to be alone."

She slumps back down.

"Maybe you should get dressed and go outside for a bit. You know, get some sunshine," I say.

"Thanks, but I'm happy here, languishing in memories of forgotten glory and past tri—"

"Mum," I interrupt. "It's impossible for me to work on my novel when I know you're in here like this. So, for your sake and mine, I want you to go outside today."

I clear a spot on the nightstand and put the breakfast tray

on the bedside table. As I stand up, Mum's lighting a rolled cigarette.

"Mum, I told you Katharine doesn't like cigarette smoke."

"Relax. It's marijuana," she says, trying to hold the smoke in.

I yank the joint out of her hand.

"What?" She exhales defensively. "It helps with my appetite. You said I needed to eat something."

"Fine," I say.

I offer her the joint. She reaches for it, but I pull it away.

"But you have to smoke it outside. So you can get some sunshine. Then you have to eat something real. Not Toblerone."

I want to protect her, love her and help her, but she's driving me crazy.

I take a hit off the joint and pass it back to Mum. Then make my way back through the briar patch of bottles, suitcases, and discarded Swiss chocolate triangle tubes.

Katharine is waiting outside the door when I come out.

"So she's ok?" Katharine asks.

I shake my head 'yes'.

"Ok. I'm late for the clinic. You've got basketball tonight?"

I nod my head 'yes'. Katharine kisses me goodbye. She's about to leave but hesitates.

"Do you smell pot?" she asks.

I shake my head 'no' and look bewildered. Katharine goes out the front door which is right next to the spare bedroom. As the door slams I exhale a plume of smoke.

I go to my study and face the blank page.

I try to get into the zone.

The cursor blinks.

I blink.

I can feel the sinking feeling of my deadline getting closer, and the money from my advance running out.

My approach to my new novel so far has been like my room decor, Zen and minimalist. I've basically done nothing. So, extremely minimalist.

My Zen state of mind is disturbed with two equal parts of panic: the novel and Mum. If I can't get cracking there's gonna be trouble. With the publisher, with myself, with my life dreams, with Katharine.

I can't write with her in the house and I can't get her out of the house. I'm suffering in here while she's suffering in there. Alone together. If only there was some way I could take away her pain, so that she could take away my discomfort, and I could write. I'm in a limbo world between failure and success and the thing standing in the middle of the two is my mother.

Then the thought comes: *If she had just killed herself then I wouldn't have to worry about her and I'll have something to write about.*

The sting of guilt is instant. How could I even entertain the idea? Where do these evil thoughts come from?

Say that's an idea, where do they come from ...

My fingers begin tinkling the ivories of the qwerty keyboard:

Where do bad ideas come from, thought Reid McGowan, private eye. They must be cheap, he mused. The market is flooded with 'em and sellers are happy to offload them at a premium. But with anything that comes cheap and easy in this life, there's always a caveat emptor: let the buyer beware.

The words start coming. Suddenly all the problems of my

world evaporate, Mum, Katharine, everything, as I get into the zone. Maybe this will be easier than I thought.

Episode 7

I dribble down the court after taking a rebound. I pass to Anthony, who fires it back to me at the top of the key. I fake left on my defender, and then hit a fade away jump shot.

The whistle blows for half-time, with the Brunswick Peewees leading the Fitzroy Barking Owls, 31–27.

All the Northside Co-ed Community Basketball teams are named after domestic bird species. There's the Coburg Kestrels, the North Carlton Darters, the Thornbury Thrush, and the Moonee Ponds Diamond Firetails. The name Peewees doesn't exactly strike fear into opponents hearts, but I suppose it's better than the Mudlarks, Figbirds, or Crested Shrike-tits.

The rest of the Peewees all congratulate me as we gather on the lower stands for halftime. We're a ragtag group of white collar types including an accountant, a public servant, a dentist, a drama teacher, and, as of today, a professional writer. My artistic energies came alive today and I crushed it like a clove in a garlic press. I could practically smell the juices of the stinking rose of creativity.

Anthony, the tall handsome teacher, slaps me on the back. "You're in the zone tonight, dude."

Joanne, the short accountant, says: "The zone!"

Edina, the well-groomed dentist, slaps me on the back.

Callum, the portly public servant, playfully punches me in the arm, a little too hard. "You're superhuman."

Several other league games continue while we're on half-time break. Basketballs bounce around the gym like molecules in a vacuum. The symphony of the court is a glorious ode to the competitive spirit still burning in men and women of all ages.

We all sit down on the bench.

"It's a team effort guys. We just gotta stay hungry," I say.

"Anybody bring snacks?" Callum says.

"Just stay in the zone, it's what I tell my drama students. In the zone," Anthony tells me.

"Don't worry. Nothing can break my concentration," I say.

"Daa–vid!!!"

The syllables of my name pierce through the bouncing rubber and shoe squeaks on varnished wooden floors. It echoes around the cavernous gym and pierces my eardrum like an arrow hitting a bullseye.

Emerging from nowhere comes my mother. She strides right through all the games as if they didn't exist. Her metamorphosis from depressed caterpillar to confident butterfly is total: Prada pumps, blonde hair straightened, big dark sunglasses, alligator purse, with a knee-length Burberry overcoat.

A point guard, with sports goggles, is so distracted by Mum that he takes an inbound pass to the face, knocking him flat on his back. The rest of the Fairfield Kookaburras are oblivious to his pain.

"Who's that, Dave?" Anthony asks.

I'm too stunned to answer.

I'm glad she's feeling well enough to come out. I just wish

she'd dressed like some of the other mothers.There aren't any other mothers here I realise quickly. Except for the ones playing basketball right now.

I'm focusing on the positive; like Katharine does. Mum is up and feeling good enough to wear clothing that is totally free from vodka and chocolate stains.

Mum reaches the team bench. "Hello darling," and gives me a kiss, getting lipstick on my cheek. "Hi, I'm David's mum. Just thought you kids might like some refreshments."

"Oh, Mum you didn't have to."

Susan dumps some drink boxes and muesli bars out of her purse onto the stands. The team descends like a synchronised diving event.

"It's good to see you fully clothed Mum." I say, as she removes her overcoat, "…ish."

She's wearing a tightly hemmed, low-cut dress that she's practically vacuum sealed into.

"Well it's been great, Mum. Thanks for stopping by–"

"David, I'm here for support."

I pull her aside. "If you want support you could start by wearing a bra," I say.

"I know, but darling, I didn't know if it was formal attire or smart casual for a basketball game."

"Yeah, a lot of people get confused by that," I say, walking further away from people. "The team really needs to focus on the game right now. But, I'm glad to see you're feeling better."

"I am. I got a call from my agent here and I've got an audition with the Victorian Theatre Group."

"That's great. Look at you; VTG is very prestigious."

Mum stares back at me blankly, then says. "It's a whores' nest of actors, David. But it's for a leading role so I couldn't

71

deny them. I'm reading for the part of ... Mrs. Robinson."

"Who?"

"From *The Graduate*, it's a stage adaptation of the movie. Mrs. Robinson, the seductress, the enchantress, the quintessential older woman. I know you are thinking, *she's too young* but this part was made for me."

"That is the best news I've had all day." My instinct is to try and temper her exuberance, to avoid another crash, but I learned from a young age that trying to add a dose of reality to my mother's dreams is dangerous. Mum would accuse me of being a *professional dream squasher*, which seemed to be as horrid a job as being a Nazi or ticket inspector on the train.

"I feel alive again. And I've quit all mind-altering substances. Except white wine ... and Xanax ... and Percocet and valium. But everything else unhealthy, gone," Susan says while she lights a cigarette.

"Mum, you can't do that in here."

"David, I need *some* indulgence, now I've given up everything else. Do you want me to be Amish?"

I look at her, imagining her with a bonnet, a blue dress and a white apron milking a cow. My hopes of her coming back as a humble, nurturing Amish mother disappear into a barrel of churning butter. She's Susan Wilde again. That's for sure.

She drops the Dunhill into someone's polystyrene water cup, as we walk back over to the Peewees.

"Thanks for the bars and juice, Mrs. Hawkes!" Edina says.

"It's actually "Wilde". Ms Wilde." Susan extends her hand in princess handshake to Edina.

"Edina, Joanne, Callum, and Anthony, this is my mother, Susan. She's just gonna watch the game if that's ok."

Everyone nods in agreement.

"Do you have any more snacks?" Callum asks.

"You've had enough, Callum," I say.

"I thought we had to "stay hungry" though?"

"I meant metaphorically," I say.

"I'm feeling ravenous," Edina says, still looking at my mother.

"Ok! So, strategy for the second half, what do you reckon, captain?" I say looking over to Anthony, hoping he'll refocus everyone on the game.

But he doesn't.

"Haven't I seen you somewhere before?" Anthony says to Susan.

"Oh, I don't know … probably," she says coyly.

"You used to be an actor, right?"

The carefully constructed façade Mum put on tonight is holding strong, but I can see the cracks. Her left eye twitches slightly.

"Yeah…" says Callum.

"That's right," Edina chimes in.

"Would I have seen you in anything?" Joanne asks.

More eye twitching.

This is bad. She's gonna spiral again. But I can save this, I've got time.

The whistle blows. The team turn their heads.

"Second half!" the Ref shouts.

"Let's do this!" Anthony shouts.

The team cheers as they run out onto the court.

Mum grabs my arm as her legs buckle.

I sit mum down on the bleachers and run onto the court.

"Ok everyone, let's just keep it together," I say looking back at Mum who's staring into space like an amateur astronomer.

* * *

Katharine is pulling down the blankets to get into bed, as I enter our bedroom. I'm still wearing my basketball clothes and carrying my gym bag. I'm exhausted but it's the good kind of tired.

"I've got good news," I declare.

"First win of the season!" Katharine says hopefully, kissing my cheek. "Congrats."

"No ... no" I sigh, "We got close though." I collapse onto the bed. It feels so good to be in this bed with Katharine. She has the fresh look of just having just removed her makeup and washed her face. She's taken off her mask for the day and is even more beautiful and vulnerable without the protective layer of cosmetics. I see the person I love and gratitude fills me.

"What are you looking at?"

"Oh nothing, sorry."

"Do I have something on my face?"

"No, it's just..."

"Why are you staring at it then?"

"I'm not, I was just ... look, it doesn't matter. The good news: Mum's got an audition," I say excitedly.

The news doesn't land the way I expected.

"I said she has an audition."

"Uh-huh."

"If she gets this part, she'll be performing every night, and a matinée on the weekends. No more drinking, no more crying; no more crying and drinking. She'll be back on her feet again, we won't have to worry about her."

"We can get our life back on track. I can host my Podiatry

meet-ups, we can talk about kids, and you won't be blocked creatively."

"Already happening. I had a major breakthrough today."

"That's wonderful babe. See, you don't have to be controlled by your mother's moods after all."

She kisses me like she thinks she's given me a compliment. But it's really not.

"What the hell does that mean?" I say.

"It just, I mean," Katharine stammers. "It's just that, you are, how do I put this, very sensitive, when it comes to how your mother's feeling."

"Is trying to be a loving son so wrong?"

"No, it's just–"

"Do you think I'm some sort of hostage to my mother's emotional state?!"

"That wasn't the precise sentiment I was trying to articulate with my inference," Katharine says, in her nervous technical-speak.

"I'm my own man. I do, and feel and behave exactly how I want. I'm me, I'm David Hawkes."

"I'm just trying to help you find a new way to look at things."

"I'm looking at things!" I'm getting way more worked up than I wanted to tonight. Maybe it's that we lost the basketball game after giving up 27 unanswered points, or the fact that I couldn't make a single bucket in the second half, or maybe because Mum distracted everyone by showing up dressed as if it was Fashion Week in Paris.

As my father always used to say: "Just apologise son."

"Look, I'm sorry. I just thought you'd be more excited with the news about Mum. I'm sorry."

"David, you can't have an expectation of how I'm going to

react to things. We've talked about this. Remember that for next time."

"You're right. Sorry."

"Plus, it's just an audition. And you can stop apologising."

"Sorry, I'll stop." Then I add, "But, it is a start. If she gets the job she'll get her own place, we can have our place back to ourselves. We can all be happy together … separately."

Katharine says strokes my hair. "That would be good," she says.

"It's a start."

"So we can make noise again?"

"As much as we want."

"Is she home now?"

"No. She went out for a drink with the guys after the game." I say, rolling my eyes.

"You know, I think I'm starting to *unclench*."

Katharine starts kissing me. I touch her shoulder and lean into the kiss. It's been too long since we kissed like this. I'm reminded of the time we first kissed in my old Mazda. I leaned in for the goodnight kiss but forgot to take my seat belt off and got caught halfway, lips pursed, looking like a freeze frame at the end of an 80s movie. She met me halfway and I knew I'd found someone special.

We caress each other, lean back, and get ready to have a combination of make-up sex and reunion sex.

"David, darling!" Mum sings out, as she barges into the room without knocking.

Katharine is so startled she falls off the bed.

"Jesus, Mum. Can I help you?" I say, startled as well.

"Yes, thank you for asking," Mum says, and sits on the bed. She hands me some papers.

I awkwardly cross my legs. Basketball shorts are the worst clothing to hide an erection.

Mum is still wearing the same outfit.

"What's this?" I say, strategically placing the papers on my lap. I look down and see lines of dialogue.

"Preparation. I need to get started right away," Mum declares looking at her nails.

"I'm fine. Thanks for asking," Katharine says, getting up from beside the bed.

"I can't now. It's our bedtime," I say.

"This'll be fun. Remember the joyous times we had when you were a child, I would let you stay up late so you could help me recite lines?"

"I remember me reciting lines while you snorted lines," I say.

"What was this?" Katharine asks.

I must not have told Katharine these little episodes.

"It was just a little Adderall to help me concentrate," Mum says as an explanation to Katharine. "After all, that Psychiatrist boyfriend I had in LA thought I had undiagnosed ADD."

"He said NPD: Narcissistic Personality Disorder. I told him I knew I—"

"I, I, I, can you talk about anyone but yourself, David? You are just like him. That's why I stopped seeing him. And broke up with him."

I take a deep breath.

"Mum, I'm not doing this now. I'll help you in the morning."

Katharine resumes her place on the bed, as Mum looks directly into my eyes. Her voice goes quiet.

"David, I ask for so little. I need this part." she works her way up into a pleading crescendo. "Please, David, please,

please, please–"

"Fine! Once through, then bed." I'm placating her, but I'm only doing it because it's the only way to get her out. I make my own decisions.

"Katharine, if you could be a doll and read the stage directions," Mum says. She stands up quickly and starts doing lip trills, rolling her shoulders, and shaking her hands like a sorceress who can't get the magic spell to come out of her fingers.

Katharine can't believe the circus side show that has invaded our bedroom.

"Ok," Susan says, putting her left hand just beneath her breasts.

Katharine starts: "Um … Exterior, a poolside setting–"

"I meant 'ok', time for my breathing exercises," Mum snaps and breathes in sharply with her stomach muscles.

"Mum!"

"You know I have to warm up my diaphragm, David."

Dammit. She's right, but I can't let her know it. She botched the audition for a *Mad Max* movie because she didn't warm up properly.

"Do you have any idea how uncomfortable it is to have a cold diaphragm inside you?" Mum continues.

"Let's leave it to the imagination," I say. I want to help her but I also want to get to bed before 2am. Plus there might still be sex still on the table. Though my hope is waning thin.

"Let her warm up, David," Katharine says, defending Mum for some reason.

"Thank you, Kathy."

Mum inhales deeply and holds it, while Katharine bristles at being called 'Kathy'.

We all wait with bated breath for what seems like an eternity.

"Mum. The scene. Now."

"Fine, we'll blow off the breathing exercises," Mum exhales. "Carry on Katharine love."

Katharine starts in again: "A poolside setting–"

Susan's phone rings.

"Sorry, I have to take this," mum says, sticking the phone to her ear, walking out, and closing the door. "Arnold, dearest; tell me good things," we hear echoing down the hallway.

There is a moment of stunned silence.

"... Is she coming back?" Katharine asks.

I give her a look to say, 'I don't know'. I go in for a kiss. I get one. I go in for something more and get denied.

"The moment's lost, isn't it?"

Katharine gives me a look of sadness and nods her head 'yes'.

"No chance of getting it back."

Katharine grimaces and shakes her head 'no'.

"So you're clenched?"

"Yeah."

"Please?" I beg.

"Go take a shower," she says gently pushing me.

I grab my towel and she grabs the novel she's reading, *My Left Foot*. One of several books on her nightstand she's working through.

As I take a cold shower it occurs to me that living with my mother and girlfriend may pose more challenges than previously thought.

It also occurs to me that I may never have sex again if I don't find a way to help her get this part in *The Graduate*. I'm already suffering from a medical condition known as DSB (Debilitating Semen Backup) which causes the male mind to do stupid things like thinking that begging for sex is a turn on, or that whispering 'are you awake' amounts to pillow talk.

If the DSB gets worse though I might not be able to focus and write like I did today. I can't miss my deadline. The money I have saved up from my advance and from lawyering will only last me about a year.

I can't be like my mother with her career in a state of crisis. I've got to get her back on her feet for both of our sakes. I think of a mantra. By helping her I am helping myself.

If she fails then I fail. And that can't happen. Mum is going to get that part.

Episode 8

I am sitting at the computer typing away. I got up early this morning to start on the novel. There's nothing more inspiring than seeing dark skies, hearing chirping birds, and feeling the rumble of the rubbish collector's truck to get the creative juices flowing.

As my father used to say: "Writing is hard work, but it beats working."

It also helps to have a full bodied Panamanian coffee blend fueling me. I'm on my fourth cup already and it's not even 10 o'clock. Maybe I need to slow it down. Or maybe I need another coffee …?

The combination of caffeine and fingers tinged in butter from the cold toast I'm eating are a potent potion for productivity.

My phone rings. I answer without looking at the number.

"How's my favourite author doing?" A Northern Irish voice booms down the other end of the line.

"He's busy writing," I say.

"That's what I like to hear."

It's my Belfast-born editor, Deirdre Slocum. She's the most supportive, nurturing, caring, and completely impatient person I've ever had the pleasure to displease. She championed me at Hepburn Publishing and was the first person in the literary field to identify me as a 'talent'. She was also the first person in the literary field to throw a book at my head. She was pissed off because I missed a manuscript deadline. Supposedly the level of anger is directly proportional to the size of the book she throws at you. Slightly miffed equals a children's book; a Maurice Sendak or a Bill Peet. Peeved, a shorter novel, *The Great Gatsby* or *Animal Farm*. Really angry, *Catch-22*, or *The Thorn Birds*. The classic Russian authors were reserved for apoplectic rage. I recently got hit with *Notes From Underground*, a novella by Dostoyevsky. So, a bit of a mixed message there.

I've never met anyone like Deirdre who cares so deeply and passionately about literature and the process of writing prose. I also suspect she's a former member of the IRA.

Her personality is like a car bomb in a Porsche. Amazing exterior but you never know what's going to happen when you turn the engine over. She is encouraging and insightful as an editor while also teetering on the edge of a conniption fit if drafts are turned in late.

"I'm expecting those chapter outlines on my desk in a fortnight," Deirdre says, biting into what sounds like an apple.

"The plotting is going great," I lie. Deirdre likes things to be done in a very logical fashion. If I told her that I sat down at the computer yesterday when inspiration hit and started typing with no plan, she'd remove my pancreas with a claw hammer. Probably without sterilising the area beforehand.

"That's grand," she says, crunching into the apple again. "People say the second novel is the more difficult novel, but they can just blow it out their arses. The Reid McGowan character is great and if anyone says anything different, you just make sure and tell me, cause, I'll be paying them a visit and yanking their balls like a bell chord."

She takes another chomp into her apple.

"That's … reassuring."

"I just want you to know I'm in your corner."

I've never known anyone who related books to battle as much as Deirdre Slocum does.

"This book's gonna be deadly," Deirdre says, which I think means good. "By the way, have you ever had a jazz apple before?"

"I don't think so."

"Jazz is musical wankery but their apples are good craic. Anytime I meet someone who listens to jazz I want to put some gelignite under the bonnet of his car. Now, I want you to give me a synopsis of the book so far."

Shit.

"David! Daa–vid!" I hear from another room.

I've never been so glad to hear my mother's voice.

"Hold on a tick," I say to Deirdre, "What is it mum? This better be important. I'm on the phone with my editor."

I cover the receiver with my hand.

"Darling, I need help making an espresso."

"Deirdre, I've gotta go. My mum needs me for something that just can't wait."

"You're living with you ma, Dave? I thought you'd saved enough to take time off."

"No, no, no. She's moved in with me," I say. "Temporarily. She's had a health scare."

"I hope she's ok? You know you never talk about her."

"David!" I hear again.

"I've got to go, Deirdre."

83

I hang up and go to the kitchen.

Susan Wilde is sitting at the dining table with three cups of coffee in front of her smoking a cigarette. Smoke and steam curl up together towards the ceiling creating a double helix of Java and tobacco. The DNA of my youth.

"Hello darling," she beams at me. Mum has on a black dress with a white trim around the edges.

"You can't smoke in here, Mum."

"That's fine. I decided to give up. One must be in one's best shape for an audition."

She takes a drag and drops it into one of the cups.

"I thought you needed help with the stovetop?"

"Come on David, I'm not completely clueless. Remember I used to send you to school every morning with a double shot mocha in your thermos?"

"Yeah, my kindergarten teacher thought I had ADD."

"And I was so grateful you shared your Adderall with me. Now let's rehearse, like you promised."

Mum slides some papers to me across the table as I sit down.

"You didn't have to trick me into coming out here. I'm happy to help."

"You always were such a good son. How did I get so lucky?" She puts her hand on top of mine.

Sunlight streams through the glass window illuminating the kitchen.

This takes me back. My entire youth I was her scene partner, as we moved back and forth from Australia to England to America. I learned to read using scripts from the various soap operas, plays, and movies she was in. They were always around the house. Mum venerated writers, and she treated their words like religious texts. And because our membership and attendance at various synagogues around the world were so haphazard I often conflated the two. I recall going between studying my haftorah portion for my bar mitzvah and Shakespeare's 'Battle of Agincourt' speech from *Henry V*. I think I was the only kid in my bar mitzvah class who said 'Shalom my band of brothers' from the bimah.

Susan slides a cup of coffee over to me.

"Just a pinch of sugar, to take the edge off," she says.

She's right. I'm surprised that she remembers this. She can't even remember Katharine hates being called anything but Katharine, but she remembers this intimate little detail.

I take a sip.

And gag.

"Sorry, that's mine with the sweetener in it."

I can't stand artificial sweeteners, they taste like candy coated flecks of rat bait.

"That's ok, Mum. I probably don't need another coffee right now anyway. I've had three already this morning."

"True. Coffee is not good for your ADD love, remember what your teacher said? Now, you're reading the part of Benjamin Braddock. I'm playing Mrs. Robinson, his father's business partner's wife who is bored with her safe suburban life. She hates the middle class repression and is aching to break out of her stultifying conformity and really live."

"Yes. I kinda remember the movie."

"This is the scene where I, as Mrs. Robinson, am seducing you, Benjamin, for the first time. Now, my dearest, I know you're not an actor, but it would help me if you could just try to pretend that you're uncomfortable with this situation. Sexually speaking."

"It shouldn't be hard."

I say my new mantra: by helping her I am helping myself.

"Have you done your warm ups?" I ask.

Mum sits, shoulders back and down. "Vocal cords lubricated, diaphragm warm," she says. "And … curtain up!"

I read from the script: "You've got me into your lounge. You're giving me drinks, and you say your husband won't be home 'til later. Are you trying to seduce me, Mrs. Robinson?"

"Cut!"

"What's the problem?"

"I forgot my Meisner warm-ups," she says, pulling her hair back and standing up.

My shoulders slump down. Mum stands up. I look at my watch, it's not there. I forgot I gave it to Katharine to hold when I went into the emergency department. I repeat my new mantra: by helping her I am helping myself.

"You said you did your warm-ups," I say.

"This is called the Repetition Exercise."

"The what?"

"Do I have to say everything more than once?"

I roll my eyes.

Mum motions for me to stand.

"It's simple," she continues, "I am going to 'come in' and you are going to say something about my physical appearance, then I'll repeat it, then you say the same line again, and I repeat it again, etc. etc. And we have to stare directly into each other's eyes."

Susan mimes coming in a door and looks at me.

"You … have a black dress on," I say.

She hesitates.

"Don't you want to say something about how I look? Maybe something about how amazing my hair looks today." It's a question that's not a question.

"Your hair looks amazing today."

"My hair looks amazing today."

"Your hair looks amazing today."

"My hair looks amazing today."

"Your hair looks amazing today."

This is getting truly tedious.

"My hair looks…" There is an extremely long pause, "amazing today."

"How long are we gonna do this for?"

"Until the exercise is complete, David," she snaps at me.

"My editor is pressing me for chapter outlines which I haven't even started. So if we could just maybe hurry this up a bit!"

"Hurry? David, we have a full rehearsal today. Six hours, then notes, then a glass of red at Pollock's on Little Lonsdale. Now again. 'My hair looks amazing today.'"

"That is ludicrous! I'm not spending the whole day repeating a phrase about how amazing your hair looks–"

"We can use that anger."

"I'm not angry!"

Susan Wilde instantly snaps into character.

"I just want to tell you something."

She throws herself against an imaginary door, blocking my exit.

And I'm in the scene, before I could even realise it, I'm in it, and in deep.

Mum runs her hand across my chest.

"Benjamin, just know this, I am available … to you."

"Oh my god."

"We can make some other arrangement, if you're not

comfortable sleeping with me now."

"Oh ok."

"Understand me?"

"Yes. Now let me out."

I go to leave. Mum keeps blocks my path.

"Do you get what I'm saying, Benjamin."

Mum touches my face in a very sensual way.

"Let me out! Let me out!"

"You're very attractive to me."

"Let me out, Mum," I say, trying to get around her again.

"Don't break character, David."

"I mean let me out of this scene!" I say sitting down and panting for air. This is too weird even for our fucked up family. "I can't do this."

"This scene is vital to my audition and we were just about hitting the climax. You can't pull out at the last second."

"I'm aware of that," I say, avoiding eye contact.

I repeat my mantra: by helping her I'm helping myself. I just didn't realise that helping myself would border on incest. I've got to help her land this part, but I also can't afford to run lines six hours a day. If I fall behind on my manuscript Deirdre will hit me with a barrage of *War and Peace*, *Brothers Karamazov*, *Anna Karenina*, and the Macquarie Dictionary. What's scarier? An irate ex-IRA editor hounding me for the draft of a book I'm behind on, or the prospect of my mother living with me for the rest of her life?

Sisyphus had it easy. He only had to push a rock up a hill in Hades for all eternity.

"I can't do this on my own, David," Mum pleads with me, desperation in her eyes. "I'm like a ship without a rudder, drifting upon a sea of uncertainty; purposelessly floating to nowhere, without a compass to guide me. Seagulls and albatrosses circle above."

"I get it. Just, stop the metaphor already. I'll pay for an acting coach."

The face of Susan Wilde transforms from sadness to joy in an instant.

"Oh, brilliant. I shall also require a dialect coach, a scene study partner, and a dramaturg."

"You can have *one* acting coach. My friend, Anthony, from basketball, he's a drama teacher."

"You mean that insolent little twerp with the brain of a platypus?"

"He's on school holidays at the moment. Plus, he's getting divorced so he could probably do with the extra money."

I don't really have the money to spend on hiring an acting coach but I'll do this for her. This shortens my runway financially but it may lengthen my lifespan.

"I'll only work with someone proficient in the Meisner technique," Mum says, turning her back on me and crossing her arms. "Does he know the Repetition Exercise?"

"I'm sure he'll repeat stuff to you all day long as long, as he's getting paid."

"Pardon?"

"I said, I'm sure he'll repeat stuff to you all day long, as long as he's getting paid."

"What?"

"I said, I'm sure he'll—ok —I see what's happening here. I'm calling Anthony now," I tell her. "No more repetition. Don't make me say it again."

By helping her I'm helping myself, I say to myself over and over again.

At least this will solve the problem. She gets the help she needs and I get to write.

* * *

I'm back to work now.

I am sitting at my computer. Staring.

The computer is on, the screen is on, my brain is off.

I'm finally free to do exactly what I want and I can't do it.

I feel guilty that Anthony is in the other room with Mum helping her with the audition.

I know Anthony will do a good job with Mum. He's a good drama teacher. I saw the student production of *Fiddler on the Roof* he directed and it was one of the best high school performances I've ever seen. I've got to let go and let Anthony do his job with Mum, even though he probably doesn't know that she likes her scene partner to leave a little gap after saying their lines and to always have a pot of chamomile tea (with honey) ready in case her throat gets itchy.

No, let it go.

She's had her time, now it's my time.

It's time to focus on me and my career. She taught me to follow my passion no matter how hard things seem at times. I've put my dreams on hold for too long now. I'm following my passion in my room, while she's following her passion in her room with a guy my age who can do what I used to do with her but only better because he's a qualified dramaturg.

Back to work.

I hit the "J" key on the keyboard with a dull thud of my index finger.

The sound isn't inspiring.

I sometimes wish that I could have been a writer during the age of typewriters. The squeak in keys, the splat of ink staining the paper, the ding of the carriage return reverberating in the Bakelite body. The writer as the conductor of the symphony of prose.

Whenever my mind wanders to typewriters, it makes me think of the intense focus required to work on them. There is something single minded about typewriters. They only do one thing. There are no distractions on a typewriter. You push a key and that mechanised hammer is propelled out from the primordial soup and … WHAM … there's a letter …on the page. It's there. It exists. Forever. You can't erase it. There's no spell check. There's no delete key. If you forget to put the 'p' in pneumonia you have to retype the whole page.

I just talked myself out of my own nostalgia.

Back to work.

On my computer. That has spell check. But just in case I have a dictionary. Where is it? I look over to the bookshelf.

Back to work!

Looking down from the screen I see a little green figurine. It's Amoghasiddhi, a meditation Buddha that Mum got me when we were in Vietnam. He's been on my desk the entire time, but he's just been covered up by notes and papers and other pieces of desk detritus. I move my lamp out of the way and put Amoghasiddhi front and centre underneath the computer monitor.

I'm finally getting started on the chapter outlines that Commander Deirdre ordered me to get done. I take a sip of water and start in.

"Red lorry, yellow lorry, red lorry, yellow lorry."

Vocal warm-ups penetrate the walls from my mother's

room.

"Lipity tippity lipity tippity!"

The noises continue.

"Irish wrist watch."

We're onto the tongue twisters now.

"Should saucy sharks seek shelter soon?"

Every time I am about to start typing something. I hear another vocalisation from the other room. Years of smoking have done nothing to diminish my Mother's lung capacity or projection. Her voice cuts right through the sheetrock and insulation, and reverberates around in my study.

Susan Wilde is now a weapon of mass disruption.

The warm-up exercises continue into the afternoon as I try to type in vain. Every keystroke is followed by some new sound. Animal sounds, machine sounds, imitations of musical instruments. Does Anthony even know what the hell he's doing? Enough with the warm-ups already. She's warm, in fact she's probably blazing hot by now. Why the hell don't they just run the lines? I prepared her for a Shakespeare audition with only a day's notice. Has he even given her any chamomile tea?

It's just a basic lack of respect for her ... and for me. I'm trying to follow my dreams here and it's impossible with Anthony wearing out Mum's vocal chords and making her do spirit animal exercises.

Every wasted minute getting me closer to Deirdre's wrath by projectile paperback.

I punch the keyboard.

Alhfketawiorufjwefinobwpergh. It's the first thing I've written all afternoon.

I march down the hall.

I need to say something to someone.

Episode 9

I knock on the door. It opens.

"Unbelievable!" I say, as I barge in.

Katharine is taken aback as I brush past her into the consultation room.

I am at Katharine's podiatry surgery. I had to get out of the house and talk to her otherwise I was going to do something that I would regret.

Katharine looks professional, wearing her freshly starched white coat, hair pulled back tightly in a Japanese topknot held together with large decorative chopsticks.

"I can't get any work done," I carry on. "None! The interruptions are constant. It's a total invasion of my work place; do you know what that's like, Katharine? Do you know?"

Katharine just stares at me.

"Mr. Weir, this is my boyfriend David. David, this is Mr. Weir … my patient."

I notice a portly, balding man, sitting in the examination chair. Socks and shoes off. His toenails are blacker than the blackest black.

I adjust my horn-rimmed glasses.

"Pleasure to meet you."

"Same here, mate."

There's an awkward pause. He picks at his toenails

"So that fungicide should clear everything up, Mr. Weir," Katharine says, taking off her latex gloves with two clean snaps.

"Thank you, Doctor." Mr. Weir puts on his shoes and socks. There is complete silence as I stare at the ground and Katharine stares at me staring at the ground. He goes to leave.

"Nice to meet you," I say.

"Same here, mate."

We both stick our hands out and shake as he heads out the door.

The second he's gone I rush over to the little sink and start doing my best Howard Hughes impression under the running water. I work the soap into a furious frothy lather and go at it with the nail brush.

"Katharine, I am so sorry."

"That's ok. It's only highly unprofessional."

"I shouldn't have barged in like that."

"I'm getting used to it."

"It's just Mum. She's rehearsing in the house with Anthony and I can't focus to save my life."

I dry my hands with a paper towel and toss it in the bin.

"Why don't you just write in a café."

"I can't write in a cafe, it's too distracting, with all those other wannabe writers sitting around with their laptops and lattes pretending to be working. I need to be home."

"Well, there's the other obvious solution."

"Fire Anthony and do it myself."

"'Fire Anthony'? Are you paying him?"

"Yeah, I hired him as an acting coach. His school production of *Fiddler on the Roof* was really good."

"You didn't think to consult me about this?"

"Katharine, I did it for us. I want Mum to get this part so she can get back on her feet financially. So we can get on with our lives. Together."

"And we can look at potentially buying some property ... together."

"Sure. Maybe. I don't know. Like, whatever. The main thing is that Mum gets this part. Maybe you're right, maybe I should be the one to help her prep. It would save money."

"You could just try talking to her. You know, work through whatever feelings you're both having about the situation in a calm, rational manner."

"Oh, when did that ever solve anything?" I say despondently. I perch on the front end of Katharine's blonde oak desk and look at my shoes.

"David ..."

"Ok, I'll talk to her." I know she's right. "But Mum's in a vulnerable place. I don't want to push her too hard after she tried to take her own life."

"Don't worry about that right now."

I look up and see Katharine has unbuttoned the top of her blouse and pulled her white doctor's coat back.

"You just need to relax. You're pent up." Katharine removes my glasses and plays with my dusty blond hair.

We kiss. She pushes back from me and removes the chopstick from her hair like a samurai warrior unsheathing swords from behind their back. She shakes her head, allowing her brown locks to fall around her shoulders.

Katharine is rarely ever this forward, sexually speaking.

"You're right," I blurt out. This is definitely what I need to regain focus. "I'm pent up."

"We both are," she whispers in my ear.

"What do you suggest, Doctor?" I say coquettishly.

I give myself a mental high five for saying the smoothest thing that I have ever said in my entire life. I can't believe this is really happening.

"I think you're going to need a full pelvic examination, Mr …?"

"Johnson," I say, "Ace, Johnson."

"Well, Ace, can I call you Ace?" Katharine says as she yanks the tong out of my belt loop and unzips my trousers. They fall to the ground with a clink. "I think a thorough examination is the only thing that's going to relieve your throbbing tension."

"I don't know if we should be doing this Doctor. It seems 'highly unprofessional.'" I say going to work on the remaining buttons on her blouse.

"What the APA don't know won't hurt 'em."

"APA?"

"Australian Podiatry Association."

"Yes … of course, them. Do they punish naughty doctors?"

"Only ones that are clenched. Fortunately, right now, I'm completely unclenched."

I begin to grow beneath my boxer shorts.

She undoes another button and rubs my face against her breasts. It feels like my face is going over speed bumps, but I don't want to break the flow.

We kiss like high schoolers behind the bike shed. Barely coming up for air.

"Wait," I pant, "Someone could come in."

"Lock the door, Ace," Katharine orders as she unhooks the front clasp on her bra.

I push myself off the desk and shuffle over to the door, my pants around my ankles. As I move my penis pokes through the hole in my boxers. I reach for the knob, the doorknob that is, with eyes zeroed in on the lock button.

Suddenly the door swings inwards.

My jungle cat-like reflexes kick in and I leap backwards. I neatly evade my hand, or any other part of my body, getting hit by the door.

However while stumbling backward, pants around my ankles, I step on Katharine's chopsticks and I slip and fall to the ground.

I lie with my hard wood on the hardwood. At least I've been able to maintain my dignity. I feel a cool rush of air blowing in along my backside.

"David, darling?" My mother's voice. "Oh my stars, David! Did I hit you?!"

I grunt something, but it's not English.

"My dearest," Mum says, as I feel her hand touch the small of my back. "Why are your pants— Oh dear, have interrupted something?"

"No!" Katharine stops Mum from finishing the sentence. "We were just … um …" Katharine can't finish her sentence.

The commotion attracts the other podiatrists and patients. I hear their footsteps as they gather round. Murmurs of 'are you ok' and 'is everything all right' come drifting in. I look up at Katharine, who has covered herself strategically with her white coat. I can tell she wants to come and help me off the floor, but if she uncrosses her arms her coat will open exposing her chest. So she stands there hesitantly shifting her slight frame back and forth, not knowing how to deal with this Susan Wilde situation.

"My beautiful boy. How can you ever forgive my unpardonable intrusion? I've interrupted your lovemaking."

"That's not what's happening," Katharine lies.

"No, she's right," Susan chimes in, "I'm just here because I need cash."

"He was just, um, he wanted my medical opinion on a fungus he has on his, on his, on his, penis. And then he slipped on this chopstick," Katharine explains to the growing crowd in the hallway. She reaches down with one hand and holds up the chopsticks. Ladies and gentlemen of the jury, Exhibit 'A'.

"David, do you have penis fungus?" my mother asks.

I can either admit that we were about to have sex in Katharine's office risking her career, her reputation, and our financial stability, or admit to her colleague's and clientele that I have a fungal growth on my nether parts.

"Yeah, I do," I mutter.

"What was that honey?" mum asks.

"I said I do have fungus penis!"

"You better let me see it."

"No!" I shout. "I mean, that's ok. It's nothing really."

Katharine looks at me, wide eyed, pursed lips.

"I mean, it is *something*," I stammer, "It's pretty disgusting, actually."

"It looks like lichen spores on an acorn," Katharine blurts out.

A nauseous collective groan comes from the crowd who slowly disperse.

Susan pushes my legs inside the door and closes it. "If you'll excuse us, this is a private matter."

A patient hangs back. "Don't I know you from somewhere?" the woman says to mum. They talk through the partially open door.

"Potentially."

"You used to be on TV."

"I admit I have graced the small screen on more than one occasion," my mother glows.

"You were in those Polaroid commercials with Jack Thompson."

I wait to see how Mum reacts to this one.

Those commercials ran for years and were so popular for their on-screen chemistry, so palpable, that people actually thought the two of them were romantically involved. A rumour my mother never bothered to deny even though it wasn't true. The truth was she hated doing them and hated Jack Thompson. Mainly because he refused to sleep with her. Apparently his polyamorous relationship with the King sisters was monogamous.

But those commercials paid for my braces. Mum always reminded me that if it weren't for Polaroid I would not have a smile worth capturing on film.

"You never focus, you just press the button," says Mum, sponging on the attention.

"It's so easy," the woman chimes in, quoting Jack Thompson's tagline.

If only that were the tagline for the relationship with my mother.

"Are you still in touch with Jack?" the woman asks.

"Christmas cards mainly," my mother lies. She closes the door.

Katharine has buttoned herself back up, but I continue to stare at the parallel grain running through the hardwood floor. My hip is aching from where I fell on the ground.

Katharine and my mother lift me under my armpits and sit me in the examination chair. "No mum!"

"Oh please David, I've seen it before."

They help me get my trousers on. I don't fight it.

"Oh my," Susan says with astonishment. "David, I don't know if you know this, but you have a rather large penis."

"Mum!"

"Can't a mother be proud of her son?"

"It's not that big."

"Trust me, it is," she says.

"I don't think this is an appropriate discussion to have in a doctor's surgery," Katharine says.

"You mean the type that you have sex in during the middle of the working day?" Susan says.

Katharine blushes.

"I'm only joking, love," Susan continues.

"Why are you even here, Mum? How did you know I was here?"

Susan doesn't answer me. She sits on the desk, checking her nail polish using Katharine's magnifying glass and changes the subject. "You know when you're so close to something you can feel it. But then it slips away."

Katherine looks at me. "Vaguely …" she says.

"This audition, I'm having doubts. I can see myself as Mrs. Robinson, the sultry siren, the alluring embodiment of raw sexual power, but …" she sighs.

"What can we do to help, mum?" I sigh back. I know this script.

"No, no, I've imposed too much upon you already."

"It's fine, Mum, what is it?"

"No, no, I'll let you get back to your passions. The kind I

can only dream of recreating in front of people … on opening night."

She heads for the door and reaches for the knob.

"We're happy to help, Susan," Katharine chimes in.

Susan wheels around on her heels.

"Just two hundred dollars, for some more coaching sessions."

I pull out my wallet and hand her cash.

"And another 50 for cab fare," she adds.

"I'll drive you home," I say standing up. I pull Katharine to the side and go to kiss her goodbye. "We can pick this up later can't we?"

"Let's talk when I get home," Katharine says, which is her way of saying 'no'.

I'm crestfallen.

"Now that I know you have penis fungus I'm not sure that I'm as attracted to you as I once was," Katharine smirks.

"It's good to know that my humiliation is your punchline."

At least we can laugh at the pain and suffering which is family.

Katharine kisses me goodbye then pulls me close. "Just be ready, later" she whispers in my ear. Then Katharine says, "I think we'll have salad for dinner tonight, is that ok Susan?"

I look up to see Susan taking Katharine's cruelty free perfume from the top desk drawer, sniffing it and spritzing herself with it.

"Sounds divine, dear. Shall we go David?" Mum says, walking out the door and continuing to sniff her wrist.

As we're in the car driving home I ask Mum: "How did you even know I was at the clinic?"

"I put the Find My Friends app on your phone," she says

matter of factly. Mum puts down the sun visor and uses the mirror to touch up her makeup.

"But I have a—"

"3875. Your Starfleet Academy badge number."

Dammit. Am I a lot more predictable than I think?

"It's not that I need to know where you are at all times, I just need to know where you are when I need you," she says, reapplying her lipstick.

I feel the sudden urge to swerve the wheel so her lipstick goes all over her face. But I restrain myself. Lashing out randomly isn't going to make me less predictable, it's only going to make me vindictive.

"I can almost see my name on the marquee now. You have to really see yourself in the role. That's one of the visualisation exercises Anthony has me doing."

"Is it a silent visualisation?" Because otherwise you need to find somewhere else to practise."

"It's called rehearsal."

"It's called loud."

"You have to block out everything when you're doing your art, David. When you're serving the higher purpose of expressing your soul you have to ignore the purely superficial. Now how does my makeup look?"

"It looks good," I say genuinely. Mum was always good at applying makeup in the car. I remember many mornings when she'd be driving me to school while using the rearview mirror to apply her makeup. I never realised how unsafe that was until right now. "I'm just asking you to tone it down a little, while I'm trying to write."

"Don't you get it David. I'm fighting for my life out there as a woman over a certain age. You have no idea the prejudice

I'm faced with on a daily basis. I'm a minority now that I'm old-er."

"You are not a minority, you're just overreacting."

"Don't gaslight me, I have been dealing with this for decades."

"You can't have been dealing with this for decades."

"Time is an illusion when you're being discriminated against, David."

Time. I look down at the dashboard clock, which for some reason, isn't working. I tap on it. But it's broken.

"Plus, we're Jewish, which is a minority."

"Fine. You're a minority. We both are. But I have to put my foot down on this, Mum. You can't rehearse in the house anymore."

We sit in silence for a few minutes as we drive past the Northcote Cemetery. As the light comes through the car window Mum looks like a broken doll. My heart breaks a little bit seeing her like this, the weight of her own expectations on herself is like gravity crushing the mass of her fading stardom.

Mum breaks the silence.

"No, no, it's all clear now. Susan Wilde's best days are behind her. Pull the car over here."

"Why?"

"It's a cemetery. I'll just lie down there until I die."

Mum grabs the wheel and pulls it over towards the curb. We scare the living daylights out of a jogger who jumps out of the way.

"Jesus Mum. Fine. You can use the house, just keep it down."

"Ok, David, I promise. We're finished warming up now anyway. The next few days we're really going to attack the text."

This is meant to reassure me, but it doesn't.

To her credit though my mother keeps her word and I don't hear much for the rest of the afternoon. I am able to write and get back on track. We have a pleasant dinner of Caesar salad, one of Katharine's specialties. We avoid any discussion of what happened in the podiatry clinic earlier today.

Later, when I'm brushing the anchovy out of my teeth, I hear Katharine calling: "How's that new toothpaste?" from the bedroom.

I come in to see Katharine, in her silk pyjamas, sitting up in bed reading *Feet First,* a biography of Everett Dunbar, the inventor of orthotic inserts.

"It tastes like bat guano."

"It's cruelty free."

"Not for the people using it," I say.

"It means it's not tested on animals."

"Probably because the animals refused to put it in their mouths."

"How about I knock your teeth out and you won't need to brush anymore?" she says smiling.

"Genius."

I jump on the bed and go to kiss Katharine, but I land on my hip and wince in pain.

"What's wrong?"

"It's just from where I fell earlier."

"Do you need the doctor to take a look at it?"

"I might…"

We start kissing.

Katharine unbuttons my pyjama top.

"You have just the perfect amount of chest hair," she tells me, as she curls her fingers around the follicular fibres of my upper torso.

"Glad to know you approve."

We start kissing some more. It starts getting hot and heavy. I'm able to ignore the pain I feel in my hip because I know sex is on the way.

Just then Katharine breaks off the romance.

"Hold on, I gotta go wee."

"Ugh," I flop back. This is my least favourite of Katharine's love making rituals. The pre-coital urination.

"Don't 'ugh' me. How would you like to have something repeatedly poking you in the guts when you have to pee?"

Katharine's up and out of bed.

"It's fine. I'm gonna take a pain pill."

"Good idea. I need your hip to be at full power."

Katharine throws the box of Panadeine at me. I pop two out and try to enter the bathroom, but Katharine blocks my way.

"I just need water."

"Just go to the kitchen and use a glass. And don't suck the faucet." Katharine hates that I just angle my mouth under the tap. "I'll see you out there in a minute," she says coquettishly as she pushes me gently back and closes the door slowly.

I go out into the kitchen. It's dark, but the moonlight shining through the window is bright enough for me to barely see the sink. I consider just drinking from the tap out of spite, but I grab my heat sensitive Doctor Who TARDIS mug off the kitchen bench. You put hot liquid in and the TARDIS disappears. Wheezing/groaning sound not included.

I swallow the pills and wash them down with some water.

Then I feel a familiar body push up against me from behind. She's put on her cruelty free perfume and the scented aroma of unharmed animals fills my nostrils. She gently bites/sucks my ear lobe, reaches into my pyjama pants and starts tugging gently on my bits.

"I see you're ready to go again."

"Again?"

Just then I hear the toilet flush.

I turn my head and see my mother, Susan Wilde.

Mum screams so loud it pierces my eardrums and throws me off balance. I fall to the floor and hear my mug smashing on the kitchen tiles. Both my dignity and the TARDIS mug dematerialise in an instant.

Katharine rushes in and flicks on the light. My mother backs away slowly, her hands cupped over her mouth, breathing heavily. I've heard the term "abject horror" before but now I know exactly what it looks like.

My mother has just touched my partially erect penis for some reason.

"What was that?" Katharine asks.

My mother and I make eye contact.

Just then a man comes in wielding an empty bourbon bottle.

"What's happening!" he shouts.

It's Katharine's turn to scream.

"It's ok, I'm her acting coach."

It's Anthony. Wearing a pair of *my* pyjamas.

My mother and I make eye contact again. A lot is exchanged in this momentary glance. I know what's going on now. She knows that I know what's going on now.

We both know that there's a time for frank and brutal honesty … and that this isn't that time.

Family survival instinct kicks in.

"Everything's fine," I say.

"I just came in to get a glass of water–" Mum continues.

"And I startled her–" I say.

"Which is when I screamed–" Mum jumps in.

"That's when you dropped the mug–" I add.

"And it shattered–" she offers.

"Then you came in and flipped the light on." I conclude.

We fib in tandem, like an Olympic Sport. Synchronised Deception.

Everyone looks around and seems to come to the conclusion that we are telling the truth.

"But wait," Katharine interjects. We are going to have to wait for the judges' scores. I look at Mum, she's ready. Her confidence gives me strength. "No one is allowed to use that mug but David. It's his special Doctor Who mug."

"You're right, Katie," Mum says, not missing a beat. Katharine bristles. She hates being called Katie. "But it was dark and I couldn't see properly."

"So you just grabbed the special Doctor Who mug accidentally, right?" I say.

"Yes it was a total accident. I didn't mean to touch it without your permission."

"Well, you know that I would never give you permission to touch my special Doctor Who mug."

"And that's why I am so sorry David. I should have known the instant I touched it that it was your mug by the size and girth." She looks over at Anthony.

"Yes, fine, that's settled then," I say.

"Can you ever forgive me for touching your special Doctor Who mug, David?"

"Let's just forget that you touched my special Doctor Who mug, and never speak of it again, ok?"

Katharine and Anthony are perplexed by what's just been said but they aren't asking any follow up questions which is a relief. However my sense of ease and comfort quickly dissipates as I stand up to full height and slowly step towards my basketball teammate. "The real question is though, what is Anthony doing in my pyjamas?"

"It's not how it looks," Anthony says.

Anthony and Susan trade a sideways glance.

"Ok, it's exactly how it looks," he says.

"You're a scumbag. No wonder Diane left you."

Anthony interrupts my rage with his own. "Hey, leave my wife out of this."

"Alright that's it!" My mother's voice cuts through our bickering. Her stage projection is astonishing. Those vocal warm-up have paid off, they'll have no problem hearing her in the cheap seats. "Outside! Right now, young man."

Anthony and I both start to go outside.

"Not you," Susan says to Anthony. "Go to my room and wait for me," she says.

Mum and I head out the front door into the cool night air. She closes the door behind us.

"Mum, what are you doing with him?"

"Having sex," she answers in such a straightforward manner that it throws me off.

"Well, yeah, I can see that. Are you sleeping with him to get back at me? That is so vindictive, Mother. I'm never going to be able to show my face at basketball again. I'll have to change teams. I won't be a Peewee!"

"Shh, shh, shh," Mum says, grabbing me around the neck and pulling me towards her shoulder. She strokes the back of my hair like she used to when I was a kid. "You'll never be a peewee, trust me," she whispers in my ear.

I pull back. This is beyond disturbing.

"Yes, yes I know, never mention it … blah blah blah"

"How could you do this to me?"

"Not everything is about you, David. I don't know where you got this narcissistic streak from. Probably from your father."

"Father …?"

"I need Anthony if I am to become Mrs. Robinson if I'm going to nail the audition."

"He's really that good of an acting coach?"

"No, he's a terrible acting coach."

"Then why–"

"Don't you see, darling? I'm Mrs. Robinson; he's Benjamin Braddock. I need to be the seductress. I need to know I can still be attractive to a younger man."

"So you're just using him for sex?" I stand there staring at her. This is wild even for Susan Wilde. "He's my friend, plus, he's going through a really painful divorce. His ex-wife is a loony." I take a breath, then say, "Mum this is wrong on so many levels. You can't do this."

"Do you think I want to? Do you think I enjoy getting repeatedly pounded by a young stallion at the peak of his sexual prowess? But it's a sacrifice I have to make. Like in chess, darling, when you sacrifice a prawn."

"You mean, pawn."

"Whatever. It's not important. What *is* important is that you refrain from interfering in my process. If I get this part I'll be out of your hair, I'll get my own place. You can get on with your life without your mother hanging around. Maybe you and Katharine can get married, go on a honeymoon, conceive a child."

"Ok mum, stop!"

"I'm just saying–"

"You've said enough."

"Surely you and Katharine have discussed your relationship moving forward."

"Of course we've discussed it … at length," I say, my voice wavering.

"I just don't want to be the one who's standing in the way of you and Katharine achieving your shared goals of having a family in the suburbs."

"You're not, Mum. Katharine and I are on the same page about everything."

"You two are so good together. And for each other. I'm envious of your love. I only wish that I had something like it."

"Yeah we've got something special," I say.

I don't know what's more frightening, having my mother living in the house, or the fact that she may be my last line of defence from having to move to the outer suburbs and start a family when I'm clearly not ready. What's a man to do when he's happy with his relationship the way it is?

My musing is interrupted by a man delivering a pizza.

"Susan … Wilde?" he says.

"Yes, I admit it, it's me," Mum says with faux-embarrassment.

"Yeah … medium Hawaiian?" the delivery guy says, looking at the docket.

I sigh. At least she's eating again. "Do you need cash?" I start to go back inside to get my wallet.

"No, I used your credit card."

"Mum!"

"What? Mine are maxed out. Anyway it's a business meal

so I can write it off on tax."

"Not if it's on my credit ca— never mind." I take the pizza box. "Thank you," I say to the delivery man as he leaves.

"Just promise me this whole thing with Anthony stays under wraps. I don't want the rest of the basketball team knowing about this."

"David, I would never do anything to publicly humiliate you."

I let that one go as we head back inside.

Anthony is standing at the door of my mother's room.

"Now what did you want to say to Anthony?" Susan says to me.

"Sorry," I mumble.

"What was that?"

"Sorry," I say, in a clearer voice.

My mother looks at Anthony expectantly.

"I'm sorry too, mate," he says.

We shake hands.

I walk back to the kitchen to clean up the remnants of my special Doctor Who mug, but Katharine has already done it. She's a treasure.

"What's going on with your mother?" Katharine asks me as I flop down in bed.

"Oh, her... yeah, um, well, she's in there, currently, um... having sex, and pizza, with Anthony."

"On the new sheets?"

"Yeah. And, she's just using him for sex. To get into the role of Mrs. Robinson. It's Method acting, or something," I say, rolling my eyes.

"Does he know that?"

"No."

"Poor man. Does she know he's vulnerable? He's getting divorced, you know. And his wife, Diane ..." Katharine shakes her head and looks into the distance. "I only hung out with her at your basketball games but she thought I wanted to sleep with Anthony just cause I clapped when he made a jump shot. She's a bit scary and possessive. Should we call her and see if we can get them back together?"

"Look, it's gonna be fine. The audition is in a few days, it'll all be over then. We can get back to normal."

"'Normal' normal or 'Susan Wilde' normal?" Katharine says. She's learning the lingo.

I look deeply into Katharine's eyes and decide that I am not going to lie to her any more tonight. So I just keep silent and nod my head.

I'm saved from my idiotic tactic by the sounds of lovemaking emanating from my mother's room.

We stare at each other and shake our heads.

"What really happened in the kitchen tonight?" Katharine asks.

Katharine isn't making this whole 'not lying' easy on me.

"Nothing happened."

"Nothing...?"

"Nothing, Katharine."

I don't want to tell Katharine the truth about my mother touching my penis because I'm afraid that if she knew she'd never want to touch it again.

The lovemaking sounds continue.

"We'll just have to block it out." I'm speaking just as much about my shame at having my mother grope me as I am about the lovemaking sounds.

"Well ... goodnight."

113

"Goodnight," I say and switch off the lamp.

As I lie in the dark I churn over all the conflicting thoughts, feelings and shame triggers. I'm being pulled in more directions than there are directions to be pulled in. But I land at one important conclusion: I don't want Anthony to get hurt by my mother. I've got to protect my friend, for his sake. He's an innocent victim in this. I've got to warn him that he's being used by a person who has no regard for his emotional wellbeing and is thinking only of themselves.

I close my eyes but I can't sleep.

Episode 10

It's funny how the world looks different when you're sleep deprived. The sunshine hurts my brain. The sounds of the birds chirping are like needles on my ear drums. The space right between my eyes aches. It's like my eyes are two ends of a vice pushing the bridge of my nose together.

I feel like a zombie on heroin.

And I look like one too. Unshaven, bags under my eyes, hair uncombed.

I grab my second favourite heat sensitive mug from the cupboard. It's a self-portrait of Vincent Van Gogh. Hot liquid goes in and his ear disappears. If only he had a hot beverage in him he wouldn't have had to hear the sounds of my mother and my friend having sex through the night.

For the past three days.

I've been writing but I have no idea whether the material is any good or not. The evaluating part of my brain has been shut off from lack of sleep. I emailed the pages to Deirdre last night in preparation for the meeting we have later this afternoon. If Deirdre hates the pages she'll chuck a book at my head. Maybe that will wake me up. I need a high voltage dose to snap me back from my semi-conscious state.

I pour myself some coffee from the large French press

Katharine bought me for our 5th anniversary. That year I got her a pair of nice designer sandals, which she said she loved despite the fact that they offered no arch support. She wore them once when we went to Bali and now they're decorative additions to the back of her closet. But she refuses to throw them out because they were a gift. That's love for you.

Fortunately this will all be over soon. The audition for *The Graduate* stage adaptation is today.

Anthony comes into the kitchen, bright eyed and bushy tailed, wearing Susan's monogrammed robe. This is the first time I've laid eyes on him in three days. I've heard him but I haven't seen him.

"Hey David. No Katharine this morning?" he says.

"She couldn't sleep so she went to the surgery early."

"Actually, I'm glad I caught you. I thought we should have a little chat. Man to man."

"I've been meaning to talk with you too." How do you tell your friend that your mother is using him for sex? It's one of those situations that isn't covered in the manual to life; like a lot of situations I find myself in with my mother. Such as being your mother's designated driver ... when you're thirteen ... for soccer carpool.

The trick is going to be introducing the idea subtly so I don't make it obvious that I am trying to help him see the truth. I don't want him to get mad at me for delivering the message.

Anthony helps himself to coffee. He grabs a floral mug and adds milk and enough sugar to give him type two diabetes.

"I can understand if you're mad at me for having relations with your mother. We didn't plan any of this, it was just business. It was all totally innocent, in the beginning," he says.

I breathe deeply. None of this is easy.

"Are we ... are we ok?" he says earnestly. "I don't want this to affect us being friends."

"I'm ok. But are you ok? I know the separation from Diane can't be easy."

"Being with your mother really clarified my feelings about the whole situation and helped me to understand the very real feelings I have for her."

"For Diane?

"No, for Susan."

"This isn't just rebound sex?"

"I see what you did there. 'Rebound sex', cause we play on a basketball team," Anthony laughs. "No, there's something about Susan. It's that caring, nurturing spirit of hers that's awakened something in me that I didn't even know was missing. With Diane it was stormy and tempestuous. Hot and cold, on and off. You could never gauge her emotional temperature. That's what was so exciting about her. But with Susan there's none of that. Your mother has a real mothering quality. You must have felt it too," Anthony says.

"On occasion. But, you do know she's an actor–"

"And a great one," Anthony interjects with a big smile and a twinkle in his eye.

"Mmmm. And you know, she likes to, you know, *act*."

"Well, she wasn't acting last night, when she had her hands around my–"

"I don't wanna know–"

"Face, and told me she liked me too."

"Wait what?" I can't believe what I'm hearing. Why is my mother making this so hard on me?

"She confessed her feelings too."

"Last night? When exactly?"

"I don't know. Time stood still."

I look down at Vincent on the coffee mug. The coffee is hot and his ear is gone. He's lucky he doesn't have to hear this lunacy.

"I just don't want our friendship to be hurt," Anthony says.

"Yes, I feel the same. I don't want to see anybody get *hurt*."

"And me dating your mother is not going to change our relationship one bit." Anthony looks at his watch and downs his coffee. "I gotta run to class. I'm doing Shakespeare's *Macbeth* with my students. But get this, instead of Scotland it all takes place in fast food restaurants."

"Fresh take," I say, genuinely surprised.

"Yeah, I stole it from a Christopher Walken movie. Plus most of the kids have after school jobs at McDonald's or KFC, so it helps with their character motivations. But, I do have something I need to bring up with you, which is a bit awkward."

"You mean this wasn't it?"

"I still need to be paid for the last two acting sessions with your mother."

"I don't have any cash on me."

"That's fine, just pay me at basketball tonight," Anthony says, and leaves for the shower. "I trust you, we're friends."

I go back to my study and sit down at the computer. My head is spinning from Anthony's revelation. How could he have feelings for her? Anthony has cheated on his soon-to-be ex-wife with more women than I can count. He never had feelings for any of them. What's different about my mother?

On a certain level I get it. Susan Wilde does have the ability to make you feel special, like you're the only person in the world that matters. She does have a caring and nurturing spirit that comes out when you get past the mask. I've been there when the walls have come tumbling down and felt that genuine connection. Except that Anthony is in the way now.

No, I can't think like that. As my father used to say, "Don't be envious son. Or you'll get what they got. Which is usually not what you think it is."

Say that's an idea.

My fingers begin tinkling the ivories of the qwerty keyboard:

'Where does envy get you thought Reid McGowan. It might get you to Carnegie Hall, divorce court, or dangling on the business end of a noose. Envy can be a sweet little indulgence, like liqueured chocolate. But swallow too much and you might get sick.'

I write in the flow state in my study until my mother enters without knocking. "It's time," she says, and goes back out.

I get up, rub my eyes, grab my keys, wallet, pen, and stick them in my pocket along with my self-determination. I've got to do something which I've never done before. I have got to confront my mother while we take part in the pre-audition ritual of having a coffee and running through her list of insecurities while I refute them.

It started when I was a kid and is one of the most enduring aspects of our relationship. The ritual is like Shabbat dinner on Friday night, an obligation but also strangely comforting. It's also one of the only times my mother never drinks. So I have her stone cold sober attention.

We sit at the back of the café so as to avoid any unwanted attention. It's the one time she doesn't want to be noticed by fans.

We sit across from each other at Ray's, the hippest of the hip cafes in the inner north of Melbourne. The unofficial staff uniform consists of skinny jeans, a non-earlobe piercing, and a T-shirt of a band from the 70s. Mum's dressed in a leopard print dress, adorned with pearl earrings and necklace. She's checking her makeup in a compact.

"I don't know all my lines."

"You know all your lines," I reassure her. The ritual begins.

Mum is mid-neurosis as Sophie, the Swiss-French waitress, with the side ponytail slides our cappuccinos onto the round table. When Sophie took our order mum discovered she was from Geneva, a place where we lived while mum was filming *Heidi: Diary of a Mountain Seductress*, about a grown-up Heidi who battles not only Nazis but loneliness alongside her trusty St. Bernard dog imaginatively named Bernie. A landmark in Swiss Cinema, it was not. A staple of late night basic cable, it was.

"*Merci vielmal*," Mum says to the waitress, using the uniquely Swiss-French term for 'thank you.'

"*De rien*," the waitress says, and slips away.

"I'll probably forget them."

"You won't forget them."

"The producers are going to see through me. They'll see that I'm a fraud."

"They won't see through you and realise you're a fraud."

"So you admit that I am a fraud, I'm just better at hiding it than most," Mum says.

"No, I'm saying I understand your fear. The sense that at any moment people are going to pull back the curtain. No matter how much people liked my first book I thought they were lying. Praise is fleeting, insecurities are forever. Like diamonds."

I adjust my horn-rimmed glasses.

"You're right, David, as always. You always know how to reassure me. Now my crow's feet–"

"Mum, you have got to come clean with Anthony," I blurt out. I would have liked to be more tactful but it's out now. I don't want to upset her before her audition. If she blows this one who knows how long she'll stay in her room sulking and drinking. But I can't help myself.

"He knows I'm not really 47."

"No. I mean, you need to tell him that you're just using him. You've led him on and now he thinks you really like him."

"He said that?"

"Yes, this morning he–"

"That's wonderful."

"It's not! You're playing with his emotions. He's all screwed up right now. And I'm sorry that I had to bring this up right before your audition, I just had to say something. You know, for his sake." I finish my diatribe and take a sip of my cappuccino.

"David, I'm not mad, I'm over the moon. I love him too."

"Wait, what?"

"He's awakened something in me."

"Anthony?"

"It's more than just lust, David. I haven't felt that way since I fell in love with that reclusive art dealer who was forging valuable paintings to pay for his wife's life support."

"That wasn't real, that was *Destiny's Hope*."

"Yes but I *felt* it. It was through my art that I truly felt something. And the same is true for Anthony. I was pretending until it felt real. But now it is real. Don't you see?"

This is really messing with the pre-audition ritual.

"He makes me feel, so … so, um … what's the word …"

"Inarticulate?"

"Well, for want of a better term."

"Mum you can't date him for real."

This is starting to get critical.

"Darling, I think I might be falling in love with him."

Ok, now it is critical.

"It's like we're in some great historical romance like *Antony and Cleopatra*."

"That story doesn't end well."

"I meant more like Elizabeth Taylor and Richard Burton."

"They got divorced," I exclaim. "Twice! You're delusional if you think this makes you younger. You've got to start thinking about the future, find someone you can settle down with, where it's not about compulsive fornication all the time."

"Don't you dare try to desexualise me David. I thought I raised you right, but you're just like every other man who wants to stick women my age in a box and forget about them. But you know what? I'm going to stick myself in my own box," Susan Wilde says, as she sucks down the rest of her cappuccino and slams the cup down on the saucer.

A few faces turn towards us.

I adjust my horn-rimmed glasses.

"You just want me to be a normal mother."

"Would that be so bad?"

"The traditional role of 'mother' castrates women. I read it in that Germaine Greer book, *The Female Munich*."

"It's 'Eunuch' not Munich."

"I don't care which German city it is. It is still a hate crime."

I drain my cappuccino and inhale sharply through my nose. I smell powdered chocolate and years of simmering resentment. "Mum you can't–"

"David, you're foaming at the mouth."

"Well I'm angry."

"It's from the cappuccino."

I forgot how my unshaven face is like Velcro for caffeinated milk foam.

I survey the rounded plywood table for something to wipe my face with, but before I can find something Mum reaches across the table with a napkin and goes for my upper lip. I pull back instinctively.

"Hold still, David."

I grab her right wrist and immobilise the incoming napkin, but she quickly attacks from the flank with another napkin in her left hand.

"No— Mum!"

People are definitely looking now.

I give in and get my face wiped like a child.

Sophie, the Swiss-French waitress with the side ponytail comes up, "Another round?"

"Just the bill," I say.

"We'll take two more cappuccinos thanks," Mum corrects.

The waitress leaves.

"Now where were we? My crow's feet. You don't think they're too hideous or noticeable?"

"I don't know Mum. Why don't you ask Anthony? This whole situation is wrong."

"No David, it is totally right. Everything is going to work out. I am going to get the role of Mrs. Robinson today. I will move out on my own and reestablish my career here in

Melbourne. This is all part of the plan."

I breathe deeply. Mum puts her hand over mine.

"When the play is over I shall take us on a Pacific holiday so we can spend some quality time together. Just the two of us … and Anthony."

I roll my eyes.

Sophie, the Swiss-French waitress with the side ponytail arrives with the coffees. She's about to leave, then stops, and pulls two more napkins out of her apron and quietly slides them onto the table.

I can't take any more of this. I get up and leave.

"David, wait!" she calls after me.

"Yes Mum?" I turn around, hope on my face.

"I need cab fare."

I throw a fifty on the table and leave.

"David, I'm sorry–"

I turn around again.

"But can I have your coffee?"

I look directly in her eyes, grab my cappuccino off the rounded plywood table and down the entire thing in one gulp. I go to the front counter which is also made from varnished plywood.

"Oh, you have foam." Sophie says and indicates on her upper lip.

"I don't care."

I slam twenty bucks on the counter and walk out. When I'm out of eyeshot I suck the stubble of my upper lip and wipe my face with my hand. I can taste the cinnamon and simmering resentment as I walk down the street.

Episode 11

I have an appointment with my editor, Deirdre, the literature loving, ex-IRA agent. Maybe she can show me how to use plastique explosives so I can blow myself up and avoid dealing with my mother, Anthony, my book, my dreams, and my impending discussion about family and houses with Katharine. I need to escape into someone else's life, someone else's story.

Maybe my legs can work out what my brain can't. I point my body towards Hepburn Publishing and keep walking.

As my Father used to say, "When you're hurt son, just walk it off."

Maybe that's the point of a pilgrimage?

My trek from Brunswick to Collingwood is hardly the Camino de Santiago but it'll do on short notice.

I head down back streets avoiding main roads. I traverse the old avenues of Brunswick, Carlton, and Fitzroy passing rows of terrace houses, old Edwardian workers cottages made from brick and adorned with decorative cast iron.

I cut through Princes Park. Even though I've lived here for years, the name still strikes me as weird. They named this park after more than one prince? It's not 'Princess Park', named for a female heir to the throne, it's not 'Prince's Park', with an apostrophe, indicative of the possessive noun. It's *Princes* Park, so it's named for multiple princes. Were there specific princes that the park was named after, and if so how many? Or is it just all princes from all time? Isn't the point of naming something after someone a way to honour them? When a prince (of any royal inclination) visits do they know the park is named for them? The more I think about this, the more confused I get.

The sky seems to be getting darker. It's either my mood or the gathering clouds overhead.

I wend my way through the streets of Melbourne's inner-north. Past cafes, pop up shops, vegetarian eateries, cruelty-free shops, bulk food stores, vintage clothing stores, second hand clothing stores, new clothing stores that look like they sell vintage and second hand clothes, vinyl music shops, more cafes and more cafes. And a place that only sells different types of Greek yoghurt.

I have successfully cleared my head. But I have no idea how Deirdre is going to greet me, with a shake of the hand or a toss of a book. Does she like the pages I sent in? I'm dreading this meeting now.

Hepburn Publishing comes into view. Their building is one of the converted brick factories that line the streets of Collingwood. They used to manufacture textiles, now they manufacture text. I climb the stairs and report to Michael Ruggles, known to everyone as Mick, the kindly receptionist, who absolutely loves me.

"David, I saw you were coming in today" he says, his smile extending like an umbrella. His desk is a shrine to his dog, Winston, even though Winston is lying behind Mick on a doggy day bed that has his name hand embroidered on the side.

Mick and Deirdre's relationship is closer than family. They've worked together for years and have a certain loving, yet antagonistic rapport. Case in point, Mick started bringing Winston, a purebred English bulldog, into the office just to piss off Deirdre who doesn't like dogs. You can gauge the state of their current relationship by the way they address each other.

"That moron's just in with another author at the moment," Mick says.

I go to an aubergine coloured leather sofa. It looks like someone skinned an eggplant and stuffed it.

"And how are you, David?" Mick asks.

"Uh, yeah, up and down," I mumble.

I slump onto the couch and stare at a framed poster of *The Blonde Wore Black* on the wall directly opposite me. It hangs there, taunting me like a bully in the school yard: you'll never match your initial success. It was just a fluke.

I keep staring at the poster of my first book's dust jacket. I just keep staring, sinking lower into the depths of the couch. I'm so tired from lack of sleep, arguing with my mother, and the fear of having to return to my law practice after taking time off to pursue a pipe dream.

"What wrong chicken?" Michael's simple question prods me from my vegetative torpor.

"Oh, it's nothing," I say.

"You look hot today," he says.

"Oh thanks," the compliment buoys my spirits a bit.

"I meant warm."

"Oh right …" Back down to normal spirit level.

"Do you need something? A glass of water?"

"I'm fine."

"A cup of tea?"

"I'm ok."

"A coffee?"

"Just had one."

"We have that Venezuelan Dark Roast you like so much."

"Thanks, but no thanks."

"Are you hungry?"

"Not particularly."

"Just a biscuit then?"

"No."

"I have Tim-Tams."

"I'll pass."

"Some saltines?"

"Not right now."

"New England clam chowder in a sourdough bread bowl?"

"I don't want you to go to any trouble over me."

"It's no trouble. I just need to hollow out the sourdough loaf, heat up the chowder and pour it in. I've been dying to make it for someone who really deserves it."

The intercom alert goes off on his telephone.

"Do you need to get that?"

"No."

"Oh ok. Can I go in?"

"Not yet."

An author, about my age, comes out from the office area sobbing uncontrollably and exits down the stairs. Her kitten heels clack on the old stone steps going down.

"She'll be ready for you now."

I get up.

Mick gets up too and gives me a big hug. He is a spectacular hugger.

"You look like you need one of those," Mick says. He studies my face. "Don't worry about going in there, she liked the pages you sent in."

"Really?"

"Yeah," Mick says, as he walks me back.

"What did she say exactly?"

"I'm not exactly sure. We are not on speaking terms today."

"How do you know she liked it then?"

"I haven't heard the shredder going all morning," he reassures me.

This isn't exactly the glowing report I was hoping for. It means that she at least wants to talk about the pages, so that's somewhat of a good sign. I wipe my clammy hand on my jeans in preparation for a handshake.

Mick opens the door for me and I am greeted by a copy of *A Brief History of Time* by Stephen Hawking. Judging by the book's mass and the impact it has on my forehead, the eminent physicist's history could have been a bit less wordy.

"David? I thought you were someone else. What the hell are you doing here?"

"Nice to see you too, Deirdre," I say, trying to hold my balance.

"Why don't you behave like a civilised human being for a change," Mick cuts in as he pushes past me.

"Why don't you behave like a proper assistant and get the appointment diary right?"

"I changed the appointments, you just didn't check it," Mick says.

"You're supposed to remind me to check them," Deirdre fires back.

Mick slams the door.

I don't want to get involved. I've learned that getting in between them is like invading Stalingrad in winter. There are no winners.

I sit down in the guest chair opposite Deirdre's desk. Paperbacks, hardbacks, manuscripts and random papers cover nearly every inch of the finely crafted blonde beechwood.

"Apologies, David."

"That's ok," I say, still dazed from the literary blunt force trauma to the head. Plus being tired, plus my mother, plus blah-blah-blah whatever else.

"Now I've read the pages that you sent. And ..."

Deirdre searches for something on her desk.

"And I..."

She keeps searching. Moving papers about, lifting books.

"And you ..." I prompt.

"Yes I, um ..."

Mick enters the room with a perfectly squared off and stapled set of papers. He hands them to Deirdre who stops searching her desk.

They stare at each other like worthy adversaries from across an Aikido mat.

Mick exits. Slams the door again.

"He's a lifesaver, he is," Deirdre says as much to me as to herself. Then mutters, "The jackass" Then to me: "Anyway, I loved what you wrote."

"You did?" I'm shocked.

"Yeah, I absolutely loved it."

Deirdre is rarely this liberal with praise on first drafts.

Editorial meetings with Deirdre are like a symphony orchestra rehearsing for a concert season. Deirdre is the exacting conductor, her antique bone-handled letter opener the baton, and the text is the orchestra. She reads through the manuscript enjoying the rhythm and melodies of the words, then erupts in anger when she spots anything derivative, boring, or inauthentic, occasionally impaling the pages. She genuinely wants the prose to sing off the page, even if she elicits that through unhinged displays of praise and derision.

But today there is no such warm-up and she calmly picks her fingernails with the letter opener.

"Normally your first drafts are pure self-conscious dreck. But this … it's like you were able to shut off the inner-critic part of your brain and write from instinct. Were there any changes in your environment that helped you get into that state?"

"Nothing comes to mind," I say.

"Well whatever it is, the main thing is that you need to maintain that atmosphere around you. Because you're spinnin' gold."

"Really? Cause don't I think the material is that much better," I suggest.

"No, it's better. Dead-on better. Whatever the recipe is right now don't change it. Normally you're faffin' about in the early stages, but this is coming out clear and concise. In fact, I want to fast track your book for an earlier publication. Get it out for Christmas, with a big marketing push. How would you like that?"

"Sounds … great," I say.

"Nothing spreads holiday cheer like a detective book about a gruesome murders. Right lad?" Deirdre smiles.

"I guess."

The thought of encouraging my mother to continually have

relations with my friend in a nearby bedroom in order for me to write better is disturbing to say the least.

"Hey, what's wrong?" Deirdre asks.

"You wanna know what's wrong?" I say, spitting the dummy. "It's my mother. She's dating a friend on my basketball team and they're having loud sex every night. It's revolting. Then when I told her it had to stop, that this was all just part of her deluded attempt to hang onto her youth, she accused me of desexualising her and turning her into a female Munich!"

"You mean 'Eunuch.'"

"Whatever!"

Deirdre looks in between the two towering stacks of books on her desk, and then turns back to me. "She's right, you know."

"Pardon?"

"She's right. You're being ageist." Deirdre considers further, "So typical of your generation."

"What do you mean?"

"You need to wake up to the fact that older people enjoy fruitful and fulfilling sex lives, David. It's especially damaging for women. Society equating fertility with social value links women's social worth to a biological imperative they're not in control of," Deirdre says, leaning forward, her Northern Ireland accent getting stronger with emotion.

"But she's my mother."

"Exactly, and you're trying to force her into a role she might not want to be in."

"You're telling me." I recall the time she took me to the Daytime Emmys and tried to pass me off as her date. I was fifteen.

"Think about how you would feel if someone tried to tell

you that once you reach a certain age everyone expects you to cremate your genitals, then place the urn on the mantle so that no one's grossed out by the thought of you ever using them again," Deirdre says, leaning back in her chair.

I ponder this for a moment. She has a point.

"And so what if she's dating a guy on your basketball team. At least it's someone you know, someone you trust; not some stranger who's giving one to your ma."

Deirdre gets up and moves to the front of the desk and leans back against it.

She does make another good point there. I wouldn't want my mother out there dating some of the psychos she's dated before. Anthony may be untalented and gauche, but he's athletic, well-groomed, and doesn't have a raging cocaine habit. He's a damn sight better than a lot of the other morons my mother has fallen for over the years.

My thoughts are interrupted as Mick comes in and hands me a hollowed out circular sourdough loaf chock full with clam chowder.

"Oh Mick, you didn't have to," I say.

"Oh, but I wanted to." Mick says looking directly at Deirdre.

She tucks a napkin in under my chin and puts a spoon in the steaming white concoction. I feel the warmth of the chowder through the bread bowl.

"Where's mine?" Deirdre snaps.

He turns on his heels and leaves. Closing the door quietly this time so as not to disrupt the contents of my bread bowl.

"Why is she so angry at you?" I break my vow of strict non-interventionism.

"Because I unfollowed his Instagram feed."

Besides being an indispensable administrator, excellent

clam chowder cook, and all around caring person Mick is also the creator of the Instagram account "Winston Reads", a light- hearted look at his bulldog's reading habits. The pictures consist of putting black framed glasses on the pup and propping a book in front of him as if he were able to decipher English, followed by a brief review. Coincidentally Winston's taste in books corresponds directly to whatever Michael is reading at the moment. He has about fifty thousand followers.

Not including Deirdre.

"Why would you do that?"

"We had a disagreement about the literary merits of *The Da Vinci Code*, and it escalated. Words were exchanged. So I unfollowed him."

"That's something a teenager would do."

"See, there you go being ageist again. Why can't an older person retaliate against another via technology?" Deirdre says, poking the letter opener at me. She even holds it like a paramilitary soldier would hold a knife.

"You're right. I am an ageist. If mum's happy then that's all that should matter. Why shouldn't she be able to express her sexuality anyway she wants."

"Exactly."

"Older people are people too."

"We are."

"They have needs."

"We do."

The intercom buzzes.

"Yes?" Deirdre snaps.

"How's the clam chowder?" Mick asks.

I taste it. It's the perfect combination of diced potatoes,

cream, and molluscs.

"Really good, Mick."

Deirdre looks over. She pensively sucks her teeth, trying not to betray her mouth-watering jealousy.

"Enjoy it, 'cause that's the last of it." Mick kills the intercom.

Deirdre sighs. "Moving hastily along," she says. "Your book." Deirdre starts going through her thoughts about the novel, but I'm so captivated by this clam chowder I can barely concentrate. I didn't realise how hungry I was, and I eat like a Viking on the Feast of Odin.

When I finally snap out of it I've eaten it down to the point where I can break off some of the sourdough.

"Sorry Deirdre," I cough out, mouth full of bread. "Do you want a taste?"

"I couldn't impose," she says as she reaches out and takes the bread bowl.

"There's only one spoon," I say, but Deirdre's already got it in her mouth. She tears a chunk of the bread bowl off and examines it like a Dutch diamond cutter taking in a rough stone.

"The thing for you, David, is to maintain your current state of mind. Your creativity right now is like this chowder and all the ingredients are swirling around. Your mind is this bread," Deirdre says, stuffing the chunk in her mouth, "It's soaking up all the influences from the environment and making it delicious. So don't change anything!"

I reach to get my chowder back.

"You need to get writing," Deirdre grunts, pulling back. "I'll stay here and soldier on with the deal memo for the new publication date."

The problem with being an only child is that sharing is

something that doesn't come naturally to me. I learned that in therapy. But I never learned how to get my clam chowder back from someone who potentially tried to overthrow a government.

"Go," she barks the order like an IRA commander. "That book isn't going to write itself, is it?"

I turn towards the door. I don't know if it was Deirdre's pep talk or the clam chowder but my feelings of doom and desperation are lifting like a hot air balloon over a touristy wine region.

If mum keeps having sex with Anthony, then I'll stay sleep deprived and I'll be able to write better. It's a win-win situation. Mum finds love, I'm successful with my book. It does mean that Anthony will be like my step-dad but, whatever, we can go on double dates. It'll be like hanging out with a buddy while also doing a family dinner. Win-win-win.

Bottom line: If I don't encourage my mother to have sex with my friend I might not get my book done in time.

Episode 12

I'm at the basketball gym in Coburg. The Peewees are facing off against our arch rivals, the Preston Powerful Owls. They swagger onto the court with the kind of cocksure arrogance that only a team made up of orthodontists can bring. Their smug grins are filled with perfectly aligned teeth. We'd all love to knock their molars out but unfortunately they all wear matching custom-made mouthguards preventing elbow-induced extraction.

The inciting incident for the rivalry came in a nail biting fourth quarter scenario when their team captain, Julian Kenner, DDS (who teammates referred to as "Doctor K"), 'fell over' and got Anthony called for a charging foul. The teams got in each other's faces, hurling abuse, and accusations of halitosis. Doctor K's two free throws after the hostilities sealed the game for the Powerful Owls.

Henceforth each game has evolved (or devolved) into a grudge match where trash talk, rough play, and jokes about dentofacial deformity are the norm.

Tonight though is sweet, sweet, cavity-inducing revenge. The Brunswick Peewees are dominating the Owls from Preston. Anthony and I are playing like a pair of Astrologers, we are reading each other's signs perfectly. Pick-and-rolls, give-and-gos, and setting screens all over the court. Anthony keeps feeding me the ball and I keep hitting shot after shot. On the last play of the game Anthony hits me in the key and I sink a turnaround jump shot right as the whistle blows at full time. Not that it matters, we're up by 19.

Our team runs off the court, high-fiving each other, as the Powerful Owls slink off the court in shame.

"You were awesome out there man," says Callum.

"In the zone," adds Joanne.

"I'm going to get a Gatorade," Anthony says, jogging off.

"Peewees rule!" Edina says, patting me on the bum. After coming home from my meeting with Deirdre I was able to finish a chapter on the novel. Then Katharine came home and we were finally able to have sex. Joyous, wonderful sex. No distraction or disruptions. We barely even talked. It was like scratching an itch. And we scratched hard, like we both had infected mosquito bites.

Romantic.

Now, as icing on the cake, a resounding win over the Powerful Owls. And I mean really grinding their faces into the dirt. Nothing can bring me down.

Enter my mother, Susan Wilde.

She emerges from in between the other team who are milling around. She's still wearing the leopard print dress, kitten heels, with a giant pair of sunglasses holding her hair up. I'm so glad to see her. This is the woman who gave me life and continues to be a source of inspiration. She was right, there is a plan. I just couldn't see it.

"Hi Mum," I say, giving her a hug and a kiss.

"Hello darling." She kisses me. "Oh …" She looks at my cheek.

"Lipstick? Just get it off," I say and point my cheek at her.

Mum takes out her monogramed hankie, licks it and wipes off the red smudge.

"Thank god you haven't started yet."

"The game's over, Mum," I say. I shrug off my normal disappointment in her.

"Yeah and we won," Joanne chimes in, "We beat a team that hasn't lost all season."

"Until now," Edina throws in.

Everyone cheers.

"Did you bring any snacks?" Callum asks.

"I got something better to celebrate with," Mum says. She whips out a bottle of

Moët from her handbag.

"We'll get some cups from the water cooler. C'mon," Joanne says, as he, Edina and Callum walk off .

"French champagne? You got the part, you're Mrs. Robinson!" I say.

"No," she says with a giant smile.

Mum cracks the golden tin and unravels the muselet at the top of the bottle.

"What?" No crying, no misdirected rage. Something must be wrong if she's this happy.

"Nope. I didn't get it," she says. "They called me about an hour after the audition to let me know."

"Mum, are you ok?" I say taking her shoulders.

Susan Wilde stops trying to pop the cork. She peers over the top of the giant frames.

"David, the sun doesn't rise and set solely on my acting career."

I have never heard these words before.

"What I mean darling, is that there's a bigger picture. I may not have got the role but I got you-know-who out of it. I know you don't like it but–"

"Mum, look, if he really makes you happy, then that's all that matters. I had a talk with my editor Deirdre, and she helped me realise I was desexualising you."

"This Deirdre sounds like a smart lady."

Mum kisses me on the cheek.

"She is. And I don't care if you date Anthony. In fact I want you to have as much sex with him as you want."

"You mean it?"

"The louder the better," I say, as I envision winning the Ned Kelly Award for crime fiction.

"Agreed," Mum says. "Now, where is my Toreador? Mon petit gateau?"

"He went to get a Gatorade."

Mum and I walk towards the vending machine area. As we pass by the stands we see Anthony kissing an attractive blonde under the bleachers. Anthony looks up and sees us.

"Susan! This is not how it looks."

"What it looks like is *you* kissing some peroxide princess," Mum says.

There's a beat.

"Ok, it's exactly how it looks. But let me explain."

The attractive blonde turns around. It's Diane, Anthony's supposedly soon-to-be ex-wife. Although judging by the lip-lock they were engaging in it might not be that soon.

"Anthony, who is this geriatric tart?" Diane says.

"Yes, um, Diane meet, Susan Wilde, my ..." Anthony swallows hard, "... acting student." Anthony's usual unearned confidence is experiencing technical difficulties.

"I'm his lover," Mum declares.

"Well I'm his wife, you hag. So why don't you take your bottle of bubbles and go christen the Titanic."

I see my mother's grip around the champagne neck tightening.

"You said it was over, Anthony," Susan says.

"Funny story–" he starts.

Diane cuts in. "She looks old enough to be your mother,"

"Hey. She *is* my mother," I say.

"You knew, David?" Diane says. "And you were ok with it? You're just as sick as her."

Mum grips the neck with two hands now.

"I don't have anything invested in this," I say. "Love is love."

"It's more like Mrs. Robinson in *The Graduate*," Diane says. "But a more busted down version of Mrs. Robinson."

The veins around Susan Wilde's eyes start twitching.

"Hey, that's right! How did your audition go?" Anthony says genuinely interested. "Did you nail it?"

The cork pops on the champagne bottle. It hits Diane squarely between the eyes, dropping her to the floor. Mum screams and leaps on Diane, dropping the champagne bottle in the process. Anthony tries to pull Mum off but slips in the puddle of carbonated wine draining onto the hardwood floor. They all fall in a heap.

"We got cups," Joanne declares. The rest of the team walk up, right as Susan attacks Diane with her kitten heel. Anthony tries to pull Mum off but cops a backwards blow to the face.

The Referee, hearing the commotion comes up and starts blowing his whistle to try and stop the fight.

"What is going on?" Edina asks, as the team pulls Mum off Diane.

"She's a menopausal maniac!" Diane shouts.

"You bitch! You don't love him like I do," Susan snarls.

Diane lunges at Susan but slips on the champagne bottle in her path and falls into the Referee. The Referee gets hit in the stomach, the expulsion of air goes through the whistle forcing a sound blast right into Diane's ear. Everyone winces. Diane falls to the floor.

Susan turns to Anthony, tears in her eyes.

"I bared my soul to you!" Susan wails.

"I'm sorry?" Anthony says, but it's clear he's not sure if he should be sorry or not.

Other players and supporters start gathering around the commotion, including some of the Powerful Owls.

"Come on, Mum."

I pull her off the ground. But she throws herself at Anthony sliding down his body. She clutches onto his ankle as champagne soaks into her dress.

"I was to be your Cleopatra, your Egyptian princess," Susan pleads.

"More like a mummy!" Diane spits.

"I just think we're on different life paths," Anthony says, trying to shake Mum loose. He tries to walk but ends up dragging Susan across the court in front of everyone. Diane pulls Susan's leg, severing Susan's grasp on Anthony's leg. Diane walks past Susan taking Anthony's arm.

"Come on, Anthony. We're going home," Diane says.

They walk towards the exit.

"See you next week guys," Anthony calls out. "Go Peewees!"

* * *

I'm lying in bed. I don't care about the thread count on the sheets. I don't care about how soft the Sealy Posturepedic mattress is or how nice the warm light is coming from the varnished teak lamp Katharine bought from Denmark. I am appreciating my hypoallergenic pillow though. Mainly because it is soft, supple and is cutting off my oxygen supply as it sits on top of my face.

I hear the front door shut. Katharine comes into the bedroom a few moments later.

"Hey babe," she says. I can hear Katharine hanging up her purse in the closet on its designated hook. "Rebecca says 'hi.' She wanted to know if we could do pub trivia at the Cornish Arms next week." I hear Katharine putting her coat on a wooden hanger. She always uses wooden hangers. "What are you doing?" she laughs.

I don't move. Don't respond.

Finally the shoes are off and put on the rack in the closet.

"Hello?" Katharine jostles my foot.

I lift the pillow slightly.

"Do you mind? I'm trying to kill myself."

"David, don't joke about that," Katharine says. "Not after your mother ... you know ..."

I put the pillow back over my face. I'm either going to suffocate from shame or lack of air. I'm putting my money on shame.

Katharine sits down on the bed and pulls the pillow off.

"Ok," Katharine says, getting all maternal. "What did your mother do this time?"

I explain the evening's entertainment. The basketball game and the ensuing floor show.

"On an unrelated note, I'm thinking of quitting the basketball team."

I put the pillow back on my face.

"Well at least you won the game?" Katharine says.

She rubs my tummy. Katharines excels at finding the silver lining. I'm so lucky to have her. She is the one saving grace throughout this whole debacle tonight. The fact that I have someone caring, sensitive and devoted makes the darkness seem lighter. As I suck in air from beneath the pillow, I realise: this is the woman I want to spend the rest of my life with.

"David, I need to tell you something. I called Diane and talked her into getting back with Anthony."

The pillow muffles the sound but I know I heard correctly. Katharine gets up and makes for the bathroom as I pull the pillow off my face.

"You what?"

"I've gotta floss my teeth."

I roll over onto all fours facing her.

"Katharine, how could you?"

"I thought I was doing us a favour. David, I need my sleep. I almost yawned into a woman's lap while fitting her orthotics."

"No, you're right, that's way more embarrassing." The sarcasm drips out of my mouth like blood from Dracula's fang.

Katharine comes out of the bathroom plinking tiny bits of food out of her teeth.

"We're both tired," Katharine says between plinks, "And I don't want this to turn into a whole big thing right before bed. I think we'll both feel a whole lot better after a good night's sleep."

"I don't want a good night's sleep, that's the whole point," I say sitting up on the bed.

"What are you talking about?"

I explain to Katharine the afternoon's events with Mum and then with Deirdre and how I got my publishing date pushed up; and how being sleep deprived by my mother's nocturnal habits was helping. It's clear that Katharine is disturbed by all of this, but I'm not sure if it's me or the whole situation.

We sit for a moment as Katharine gently rubs my back and my neck.

"Look I'm sorry I interfered," Katharine says, putting her hand on my thigh.

"You didn't know," I say, putting my hand on top of hers.

"But, hey, that's great news about the publication date being moved up."

"It's terrible. Now how am I going to make it? I've lost my secret ingredient."

"C'mon David be rational. You don't need your mother's insane behaviour to be a successful artist. You wrote your first book without her being around."

"What if that was just a fluke?"

"You don't believe that."

"I had nothing until she arrived."

"David… I don't know what to say. I think you're talented with or without your mother. Just because her arrival coincided with your inspiration doesn't prove a causal relationship. What if there were other factors?"

"Like what?"

"Like what about me, do I inspire you?" Katharine asks.

"Of course you do." I turn my body towards her and reassure her by squeezing her hand. I have no proof to back up my claim though. I'm fine as long as she doesn't ask any follow up questions.

"Really? How?"

Damn it.

"Well you inspire me by uh …" Think brain, think, I channel Winnie the Pooh. "You're a very logical and methodical person, who's really smart and beautiful, and …" I'm starting to get this now. "And in my book there's a person who's like that, and—get this— they turn out to be the killer."

"So you based a murderer on me?"

"Well, when you say it like *that* it sounds bad." This is bad. Why did I channel Winnie the Pooh? I should have channelled someone whose brain isn't made of fluff, someone whose brain is made of … brain.

"So I remind you of a murderer?"

"A 'beautiful' murderer," I change tack. "And smart."

Flattery isn't working either.

"Look, the character hardly has any connection with you."

"What does he do?"

"Well 'she' … but it's abstract. So she's not like you at all, aside from being slightly pedantic, and her methodicalism."

"Methodicalism isn't a word."

"You're right, sorry."

"Look, I'm sorry. I'm tired. I don't think of you as a murderer."

"It's fine, I'm tired too."

Katharine kisses me on the forehead and gets up to go to the bathroom. We start the pre-bed ritual: brush, floss, pyjamas, light off, lamp on, pull back covers. I go to set my alarm but the bedside clock is blinking and needs to be reset. Whatever, I'll get up when I get up.

Now sleep.

But I can't sleep. I keep turning the day's events over and

over in my head. They pile up like garbage in my mind. At first it's just a few bags, but then it becomes an avalanche of trash. The mental bags keep piling up until it's a full on landfill between my ears.

"I can't sleep," I say.

Katharine says nothing. She's asleep. It's one of the things I love about her. She's like a sprinter when it comes to sleep.

I get out of bed and go down the hall to my mother's room to get a sleeping pill off her. Assuming she hasn't taken them all already.

I see that her light is on. I knock gently and enter.

"Mum...?"

"Come in."

"I was just after a sleeping pill."

The place is tidier than the last time I was in here. The clothes are all off the floor and put away in the closet with the door shut. Suitcases in the corner, bottles gone, so it's a clear path to sit on the bed.

Mum is sitting up, propped up by a cream coloured bed rest pillow. She's in her silk robe, glasses on, she puts down the book she was reading, Uta Hagen's *Respect for Acting*. The cover is facing me as I sit down.

"How are you holding up?" I ask her.

"It's only my pride that's bruised. This old heart has withstood 400 blows, it can take one more. Your mother is a survivor. Our whole family is, that's how we survived The *Shoah*," Mum says, using the Hebrew word for the Holocaust.

"Yes we are."

"What a cliché though, leaving me for a younger woman."

"In fairness, she is his age. And his wife."

"Details, David." She waves her hand.

I notice she's taken off her makeup. It's rare to see her this real.

I've had countless variations of this conversation with her over the years. But it doesn't make it any easier. I know she's hurting and I can't take the pain away. That's the hardest part. The shame in knowing that I have to go through the motions comforting her but that I can't take away the pain.

"I know that you had a connection— or something— with Anthony," I sigh.

"Yes, the connection. That human response you find within the union of two souls. That power you feel when you walk off stage after a great performance–"

"We are talking about Anthony aren't we?"

"Yes, yes of course, darling. I just meant that great love is *like* a great performance. One day you may feel that same passion about someone."

"I do Mum. Katharine."

"Her?"

"Yes, *her*. I love her. And I'm passionate about my book."

"I am so relieved to hear that … about the book. I tried so hard to instil proper values within you. Like valuing art. But there are days when I feel like I've failed you as a parent. Have I failed you, David?"

I hesitate.

"You have to think about it?!"

"No, I um–"

"I knew it. I'm a failure at my career, a failure in love, and a failure as a parent."

"Mum you're not a failure."

"Then why don't you want to spend time with me?"

"I do want to spend time with you, it's just my book, and

everything else. We'll spend some time together soon."

"Do you promise, David?"

"Yes I promise, we'll spend some time together."

"Quality time?"

"Yes."

"And I have been a good mother haven't I?"

This is my chance to be honest. For us to have a genuine adult relationship.

"Yes, of course you have," I say, lying through my teeth. I move closer to her on the bed, and try to comfort her. I can't kick her while she's down.

"You're so sweet, how did I get so lucky to have a son like you."

"Mix up at the hospital?"

Mum smiles at me and reaches over to her bedside table and taps a tablet into her hand. She taps one out for herself and grabs one of the many glasses by her table. I grab the one glass on the nightstand that has a chapstick print on it, but no lipstick print.

That's when it clicks.

"There's just one more thing," I say.

"What is it darling?" she says, the pill between her teeth.

"Edina!" I call out, "Do you want to come out?"

There's a rustling and Edina comes out of the closet. She's in her bra and underwear and holding her basketball clothes.

"Dave … how are ya?" Edina says, "I can explain."

"How did you know," Mum asks.

Edina starts putting on her clothes.

"When I came in you had the book upside down, that's why the cover is facing towards me right now. That glass of gin has been drunk out of, but there wasn't any lipstick on it, because you only wear chapstick during games, Edina. And Mum, you never close your closet door at night, because you want the fabrics to breathe."

"Good detective work there, Dave," Edina says.

"Also, your Ford Bronco is parked outside."

"Oh, right. I might just head home then." Edina says, heading out the door.

"Go the Peewees," I call after her.

"Go the Peewees!" She echoes back.

We hear the front door slam.

"Well, I don't know about you, David, but I am exhausted," Mum says, downing her glass of gin and moving her eye mask into position.

"I'll see you in the morning, Mum."

I'm back in my room and the sleeping pill is having no effect at all. I lay in bed. At least I'll be tired in the morning. And ready for more detective work.

Episode 13

I am feeling lost. Very, very lost.

The creative blockage has come back. And it's not budging. I've spent days starting at the blinking cursor. It's tormenting me like a schoolyard bully.

Plus after promising that we'd spend more time together my mother has done nothing but go out on auditions. TV, theatre, commercials, and films. She practises lines constantly. Pretending to be someone else.

This cycle reminds me how much I hate acting and the whole profession. She always has her mind on the next thing and the next thing.

Even when we are together she isn't present.

When you share a physical space with someone you get close. I know that sounds stupid but the proximity does something to you. Because Mum and I shared apartments and hotels for much of my early childhood, we often shared rooms or beds until I got too old.

So I learned how someone could be distant while being close. How she could be totally in her own world. But she wanted to have access to me, and I wanted her near. So it became an oddly codependent world of nearness and distance.

I've dropped hints that I want to be able to spend some time with her. Casual hints, heavy hints, the whole gamut of hints, but nothing's come of it. She's constantly on the phone to her agent, booking more auditions.

She's absent while being present.

However it does give me the chance to really work on my novel. I'm trying to approach it with the *carpe diem* spirit Mum spoke about but I'm finding it hard to concentrate. With Katharine at the clinic all day, the house is just so damn quiet.

Plus there's the added pressure of my new publishing date and marketing money being spent on promoting the release. When people expected nothing of me I could surprise them, now I can only disappoint.

I just don't know if what I'm doing is any good. Am I just spinning my wheels? Is this what "real" professionals feel? The pressure to perform and create on demand is unnerving. When I didn't have a time limit I could just go at my own pace and take my sweet time.

Now the pressure's on, it's my career, it's my passion, it's my life. Now it's like being a circus seal balancing a beach ball on my nose, except when the trick is done, no one throws you a squid chunk.

The one good thing that came out of my conversation with my mother is that I've realised that I need to let Katharine know how much she means to me. Because I do love her and also because the relationship between Katharine and my mother is getting increasingly strained. Neither has said anything to me but I can sense it. The battle lines are drawn.

In this war between women, I'm in a place called 'no man's land.' There are no direct assaults. Instead it's sideways glances, disapproving facial gestures, sniping comments, and the repetition of: "Everything is *fine*." I dare not stray out into the deadly minefield between them. I'm trying to keep the peace long enough so that I meet my new deadline.

Instead of being a family I've always craved, it's increasingly feeling like three strangers sharing some carpet and walls.

It strikes me that I need to do something special for both Katharine and my Mother. Separately though. I don't want one thinking the other is getting special treatment. I've got to make a big gesture. In secret.

Fortunately Katharine loves surprises. As long as they are well thought out, organised, and highly prepared surprises.

I should be writing my new novel but instead I am planning an evening out. I get out a bottle of riesling from Forrest Wines in New Zealand. Katharine and I did a bike tour of the upper South Island four years ago, and we stopped at their cellar door one warm afternoon and split a bottle. While looking over the neat rows of grapes to the majestic tops of the Southern Alps, we both spontaneously reached for the other's hand. We both smiled, looked at each other and knew how lucky we were to have each other without uttering a word.

I find a nice French restaurant in Abbotsford called Gaul Bladder. The name is supposed to be one of those ultra hip ironic names. But I choose it because it's one of the few place in Melbourne that serves Lobster Thermidor. Katharine and I took a snorkelling trip to New Caledonia and we stumbled upon this tiny, wonderful, hole-in-the-wall French restaurant in Nouméa. We were exhausted after a day under water and had no idea what to expect, but the place was fantastic.

She ordered Lobster Thermidor, which she loved. But I have a pathological fear of crustaceans. I don't like being near crabs or lobsters, and even prawns give me the willies. It's those beady black eyes that look as if they can see directly into your darkest parts of your soul and expose it. That and the claws. Crustaceans have the rare ability to inspire both physical and existential fear in me. She wanted me to taste it so bad that I overcame my fear and we ate the Lobster Thermidor together. Since then it's been a special dish for us.

To round things off, I've booked a week at the Hotham Alpine Resort beginning the day after I hand in my manuscript to Deirdre. Katharine talked about having a ski holiday and I'm going to treat her to one. It's the next place to create a lasting memory of our relationship.

Her present is the booking confirmation for our ski holiday. I've printed the confirmation and put it in a little box with a tiny snow globe and two popsicle sticks that I've drawn on to look like skis.

Wednesday is Katharine's night to work late at the clinic. I tell her to meet me after work and to use the Find My Friends app on the iPhone to locate me and not to ask any questions.

I'm sitting at my computer and on the phone with Gaul Bladder's Maître D' organising the correct order of the surprises.

"So the wine first, then the Lobster Thermidor then the present. All good?"

"Yes, that's all fine, sir."

"Also I'm looking at your website right now and it doesn't say whether there's a corkage fee or not."

"David!" I hear my mother, Susan Wilde, calling from the other room. I try to ignore it. "David?!" She repeats louder.

"Yes, it's 20 per person," The Maître D' says.

Ouch. I look at the bottle of wine on my desk.

"What if it's a screw top bottle?" I ask.

"Sorry, what?" the Maître D' says.

"David, where are you?" She's not giving up. "David. David!"

"Hold on, Mum," I hastily cover the receiver and shout back.

"What was that?" the Maître D' says.

"Nothing, I was just talking to my mother."

"About the corkage fee?" the Maître D' asks.

"No—I just— hold on." I call out, "I'm on the phone, Mum!" Back to the Maître D' "It's a special occasion."

"David!?" Susan Wilde enters my study without knocking. "Oh, there you are, David dear," she says, switching to the sweetest tone imaginable. "Oh, beg your pardon, am I interrupting?"

"So your mother's ok with the corkage fee?" the Maître D' asks.

"Yes, yes, that's all fine," I say, trying to end the conversation fast.

"Ok. We will see you at eight thirty, Mr. Hawkes." the Maître D' says.

"No eight o'clock."

"Right, sorry, eight o'clock then, sir."

"Dinner plans for tonight?" My mother asks cooly.

"No, I mean— yes …?" I trail off as if it was a question. I don't want her to know I'm taking Katharine out. I don't want her to know I'm giving Katharine special treatment.

"Just a little something, with someone … somewhere."

My mother spies the bottle of wine on the desk. "Uh-huh?"

"Oh this, I um," I pick up the bottle. "I've just been, um… drinking. Drinking during the day. Like Hemingway. Got to get those creative juices flowing with the … the old vino." I breathe out. "You know how it is."

"Are you alright darling?"

"Everything is fine," Damn, now I'm saying it too. "It's just … you know what it is?"

"Tell mama." She puts a hand on my shoulder.

"It's the pressure. It's the pressure of this new deadline on my book."

"My god, and the pressure has driven you to drink."

She hugs me to her breast, knocking my glasses askew and gets all breathy.

"I can't help but feel that you didn't have a good role model in this department."

"I'm not pointing fingers, Mum."

"No, blame solves nothing. But I feel as if you may not have turned to drink if your father had been more present for you."

"Wait he−"

She muffles my voice as she hugs my head into her cleavage.

"You know what Mum, I think you're right. I'll give the booze a rest for a spell."

"I think that's for the best. Alcoholism runs in our family. Back in Poland when our family lived in the shtetl there were rumours of our family being drunkards. Fortunately for me it skips a generation."

"Fortunately." I say flatly. "I'll find another way to deal with the pressure of my deadline." I try to get her off the topic of booze. The only way to do this is to talk about the only other thing she cares about more. "I also wanted to say Mum. I really appreciate your work more now. Trying to be creative on demand is hard. And you've done it for 40 years."

"Thank you David, that means a lot. You know, there have been rare occasions when I suspected that you didn't respect my career. But you are right, there are days, like tomorrow at 3pm, when I have to deliver the emotional goods for a motor oil advert. And if I don't deliver on cue then someone else will have the privilege of saying the words 'Lubrication done right.'"

"Well, I just wanted to say thank you for your hard work and for providing for our family. It means a lot to me. Maybe we can talk about this a little more later. You know, so I can gather my thoughts and thank you a little more formally. Like over dinner."

"Sounds lovely," she says. "So I'll just be taking that bottle then?" she adds.

Susan Wilde latches onto the wine bottle, the way a baby does onto a nipple, but I hold onto the Riesling, and shake my head.

"Alcohol is a crutch, David, a crutch. And you don't need it. You're strong enough on your own." She lets go of the bottle and clasps her hands on either side of my head. "So, let your mother kick this crutch out from under you."

"I think I'll just hang onto it for the moment." I say, cradling the wine.

"David, you've got to learn to let go," Mum says, grasping the bottle again.

"Mum, I'm not going to drink it now, I'm saving this for later. Understand?"

"Yes I see," she says, eyeing me.

There is a weird silence as we sort of look at each other. My confusion shifts to irritation.

"What did you even come in here for anyway?"

"I just wanted to tell you that I'm leaving."

"Ok, bye."

There's a pause. She widens her eyes and turns her head ever so slightly.

I roll my eyes and take the bait: "Where are you going Susan?"

"I have a call back today for a children's film. It's something I'm perfect for, but I am not getting my hopes up." She puts her hand lightly on the bookshelf.

"It's a call back so they obviously liked you. What's the part?"

"Oh it's nothing, just a supporting role. A heavily featured supporting role, but a supporting role nonetheless. Probably the biggest small part in the whole film. It's an ensemble piece so there's no one single star per se–"

"Mum, you'll be great."

"I know I can be great, but can I be *great,* great. How great is great enough to be great?

This conversation is starting to grate.

"Can we talk about this later tonight? I'm sort of in the middle of something?"

"Yes, your book. Pardon my interrupting your creative process my darling. Of course we can speak later. I'm just going to go to my audition. Relax and have fun."

Susan Wilde leaves my study and shuts the door. A few moments later I hear the front door slam.

Alone again. With my thoughts as companions. I turn to the keyboard and stare at the blinking cursor, feeling the pressure again.

Then my mother's words ring in my ears. *Just relax and have fun...*

She's right. This is supposed to be fun. Why would I do this unless it was fun. Writing is hard work after all, but it beats working.

* * *

I have to rush to get to the restaurant early. After Mum left I got stuck staring at the computer screen for hours and I lost track of time. I didn't write anything. Deirdre is going to be so pissed. But I just couldn't come up with anything decent.

I put on the light orange button up shirt Katharine likes. But I didn't have time for ironing so I just pressed the collar and threw on black cashmere sweater my mother got me ages ago to cover up the wrinkles. While I comb my hair I accidentally touch the sleeve of my cashmere to the iron and nearly set it on fire. I throw on a bit of aftershave to hide the slightly burnt smell.

I arrive in Abbotsford, walk into Gaul Bladder, and am immediately confronted by a giant lobster tank. A shiver races up my spine and I nearly drop the bottle of wine.

"Good evening," the Maître D' says.

"Hawkes, party of two."

"Ah, yes. You're a bit early but your table is ready, if you'd like to be seated first." I was going to sit in the waiting area for Katharine but I don't want to give the lobsters more time to gaze into my soul. I realise that I'm not as over my crustacean phobia as I thought. I clutch her present in front of my chest as the Maître D' escorts me to a linen-covered table. I could swear one of those red, sea-whiskered beasts snapped its pincer at me as I walked past.

The waiter comes over. "Hi, I'll be your waiter tonight, my name is Jeffery, but please call me Jeff," says the young man who speaks like he went to a private boarding school. "While this is formal dining, I like to keep it caszh." It takes me a second to realise he means 'casual'.

Jeff pulls the chair out so I can sit down. As I sit down and he tucks my chair in at the table he sniffs several times. He's either smelling me or he has an allergy to the cashmere. That would be a posh waiter's curse, to be allergic to cashmere. Or to silk, or mink, or Burberry. Then he takes the heavily starched cloth napkin, gives it a whip, places it on my lap, and smoothes it down.

"Oh, um, thank you, Jeffery," I say.

He gives me a look.

"I mean 'Jeff.'"

'Jeff' gives me a big smile and another sniff.

"Allow me to open this for you, sir," Jeff says, taking the bottle of Riesling. He unscrews the bottle and pours a tiny bit into my glass.

"I don't really need to taste the wine Jeff, I brought it."

"We want you to get the full experience here at Gaul Bladder," Jeff says, giving me a big eager smile. Then he sniffs a few more times.

"Ok ..."

I go to drink the wine.

"Smell the bouquet first," Jeff says, giving a few more sniffs. This time I can't tell if he's sniffing to demonstrate how to smell wine or if he has allergies.

I eyeball Jeff and I smell the wine. It smells like wine.

I go to drink the wine again.

"What does it smell like?"

"Fermented grapes."

"No, you have to talk about it. The whole thing is that you're meant to describe the smell. Be creative."

"Oh right, there's, um … a scent of flowers–"

"What kind of flowers?"

"Lilacs."

"Good! What else?"

"Cardamom pods."

"Oh?"

"And a I'm getting a whiff of a dew soaked mountain pass on a summer's morn, with just a whisper of redwood bark that curls round the nose like an ivy vine through a garden lattice.'"

Now I'm just making shit up.

"You smelled all that in there?"

"…Yes?"

"Well done, sir. Most of our guests aren't as refined as you," Jeff says, sniffing to punctuate the end of the sentence.

I have the glass poised at my lips.

Jeff nods.

I empty the glass. It tastes like wine.

Jeff's staring at me. "How is it on the palate?"

"It hits the palate gracefully, like a kick from a mule." I flubbed that one. Jeff doesn't seem to notice, he's filling the two glasses at the table.

"Wonderful." Jeff sniffs a few more times. "I understand you've preordered the Lobster Thermidor."

"Yes, Jeff."

"An excellent choice if I do say so myself."

"Thank you, Jeff."

"Chef is working on that as we speak. Can I bring you a menu in case you'd like an appetiser?"

"Yes please, Jeff."

Jeff turns to go.

"Oh, Jeff. Can you take this?" I hand him the present for Katharine. "Bring it over when I give you the signal."

"Signal, sir?"

I do the 'nose tap' signal.

"Yes I see, sir." Jeff gives me the nose tap back, smiles knowingly, and sniffs goodbye as he heads back to the kitchen. I'm slightly thrown by this, but maybe fancy waiters are trained to make rich people think that what they're doing is totally normal.

There are only a few other people in the restaurant. I guessed it would be busier, but maybe Wednesday is their slow night. French food does feel like more of a weekend thing. Who really wants escargot on hump day? Wednesday feels more like an Indian or Malaysian night of the week for some reason. Monday feels the most like a fish and chips night to me, which ironically, is the one night of the week that most fish and chips places are closed.

Jeff, not Jeffery, interrupts my thoughts of the dietary days of the week.

"I think the other member of your party has arrived, sir," he says, smiling and giving me the nose tap signal.

I look over to the waiting area and that's when I see her, talking to the Maître D', my girlfriend, Katharine Nichols.

I go to stand up but someone covers my eyes from behind.

"Guess who?"

I don't need to guess.

"Mum!"

"This is a wonderful surprise David. Thank you."

Susan Wilde slips around me and sits down at the table.

"Wait— how did you?"

"Jeff and I came to an arrangement to surprise you," Mum

says, giving Jeff the nose tap signal and winking. "Thank you, Jeff. That'll be all for the moment," she says to him.

"No wait, Jeff, I need you to stall that woman with the Maître D'. Don't bring her over yet."

"Bring who over, sir?"

"The brunette talking with the Maître D'! Just tell her everything isn't ready yet, or something. I don't know."

"This is all very strange, sir," Jeff says.

"What *I'm* doing is strange? He's the weird one with all the sniffing and napkin lap stuff–"

"David. Do *not* talk about the help as if they're not there," Mum says, checking her upper lip in her compact. "Besides, the man is really quite an excellent service provider."

Susan and Jeff giggle. I don't want to know.

"Just stall," I growl at him from between clenched teeth.

Jeff leaves, sniffing as he goes.

I'm about to say *Mum what the hell are you doing here*, but realise that I've overused those particular words in recent times. As a writer I don't want to be repetitive. And you can say that again.

"I know there's a reason you're here," I say.

"For our special dinner. You've been dropping all those hints about us spending more time together. I figured out what you were planning. This little rendezvous is to celebrate me getting the role in that children's film."

"You got the part?"

"No. I should have got it. Now it's a consolation dinner."

Mum looks away and sniffs, as if she's going to cry. I've got to get her out of here before Katharine sees.

Mum takes a sip of Katherine's wine.

"Oh mum that's not for–"

163

"Magic! I just try to give people magic. But do they appreciate it?"

"What was the part?"

"It was for a witch, but the producers gave it to Claudette Carvano. Those swollen parcels of pestilence! A scurvy pox upon their houses!"

She seems a bit out of it, but she doesn't seem drunk. Maybe she's still in character. She has dabbled with Method acting in the past.

"Have you been drinking?"

"It's a children's film, David. You think I'd go drunk?" Mum sniffs like Jeff, then dips her fingers into Katharine's wine and smells it.

"Cocaine?!"

"Shh … a witch needs her magic powder … for motivation."

This wine snorting trick is something that makes cocaine absorb more quickly into your nasal passages. I can't believe that I know this. Mum double dips her fingers in the Riesling and remoistens her nose.

"I also took half an ecstasy."

"Where did you get the money for— look it doesn't matter— I need you to go, I'm meeting someone."

"During our special dinner? Rude. I can see I did fail at teaching you manners. I am getting a drink at the bar, do you want anything."

"I don't care, just go."

Mum walks to the bar, shoulders back and down. She puts on the airs of a proud woman striding off confidently.

I take a moment to catch my emotional breath, but just then Jeff brings over Katharine. She's wearing a button up white blouse, black slacks and white flat shoes with her hair in a ponytail. She's like a scene from a classic Hollywood film coming to life in front of my eyes.

"This lady says she's here to meet you too, sir. Is that right?"

"That's totally right, Jeff. Thank you," I say. He opens his mouth to speak again but I cut him off. "That'll be all Jeff, thank you, thank you very much, maybe just check to see if our food's ready. Thank you."

Katharine sits down.

Jeff whipcracks Katharine's napkin startling her, places it firmly on her lap like he's buckling a child's seat belt, then walks towards the kitchen.

"This is a very fancy restaurant David," Katharine smiles. I meet her smile. "And here I thought you'd completely forgotten about our anniversary." she says.

Wham! And not one with Andrew Ridgeley and George Michael.

"How could I forget?" I say casually. I maintain my smile, widening it, making it huge. A cold sweat breaks out on the back of my neck.

My gargantuan smile hides the abject terror in forgetting our anniversary, coincidentally creating a romantic evening for us and thereby saving myself, and the sudden revelation that if Katharine sees my mother here at our 'anniversary dinner' she might have a 'shutdown.' Katharine never gets angry, she just shuts down and refuses to talk. It's like a meltdown but silent.

"What is the deal with that waiter?"

My jaw starts to ache from holding the smile so long.

"I'm pretty sure he's on coke," I say.

"Diet or regular?"

I laugh a little too loudly.

Katharine looks at me.

"David, it wasn't that funny."

"Oh I think you underestimate yourself. You are one funny lady."

"I am one tired lady is what I am. I'm going to freshen up."

"Great idea, great idea."

Katharine grabs her purse and stands up. She notices the label of the bottle. "You got The Doctors' riesling, oh sweetie, you thought of everything."

"Not everything," I say, feeling a rising panic as I spot my mother at the bar.

Katharine reaches for her wine glass. The one my mother put her nasally infused fingers into.

"No wait, don't drink that one." I lunge at the glass. "That one's mine."

I grab the glass and drink from it.

"I switched sides of the table. I don't like my back facing the door. You know, cause I like to pretend I'm in the mafia. They never sit with their backs to the entrance in case someone puts a hit out on them. And, you know, bam!"

I mime a gun, and a head exploding.

"Are you ok David? You seem more nervous than normal?"

"Everything is fine." Damn said it again. "Everything is just dandy."

Katharine runs her hand around my ear, tucking my hair as her fingers come to rest on my chin. "This is all wonderful, and so are you." She tips my chin skyward and meets me halfway for a kiss.

Katharine leaves and goes to the bathroom. As soon as she's gone Mum comes back to the table with drinks.

"I didn't know what you wanted, love. So I ordered you a

triple vodka, neat," Mum says, handing me a tumbler of clear, iceless liquid. "Cheers." She clinks her glass against mine and downs half the glass.

"Mum, you need to get out of here."

"I might be ready for another round. How about you? Where's Jeff?"

"You need to go–"

"David, I am beginning to get the distinct impression that you don't want me here."

"What gave it away?"

"I thought you wanted to spend time with me?"

"I do. Just not like this." I put my hand on top of hers and squeeze hard to get her attention. "If you go now, you and I can go on a trip. Just the two of us. Down the Great Ocean Road."

"Oh you're wearing the cashmere I got you." Mum starts touching the woollen fabric. "It feels amazing." The ecstasy must be kicking in.

Another waiter comes by and I pull my arm away as he lights the candle in the middle of the table.

"Jeff told me the Lobster Thermidor will be out in a moment," the waiter says as he passes us on his way to light all the other table candles.

Mum pulls out a cigarette and lights it off the candle.

"Mum, you can't smoke in here," I say, grabbing her arm from across the table; she quickly switches the smoke to her mouth.

"David?!" Katharine's voice pierces through the restaurant.

Oh no. I freeze holding my mother's arm in place over the table.

Katharine is back from freshening up in the bathroom. She

either applied a lot of rouge or she's red in the face from anger.

"You look amazing Katharine. Did you brush your hair?"

"What is *she* doing here?" Katharine asks.

"*She* has a name. It's Susan Wilde," says Susan Wilde.

"Katharine I can explain."

"If you wouldn't mind," Katharine says, folding her arms in front of her.

"There was a mix-up with–"

"Lobster Thermidor for two!" Jeff announces as he approaches with a large silver tray with two dishes on it.

I can smell it as Jeff gets closer to the table. It smells like burning wool.

My mother shrieks, as she pulls her arm free of my grasp.

The cashmere has caught fire over the open flame of the candle. Katharine instinctively goes for the closest glass of clear liquid and douses my arm.

Unfortunately this happens to be the triple neat vodka.

My sweater, and arm, burst into flame and I leap to my feet upsetting the wine on the table and knocking over the Lobster Thermidor.

I wave my arm around in a panic smacking my sweater to try and muffle the flame but it's no use.

Then I see it: the lobster tank in the waiting area. I can either stick my arm into an aquarium of my greatest phobia or allow my arm to burn down to a stump.

I plunge it in and feel the sweet relief.

That is until a lobster pinches my finger.

I pull my arm out and whip the red beast from my hand.

I collapse onto the floor along the wood panelling in front of the lobster tank.

Katharine rushes over to me, "My god David, I'm so sorry.

I didn't know."

"That's ok." I clutch my hand.

Mum rushes over to me. "My baby, are you ok?"

"I'll be fine, *Susan*."

"I feel terrible. This is just like that time on your–

"10th birthday? Yes I remember," I say.

"Let's get this off you," Katharine says.

I put my arms up and Katharine begins getting me out of the tatters of my cashmere sweater.

"Yes I'd better have a look. Jeff, get me a first aid kit," mum says.

"Just let Katharine handle things," I say.

"I think you're forgetting I played a registered nurse on television," mum says.

"I think you're forgetting she's a trained medical professional," I say.

"I am a Method actor, David, she is just a podiatrist."

"I'll take my chances, thanks."

The Maître D' places the phone back on the cradle. "I've called an ambulance."

Mum puffs nervously on her cigarette. "Will he be scarred?" Mum asks.

"More than he already is?" Katharine deadpans, as she inspects my arm

"I don't need your sarcasm young lady," Susan shoots back.

"Well we don't need your …" Katharine doesn't finish her sentence, she just gives an exasperated sigh.

"What? You don't need my what?"

"We don't need you!" Katharine starts. But then sees all the restaurant patrons grouping around. "Nothing. Forget it."

"What is it Katharine? Do you have something to say to

me?"

Katharine goes into shutdown mode and buttons her lip.

"We can be honest with each other. We're two grown women. What's on your mind?"

"We don't need your, your … smoking!" Katharine says.

Susan stands up, pauses for a moment. Then exhales two huge plumes of smoke out of her nostrils like a dragon. Then drops her Dunhill to the floor and grinds it out with the sole of her shoe. Then she plunges her spike heel through the head of the lobster who is still groping around on the floor.

Jeff comes up and whispers in my ear. "Shall I bring the present out now, sir?"

I glare at Jeff.

"Wait until the ambulance leaves. Got it." Jeff scurries away, sniffing as he goes.

The ambulance arrives. A young blonde woman with hair in a ponytail and a 40ish man with a moustache in white outfits jump out. The paramedics start by cutting my sweater off me.

"Careful, that's cashmere," my Mother snaps.

The paramedics just look at her and continue to do their jobs. They get my sweater off and start to inspect my arm.

"Let's go outside and let them do their jobs," Katharine says to Mum. "They're medical professionals. Like me."

The paramedics look at Katharine.

"I'm a podiatrist," Katharine fills in the blank as she leads my mother outside the glass doors.

The paramedics go back to doing their job. The male paramedic, whose name tag reads, 'Callum', breaks from shop talk with his colleague, and says to me, "I'm sorry but I just have to ask."

"How did this happen?" I say, not wanting to reveal the truth.

"No. Is that Susan Wilde?" Callum says in a low voice.

"Who?" I say, not wanting to reveal the truth.

"It is, isn't it?" says the paramedic whose name tag reads 'Vanessa'.

My mother continues to pace on the other side of the glass doors. Unsure of what to do with her hands without a cigarette.

Vanessa watches Mum out of the corner of her eye as she starts wrapping my arm in non-stick gauze.

Callum puts a splint around my finger and then signals for Katharine and Susan to come back inside.

"How is he, doctor? Will he be able to keep the arm?" Susan says in her most melodramatic voice.

"Aside from having one hairless arm he's going to be fine," Vanessa says. "The flames went out before any real damage happened to your skin."

"Oh thank you God," Mum says, clutching her hands to her chest.

"You'll be in some pain for a week or so," Callum says. "Get some aloe vera, change the bandages daily, and we'll give you some morphine for the pain."

"Good idea, morphine, yes." Susan says.

Vanessa gives me a couple pills to swallow and hands a bottle towards Susan which Katharine intercepts.

"I'll hang on to those," Katharine says.

The paramedics get me up and out the door. At Katharine's car Vanessa finally gets up the courage to ask my mother.

"Don't I know you from somewhere?"

"Potentially," Susan says.

171

"You're Susan Wilde, from *Destiny's Hope*."

"And you used to be on *Next Door* back in the day?" Callum says. "Your character killed Gordon at his wedding and then fled the country."

"Guilty as charged," my Mother says wryly.

"What are you working on now?" Vanessa asks.

"Well just now I'm up for this big part in a children's film," mum says.

"What's it called?" Callum asks.

"I can't say. But it's a marquee role, and I'm a shoo-in."

"Is it rude to ask for an autograph right now?" Vanessa asks.

"It would be," Susan Wilde says devilishly, "But I can never say no to a fan. David, can I have your pen?"

Just then Jeff runs out. "You forgot this."

"Oh my purse," Katharine says.

"No, the bill," Jeff says. He sniffs one last time for good measure.

"Right," Katharine mutters, "My purse's still inside. Susan, can you get David in the car?"

"Of course, Kathy."

Katharine bristles as she follows Jeff in.

Mum helps me into the car and takes my pen out of my pants pocket along with my keys. I grab her hand.

"You're not driving Mum, not in your condition."

"You're right David, my nerves are shot," she says as she buckles me in. "Can you ever forgive me David? I feel partially responsible for this whole situation?"

I just look at her with beady black lobster eyes.

"You're so understanding." Mum lets go of the keys, kisses me on the forehead, and slams the car door. She goes over to the paramedics at the van. They chat and Mum signs a few papers for them.

Katharine gets back in the car.

"Are you alright honey?"

"Uh-huh," I grunt. The morphine is mixing in with the wine and making me drowsy.

"Let's just get you home," Katharine says. She pulls the car up to the ambulance and honks the horn for Susan to break off her fan club meeting.

"Sorry darlings," Mum says, jumping in the car. "I'm sorry if I interfered with your dinner plans. It was just an honest misunderstanding. Did you hear me David?" Mum asks.

My eyes get heavy and I close them. I'm too angry to talk to her right now. Plus my mouth is not really working. I keep my eyes shut and breathe. I listen.

"I think he's out," Mum says.

"Susan, I'm sorry for getting after you about your smoking. It's not my place to advise you on your health," Katharine says. "You're not my patient."

"I know you just say these things because you care so much about me."

"It's just not very healthy for your feet. You could develop peripheral arterial disease and require an amputation."

"Your concern means the world to me." There's a moment of silence, then, "You know dear, I have yet to hear the story of how you got into podiatry in the first place ... Katharine."

"How did I get into it? Well, I wanted something where I could be my own boss, something that was stable, something that would give me money to travel, and eventually allow me to have a work/life balance while raising a family. Podiatry ticked those boxes."

"You weren't pushed into it by an overbearing and controlling family?"

"No, not at all. All the women in my family are in medicine."

"So they were supportive of your decisions."

"Yeah, of course."

"That must have been nice. I never had that."

"I mean they were a little bit wary when I applied to the podiatry school."

"Why? They felt that feet were beneath you?"

"Maybe But it's not just the feet we treat. It's the whole lower part of the leg. The calf, the ankle, the toes, the toenails. And I have to diagnose what's wrong and try to find a solution."

"It sounds almost creative?"

"It is, in a sense. Like if someone is presenting with pain in the hip flexor, it could be any number of things and I have to find the solution. And the payoff is immense. If you're not walking right because of an instep, it can throw your whole life out of balance. And when I can help correct that, they walk out a new person."

"It's the greatest feeling in the world when you know that you have affected someone else's life."

"It really is. That's the joy of podiatry," Katharine says.

"You hide behind this dry, bland, boring, exterior, but I think within you beats the heart of a true artist," Susan says. Then adding, "That's what David needs in his life."

There's a pause.

Then Katharine continues: "So did you get into acting?"

"I was called to it. Much like you were called to the foot. I can still recall watching a classic black-and-white movie on TV with the most striking woman imaginable. She had gorgeous hair and wore a stunning white gown."

"Marilyn Monroe?"

"Elsa Lanchester."

"Who?"

"From *The Bride of Frankenstein*."

In my drugged out state I am not sure if I am hearing this correctly. I've heard many different versions of why my mother got into acting, but never this one. I try to ward off sleep.

"I pointed at the screen and said 'Papa, what's that'? And he said, in his thick Polish accent. 'That, my dear sweet angel, is an actor.' An actor. I rolled the word around in my mouth and spoke it aloud for the first time. 'Actor.'"

"And did your parents encourage you? Did they approve of you being an actor?"

"No, they discouraged me at every turn. They didn't have an artistic bone in their philistine bodies. Their only aspirations for me were to marry someone from their synagogue with a good job. They wanted to trap me in their suffocating suburban prison. They told me if I insisted on indulging in this deluded fantasy I'd have to do it on my own. And I did. My passion carried me."

I lived with my grandparents for parts of my childhood and they were kindly, giving, people who loved me unconditionally. I'm not sure if she's concocted this story for some purpose, or if they just mellowed out years later. They *were* Holocaust survivors and had their issues. It's hard to think with the drugs numbing my senses.

Mum continues: "I wanted something where I could be my own boss, something that was stable, something that would allow me to travel, and eventually allow me to have a work/life balance while raising a family. Acting was the thing that would allow me to have the life I wanted to live. Much like podiatry is for you."

Mum and Katharine keep chatting. I tune out.

I can see what Mum is trying to do. She's trying to get Katharine onto her side. She's building an alliance with my girlfriend for some nefarious purpose. I want to get to know my mother, the real person, the one she described in the *Bride of Frankenstein* story. Not the one covered up with the drugs and booze, and the character of Susan Wilde. I know she'll never stop for my sake, but she may stop for her career. If I can get her to stop drinking and drugging for the sake of her beloved career then she might just realise that I'm an important part of her life too.

Just before I pass out due to the morphine I decide it's time for my mother to go to rehab ... again.

She can go or get out ... she's too old to be living a lifestyle she should have grown out of years ago ... it's time for her to settle down and act her age ... be the mother she always wanted to be for me ... and be an actor that she wants to be ... for her own sake ... she can't keep doing things in the same way ... not on my watch ... not in my house ... if she wants to insist on indulging in this deluded fantasy she'll have to do it on her own ...

Now I sound just like my grandparents.

Episode 14

I wake up. Or, more accurately, I come to. I am so groggy from the wine and morphine last night that I can't remember coming home last night. I sit up in bed. I can see that I have my Star Trek pyjama tops on, glasses on the side table. It's morning; at least I think it is. I look over at my alarm clock but it's stopped.

I push myself up. My arm hurts from the burns. Some aloe vera, a fresh bandage, and a little pain medication will make it feel better. My heart hurts too. But that's the pain of being the child of a self-obsessed, substance-abusing actor who's addicted to the spotlight. No aloe vera to cool this type of blistering resentment. The only cure is to put out the fire.

The toilet flushes and breaks my train of thought. Katharine comes out of the en suite after washing her hands. She's still in her PJs too.

"Oh good, you're awake," Katharine says.

She goes back to the bathroom and gets a fresh wrapping for my arm and some lotion.

"How are you feeling?"

"I'm fantastic," I say.

Katharine just looks at me.

"I'm not being sarcastic. I *do* feel good. My arm hurts like hell, but I *feel* good." I say, sticking out my arm. "You wanna know why?"

"Enlighten me," Katharine says. She gets down on one knee, rolls up my pyjama arm, and starts unwrapping my arm.

"Because today is the first day of the rest of our lives."

"It is?" Katharine stops the bandaging and looks at me.

"I'm ready to get serious about things."

"You are?" Katharine drops the bandage roll. It spools out along the floor. It cuts in between the loose bandage clips creating an aisle in the middle.

"Yeah, of course, aren't you? I mean how long can we keep doing this?" I say.

"Does this have something to do with the present that Jeff the waiter gave me last night?"

"Wait, what? How did you know about that?" I say.

"He gave it to me when I went in to pay for the dinner we didn't eat."

"You didn't open it did you?"

"No, of course not. I couldn't open it without you being there. I'd rather wait until the right time."

Katharine points to the smallish box. She put it on my nightstand.

"Don't you see Katharine? That's my point. There's a larger life lesson here. If we wait around for the 'perfect moment' we could be waiting around forever. We've got to do this right now."

"What? Now? But, but, but, I just woke up. This isn't how I imagined it happening. Don't you think you should be the one on your knees and not me?"

"I don't care. It's time for us to get on with our lives."

Katharine seems to like this 'take charge' attitude I'm

displaying right now. I grab the little box with the tiny snow globe.

"I was going to give this to you, but now I'm going to give it to my mother," I say.

"Your mother?"

"Yes, my mother. Who else? I'm telling her that she has to either go to rehab or move out. This will be her ... going away present."

"Oh…" Katharine looks disappointed.

"What are you upset about? I thought you wanted her out?"

"No it's not that, it's just …"

I can tell something else is up. I start getting paranoid that Mum has converted Katharine over to her side.

"Did you and her stay up and talk last night?"

"Yeah, we may have sipped a few chardonnays and chatted a bit."

"Did she try to make you feel sorry for her? Because you shouldn't, it's all lies. None of those stories are true. What did she say about me?"

"She didn't say anything about you."

"No, really, what did she say?"

"Believe it or not David, women *can* talk about things that aren't men," Katharine snaps at me. Katharine softens. "She was very vulnerable. And she kept revealing stuff. Especially after she broke into the brandy."

"Yeah, brandy does that to her. I don't know what it is? For some reasons she starts to–"

"Confess. Oh yeah. I felt like I should have given her a few Hail Marys and Our Fathers to say after."

"So what did you talk about?" I ask.

"We talked about work. How hard she found it both then

and now. How she was constantly judged on her appearance. How she had to fight to get and maintain every role that she ever won. How she had to do twice the work to receive half the pay of her male co-stars. That she fought to be heard by her managers, agents, and publicity people who wanted to direct her career. She had to battle to maintain her identity outside what the men in her life wanted her to be."

"Yeah, well, things were really tough for actresses back in the day," I reflect.

"They're tough now. She's really struggling with the ageing process and how isolating it is. She's been in a profession which requires you to form relationships that don't necessarily last. All she really wants to do is get back to work. But her American agent's dropped her."

"She said all of this to *you*?"

"Why is that surprising?"

"She's never said any of that to me. How could she keep that sort of stuff from me? I'm her favourite son!"

"Only son," Katharine corrects.

"Whatever."

"She doesn't know who she is without her career."

"She's a mother, *my* mother."

"That's the point Davey, she's more than that. She's Susan Wilde."

"Not to me she isn't. Do you know what it's like to have to share your mother?" I ask.

"Um, yes, I have siblings, remember."

"That's not what I mean. I had to compete with the world for her love, you only had to compete with other kids."

"You act like you're the only person who had a mother who worked. My mum had a career too. And a husband, and kids, and a book club."

"It must have been so hard for you with your mother out discussing *Madame Bovary* with suburban housewives on a Wednesday night with supermarket-bought merlot."

"You're being a real arsehole right now, you know that?"

I breathe. Katharine's right.

"I'm sorry," I say.

"David, you act like your mother is this horrible person, who you are desperate to get attention from. Maybe you two need some family counselling."

"We've tried that ..." I sigh.

"And?"

"It was going well until Mum started dating Dr. Berkowitz. Then we had to go to another family counsellor to sort out the issues I had with my mum's new boyfriend."

"And did that resolve anything?"

"Yeah, Mum cheated on Dr. Berkowitz with Dr. O'Brien. It ended when she confessed after a few brandies, and Dr. Berkowitz brought it up in our next session with Dr. O'Brien."

"Why on earth would she tell Dr. Berkowitz?"

"She thought patient confidentiality still applied. Anyway it was a whole scene, they got in a fight, the cops got called, Mum was crying, both of them got hauled in front of an ethics committee."

"What happened to you?"

"I ended up in therapy."

"She didn't date your therapist did she?"

"Dr. Keats? No."

"That's good."

"No. She married *him*. They eloped after a Psychiatric convention in Vegas."

Katharine is too stunned to talk. She blinks her eyes repeatedly. Her lips move like a goldfish. No sound comes out. I can see she's trying to process the information I've just given her and coming up with the one maddening question that has no answer: why?

I look out the window. I see a rainbow lorikeet picking at an apple on the neighbour's tree. How simple and happy that brightly coloured mini-parrot's life must be. It wakes up, chirps a bit, eats some fruit. Flies around. Eats more fruit. It must be nice to have a brain the size of a pistachio.

I feel like I have the brain the size of a sunflower seed. The very idea that having my mother around would enable my creativity was absurd. Sure it worked for a little while but now I'm just as creatively blocked as I was before. I haven't written anything decent in the last few days and my deadline is looming.

Katharine finally collects herself. "Maybe you could just try talking to her."

"I *do* talk to her, Katharine. I try and connect with her all the time. There's just too much baggage in the way," I say. "I feel like every time I open up to her I end up getting burned." I rub my forearm. "I just wish we could connect," I mumble to myself.

"You will."

"We will when she gets off the booze and drugs. I know I've given her tons of ultimatums over the years but this is the last one. She can either go to rehab or get out. I don't care if I write better and quicker with her around. The umbilical cord is getting cut."

"Well, if you think that's the right thing to do."

"I know you two commiserate after your brandy session

last night, but I've decided, don't try to talk me out of it."

"I wouldn't dream of it. I know that once you make up your mind about something you do it eventually … or change your mind."

"Exactly," I say. "And, you know what, either way we are going on a holiday–"

"David that's not–"

"No, no, I want to make it up to you after last night. Whether Mum's in rehab or on the street, we are gonna get away together, just the two of us, without the fear of the house burning to a cinder."

I pull my feet onto the ground taking the blankets with me. "It's time."

"David, it's 7am. And she had a lot to drink last night, you might have a hard time rousing her."

"I don't care. I'm going to demonstrate my authority."

I throw off the blankets and start to get up. Katharine pushes my shoulders down and looks me square in the eye.

"You may want to put on some pants first."

I notice that I only have my pyjama tops on.

"You know, to demonstrate your authority," Katharine says.

I throw on a T-shirt and a pair of Levi's. I adjust my horn-rimmed glasses and walk out the bedroom door. Katharine follows me down the hall. I slide open the door to the kitchen, and there she is, my mother, Susan Wilde. Her back turned to us. Then she spins around so smoothly it's almost as if she's standing on a Lazy Susan.

She's dressed like an ideal mother from a 1950s advert. Hair curled, a light red dress with white stitching hemmed at the knee, a floral print two-pocket apron, and a pearl necklace lying elegantly around her collarbones with matching pearl studs to frame her face. Her eyes are clear and her makeup is perfect.

On the table a picture perfect breakfast, the type you'd find in an insurance commercial. Two place settings, on opposite sides of the table: two eggs, poached; Canadian bacon, two rashers each; orange juice; and coffee, black, steaming, with a tiny jug of milk in the middle of the table. The silverware is correctly laid out with a knife and spoon on the right, and fork on the left resting upon a red-and-white chequered cloth napkin.

A Stepford Wife wet dream.

"Wow …" Is all Katharine can manage.

Stunned silence is all I can manage. The words want to race out of my mouth but my tonsils and tongue are like speed bumps slowing my words down.

Susan smiles at us, backlit by a shaft of sunlight streaming through the windows, which appear to have been washed both inside and out.

"Wonderful, the two of you are up, I was afraid your brekkie would get cold. You had a big sleep last night mister. And you must be hungry too, missy. We had quite a night of girl talk didn't we, Katharine?"

Katharine is doing her goldfish impression again. Susan glides over to her like she's on ice skates.

"Katharine? We had quite a lovely chat, right honey?"

"I think she's talking to you," I whisper to my girlfriend.

"Yes, sorry," Katharine wakes up from her vegetable torpor. "I'm just … Susan you made this, this–"

"This hearty nutritious breakfast to get you ready for the day?" Susan Wilde smiles her trademark 100-watt beam. "Come sit. You young people never slow down enough to eat properly," Mum chuckles warmly. She pulls out the chairs and guides us each to seated positions. I'm too stunned to resist.

"You're right, things can get out of control," Katharine says.

Mum is about to place my napkin on my lap.

"I'll do that." I flashback to last night as I take the patterned serviette. We don't own napkins like this, do we? Have we owned these for years and I haven't paid attention? My head is still groggy from the morphine.

Katharine is tasting the orange juice. "Freshly squeezed?"

"Only because I had the time, love," mum says.

I turn my head and mum is coming at me with a plate piled a mile high with pancakes. She offloads a stack on each of our plates.

"*Bon appétit mes ceux chéris,*" Mum says, sitting down at the head of the table.

"Mum, I need to talk–" I start, but Katharine cuts me off.

"You're not eating, Susan?"

Susan touches our shoulders, "I made this for you two. And please call me 'mum.'"

'Mum' pops some Nicorette gum in her mouth and faces the packet so I can read the branding.

Subtle.

"This looks amazing Susan," Katharine says, tentatively digging in.

"Yes. Quite a spread Suse," I say, pushing my plate away. "You have a hidden talent."

"It was nothing," mum says, fluffing the bottom of her curls.

"I know what you're doing, mum."

"Can't this wait until after breakfast, David?" Katharine says, giving me her patented ice stare which melts into a warm bliss as she puts pancake into her mouth.

"Katharine don't you see what's—" I don't get to finish my sentence because Katharine shoves a pancake, doused in butter and maple syrup, into my open face.

My anger melts into mouth heaven.

These might be the best pancakes I've ever eaten.

"Mmm! This coffee is spectacular, Susan," Katharine says.

"It's a special kind called, *kopi luwak*. And I added some free range finger milk," Mum responds.

"Finger milk?"

Katharine looks at the cup suspiciously.

"It means no milking machine. The only middleman between that cow's teat and your mouth is a farmer's calloused hand."

"It's delish. I've got to *hand* it to you … mum," Katharine says.

Mum laughs, Katharine laughs. I don't laugh.

This is obviously some sort of trick, but I don't know where the rabbit is going to come from yet.

"That reminds me I have a surprise for you." Mum goes back around to the kitchen bench and pulls something out from behind another giant stack of pancakes. She glides back to the table and places it on a coaster in front of me.

It's my special Doctor Who mug.

It's been glued back together again.

It's full of sweet smelling strong black coffee that wafts through my nose hairs and tickles my brain. I can't believe it.

I take it to my lips like I'm about to drink from the Holy Grail.

"But wait," Katharine says, her face full of pancake, "I threw that out."

"I rescued it from the trash."

I put the now Unholy Grail back down. I snap out this maternally-induced trance and get back on track.

"This whole," I wave my hand about, "performance is all well and good, Mum. But it doesn't change anything."

"Not while I'm eating," Katharine says sharply.

"Oh, I almost forgot the surprise!" Mum says.

"Uh, no Mum, it's here, remember," I say holding up the rematerialised TARDIS mug.

"Oh that, I just did that because I love you."

"Thank you, Mum, and I really want to hear your little 'surprise', or whatever, but first Katharine and I need to tell you something."

Mum puts on her earnest voice: "No please, let me tell you the surprise."

"It can wait."

"It really can't."

"I'm sure it can."

"David, what's the big deal?" Katharine interjects, "Your mother's gone to a lot of trouble here. Just let her share her surprise first. Have some bacon, it's hickory smoked."

"Stop trying to put this off," I tell my girlfriend.

"Ok, I'll go first," Mum starts.

She clears her throat and I jump in first.

"No, Mum. Here it is: We love you but, I feel, I mean *we* feel-"

"The real surprise is that I am checking myself into a treatment facility later today."

And there's the rabbit.

Like a magic trick we just sit there wondering where it came from.

"I am ashamed to admit it, but recently I've been using alcohol and some recreational drugs in ways not prescribed by my doctors. You may, perhaps, have noticed?"

"Now that you mention it …"

"David!" Katharine cuts in. "Go on Susan— I mean Mum— *We* care," Katharine says looking at me and giving me her patented stare.

"Yes, thank you. I have been leaning on that particular crutch a little too heavily in recent months. I feel like it's taken a toll on me professionally, spiritually, and, most importantly, in my relationship to the two most important people in my world …"

The wind has literally been taken out of my sails.

"… the two of you," Mum carries on, clasping both our hands, eyes getting moist.

Katharine squeezes Mum's hand back.

"I know I could be forgiven for my overdependence on such amenities. After all, my career is on an uninterrupted downward trajectory."

"So, after a lot of soul searching, I decided it's time. Time to stop running, time to face the music, time to clear my head, time to get my life back on track, time to love my family wholeheartedly without any chemical barrier in the way. I may have lost my home and my livelihood but I am not going to lose the thing that means the most to me. It's time to turn this Greek Tragedy into a Gilbert and Sullivan musical."

Yes, it is time I think. I look up at the kitchen clock but it's not where it should be. Mum's taken it off the wall and removed the batteries for some unknown reason.

"And we support you." Katharine says.

"I can't move forward, personally or professionally, without going into the Mel Gibson Rehabilitation Centre."

"That's not a thing," I say.

"It is. He founded it after Hollywood cast him out for driving drunk."

"Mum, you can't go there, he's an anti-Semite," Katharine says.

"Yes, but the thing about Judaism is that it teaches us forgiveness and tolerance."

"Isn't that every religion?" I say.

"Yeah but Jews are better at it because we have so much practice," Mum says. "And what the industry did to Mel just wasn't kosher. Mel knows the pain of being shunned by your closest colleagues, and financiers, after years of great work. To be judged purely on the basis of ill-timed comments and not on the content of your heart. He knows the agony of not being considered for a romantic lead just because his breasts aren't as perky as they used to be."

"Yeah, poor *Mel*," I say.

"Anyway, it's the highest profile and most private facility in the country, and it's helped a lot of celebrities get their lives back on track."

"If it's so private how do you know they went?" Katharine asks earnestly.

"I just know, darling. And anyway, the time has come for me to take back control of my life," Mum says, looking me dead in the eye. "And I want you to help me do it."

"Mum, I just really want to say …" I'm playing things cautious. I don't know what her game is, but I'm gonna play along until I figure out what the trick is. "… that I support your decision and I'll do anything I can to help you."

"Anything?" Mum asks.

189

"Well, within reason," I say.

"Yes, anything," Katharine says kicking me under the table.

"But my deadline, Deirdre will kill me if I'm not work— yes, fine— anything."

"My agent made all the necessary arrangements," Susan says. "My bags are packed, all I need is a ride."

"David would be very happy to do that," Katharine says.

"I think we should do this as a family, Katharine," I counter.

"My intake is 10am," Mum says. "If I'm not there at that exact time then they'll give my spot away."

"I can't come then, I've got to shave off a patient's corns at 10 o'clock."

"C'mon, David, it'll be like old times," Mum says. "When we used to go for drives in the English countryside or Malibu canyon, or the Great Ocean Road, or the–"

"Ok!" I just need her to stop naming scenery. "I'll get my keys," I sigh.

I go to the bedroom. Katharine follows behind me.

"I'll wait outside then, shall I?" Mum calls out to us.

I dig around in my pants pocket from last night to find my car keys. But they aren't there.

"What is your major malfunction mister?" Katharine says. "This is exactly what you wanted. You're getting a chance to bond with your mother before she goes into rehab."

I look inside my nightstand.

"I don't know. Something feels off."

"You're just suspicious when good things happen. It's called foreboding joy. I read about it."

"In what? Podiatrist Monthly?"

"I know you're just lashing out because you feel uncomfortable right now. But we need to focus on the positive outcome here. We successfully circumvented a potentially fraught confrontation with *your* mother, Susan Wilde. No disagreement, no difference of opinion, no ridiculous outpouring of unnecessary sentiment."

"That is true ..."

"No smashed kitchenware."

"No. Just the opposite, repaired kitchenware."

"See, the mending process has already started."

"I'm not going to drink out of that mug–"

"No, don't ever do that."

Both of us make gag reflex faces at the thought of putting our lips on something that's been in the bin.

"I won't kiss you if you drink out of it. That's my advice as a trained medical professional."

"I better follow doctor's orders."

We kiss. I am about to pull away when Katharine pulls me back in for another longer kiss. The two of us look into each other's eyes. Just staring. I know that this is the woman I want to spend my life with. I need to tell her this.

"Hey, maybe I'll drop by the clinic and we can have lunch together. Make up for the dinner we never ate," I suggest. "There's cold cuts in the fridge I could make sandwiches and bring them over. It's not Gaul Bladder but ..."

"It's perfect." Katharine bends my head down and kisses my forehead. "As long as it's just the two of us."

She winks. Then looks at her watch. "I have to run. Mrs. Tokugawa's corns aren't going to shave themselves," Katharine says with a glint in her eye. It sometimes weirds me out the glee with which Katharine goes about her profession. I suppose it's like the same satisfaction you get from popping a big pimple. Getting that gunk out of your system feels good.

Katharine goes off to the shower.

I change out of my pyjamas. What do you wear to drop someone off at rehab? Is it formal attire or casual? Mum's in her June Cleaver outfit. I decide to go in my track pants and hoodie that I use before and after basketball games. They stink pretty bad, but then again so do I. I'll just shower when I get home.

Mum and I get into the car. She tells me the address and we drive. The Mel Gibson Centre is situated at the old Kew Cottages formerly known as the Kew Lunatic Asylum. It was a state mental institution until the city council decided they'd be crazy if they didn't sell the land off to real estate developers. The ornate old asylum was refurbished into high-end luxury apartments and condos to serve the needs of the insanely rich. Apparently the big mansion compound on the property was sold off to Mel so that he could help others like him.

I drive along the back way to Kew through winding streets of old Melbourne. I drive past the old Abbotsford Convent, which was a convent until the city council decided it would be a sin if they didn't turn it into a community arts hub.

Mum pulls down the sun visor mirror to check her makeup and hair. I suppose she wants to look her best for rehab. I'm certainly not looking my best.

I think about all the times that I pleaded with her to get help. But she would just tell me that 'this is the way the business works darling.' She had all her lines memorised: 'I need a scotch to unwind. I need a glass of Moët at award ceremonies. I need a merlot to discuss this new role with a director. It's not me, it's my job.' There were other excuses, but they were all similar riffs on the same melody. Like the Coltrane Quartet's modal jazz interpretation of *My Favourite Things*, she wove every justification, rationalisation, and explanation around one core theme: *Mummy no stop drinking*.

So much of my life has been shaped by those forces. What will our lives be like without drugs and booze? I look over at her and try to imagine. Will my character change if she gets sober? I've defined myself as being in opposition to her career and her drinking.

My mind wanders from this thought to the sad times. When I had to pick her up off the floor and carry her to bed. And the times before that, when I was too small to pick her up, so I just got a pillow, a blanket, and tried to make her comfy by removing her high heels. Actually the shoe removal was more for my benefit, I didn't want her to accidentally kick me with them as I curled up next to her on the floor. Not that she really stirred that much in her sleep but I learned early on that you needed to protect yourself.

I look down at my burned arm and see the bandage poking out from the sleeve of the hoodie. What would I be like if I didn't need protection?

I adjust my horn-rimmed glasses.

"You never told me what you wanted to discuss at breakfast," Mum says, breaking the sad reminiscence on my childhood."

"Hmmm? Oh it's, not important," I say,

"It seemed important."

"Well it's not, it's not important."

"So it was unimportant."

"Well, it was important, but now it's unimportant."

"How can something *be* unimportant if it *was* important? Isn't that the whole point of importance?"

"Fine! You want to know the truth?" I say, just to get out of this exchange of semantics.

193

"Of course honey. Have I ever been less than honest with you?"

I leave that one alone.

"I'll lead you in," Mum says. "You started by saying 'We love you but, I feel— I mean we feel …'"

Damn her acting training, it means her recall for other people's last line is impeccable.

"We feel that this has been a great experience and very much appreciate the time that you've been able to spend with the family …" I trail off as if I'm going to say something else. I'm not. I'm just realising that I've walked myself into a trap.

"… But?"

"But nothing. That was all. I love you. Katharine too."

"You think that's unimportant, David? That you love your mother?"

"That's not what I meant." Dammit she backed me into a corner. But in some ways I'm glad. I have to tell her the real truth right now. I can't hedge anymore. "You know what Mum, that's not what I was going to say at brekkie. What I was going to say is that we were kicking you out of the house if you didn't stop drinking and drugging. And if you didn't stop we would never see you again."

Susan cries. I can't tell if this is her acting training or real crying.

"I know I've caused you pain. That's why I am doing this. I am doing it for us, for our family."

"I just didn't want to say it in case you changed your mind about going into treatment."

"I know you can never forgive me. I've completely ruined your life, haven't I?" Mum dabs her eyes with a tissue.

"Well, not *completely*."

I want to forgive her but I know that if I forgive her that's just licence for her to do it again. "I think it's best that we talk about this after you've checked into rehab."

I smile and touch her shoulder, but I don't let my guard down. I want to believe what she's saying so badly but I won't allow myself to be sucked in again. I won't let her cry her way out of going into rehab and claw her way back into close quarters with Katharine and myself.

Mum reapplies her running mascara and flips up the sun visor.

"But I want you to know that I'm serious. This is the last straw," I say to her.

I look into my rearview to see if the past is getting further away. It isn't. It's still with me.

I keep driving, winding around the Yarra River, crossing over it. We're getting close now. Closer to the rehab. Closer to the drop off point.

It dawns I might be saying goodbye to my mother for the last time.

Episode 15

As we get closer to the Mel Gibson Celebrity Rehabilitation Centre I think about the nature of addiction.

She's addicted to drugs, she's addicted to alcohol, she's addicted to acting, she's addicted to men, she's addicted to praise, she's addicted to fame, addicted to her dreams. The one thing she was never addicted to: me.

I need to break the cycle of addiction, otherwise I'll never get out.

I'm wracked with shame, but I have to stay strong. If she gets an inkling of my feelings she may not go into rehab. I can't risk that, for her sake or for mine. I'll never achieve my dreams with her dreams crowding mine out. She's my mother. But she drives me insane. Would I rather be insane with a mother, or sane without one?

"Pull over here," Mum says all of a sudden.

"It's still a little further up, Mum."

"Can you do one last thing for me, please, David? If this is my last memory of you then I want it to be special."

I veer the car off on a side road into Studley Park. I know where we're going. And I know why we're going. It's the least I can do for her. For us.

"Just up here," she says.

"I know."

We get out at a parking area near Dights Falls. It's a spot we visited many times when I was a little boy. One of the few photographs I have from my childhood, that isn't a magazine or newspaper clipping, is of me and Mum at a spot along the Yarra River. It's a bright sunny day, Mum is in a sundress, with bright red nails, I'm in shorts and a Tommy Bahama shirt that is way too big for me. The picture hung on various refrigerators for years. It frayed at the edge and yellowed with time. I don't know who took the picture, probably not my father, but I hope it was.

Dights Falls is where we went to be a family. It's the only place where I ever heard my mother answer the question 'Are you Susan Wilde?' with a 'No'. It's the place where we didn't allow outsiders in. Where we could just be ourselves. Who took that picture? A stranger? My dad?

We sit down on a bench. I look into the muddy water.

It's time to clear things up once and for all.

I take a deep breath and: "Mum I think it's really good that you're getting help. But I need to tell you that if you can't ..." I look back over, she's drinking from her monogrammed flask, "I can't believe you." Actually I can believe her.

"What?" She retorts. "David, after all I've been through recently, I am entitled to one last drink for the road." She takes another pull. "Would you like a nip?"

"You want me to toast your sobriety?"

She takes a sip.

"Sorry, my rule is never before ..." I look at the tan line where my watch should be, "noon."

"Suit yourself." She takes another pull from the flask.

"Rehabs don't take you if you're drunk, Mum."

"You don't need to worry, David."

"Really? Why not?"

"Because darling, *I am Susan Wilde.*"

That statement may comfort her but it doesn't comfort me. I realise that the exact things which make complete sense to her, make absolutely no sense to me. Like taking me to Dights Falls. For her it's a reminder of my childhood, of the good times. For me it's a reminder that one blissful moment, captured in a snapshot, is bookended by all the painful memories which lay on either side.

Like drinking before rehab.

Mum offers the flask like a peace offering. Her face says, you sure you don't want any? My blank stare is my reply. She shrugs and drinks.

Looking for an explanation for my mother's behaviour is like looking for a needle in a needle stack. You know the one you want is in there but trying to find it is maddening because they all look the same and they all have the potential to give you a prick. How do you separate out all the million tiny pricks to find the one that has the meaning you're searching for?

At least with finding a needle in a haystack you know it's in there. Somewhere. My real mother, underneath the mask of Susan Wilde. I know she's in there. That's my needle. And it's a prick.

However the feeling in my chest is that this is a pipe dream. I'm kidding myself if I think that she will ever change. This is goodbye.

As my Father used to say: "the only way to get people to tell you the *liquor* is to ply them with *truth.*" I think he was drunk when he said that one.

I snatch the monogrammed flask from Mum's lips and put it to mine. I get a tiny trickle, but no more. She's drained it.

"I can't believe you."

"*Always* be prepared." Mum draws another flask out of her purse, like Arthur pulling the sword from the stone. "It's my Girl Guide training."

"You were never a Girl Guide." I say unscrewing the cap of the second flask.

"I promise that I will do my best: To do my duty to God, to serve the Queen and my country, to help other people, and to keep the Guide Law," Mum recites, holding up three fingers.

The oath sounds legit. Maybe she was in Girl Guides. Or maybe she did some straight-to-video movie where she played an adult Troop Leader trying to save her Girl Guides' Scout Hall by seducing men into buying tons of cookies. I could rack my brain for a reasonable truth, or I could just have a drink and stop driving myself insane.

I opt for the latter.

"I got a Duke of Edinburgh's Award, you know," Mum says. "Silver level."

"I'll drink to that." The gin hits the back of my throat, but not as hard as I would have expected.

"Smooth." I say.

"Only the best for my little duke."

I take another swig. Man it's smooth, but then again mum always appreciated top shelf stuff. Only the highest quality poison for Susan Wilde.

"Can you remember the last time we enjoyed a nice quiet drink together, David?"

"I remember it ended in the ER."

"Promise me that this final drink we have will have a cherished place in a hidden corner of your memory. Treasured moment shared between the two of us. You and me. Our little family."

I look over at her from the corner of my eye. I want to believe her, but I am not going to fall for any more booby traps. If she thinks she can emote her way out of going to rehab she's got spiders in her brain. I've made my decision.

I hand my flask back over to Mum. She puts it to her lips but pauses.

"This is going to be my final bow, not only to the drink."

"To the drugs too?" the sarcasm just comes out.

"To acting. I am retiring, David."

A shockwave echoes through my brain. Synapses disconnect, neurons fire in the wrong directions. I can't believe my ears.

"From this day forth Susan Wilde will no longer be a lesbian."

"What? Lesbian?" This is a gaffe, even for her.

"I said 'thespian', David, *thespian*, As in an actor? From the Athenian tragedian Thespis, who invented modern theatre, at the Acropolis?"

"Sorry, it's all Greek to me."

"Hilarious, David. But I thought you might treat this moment with a bit more gravitas."

Gravitas, more Greek. Or is it Latin? That joke was totally accidental, my head is spinning.

"My agent is putting out a press release today announcing my impending retirement." She puts her hand on top of mine and looks into my eyes. "I shall no longer be an actor, I'll just be your mother." Mum puts the flask back into my hand without taking a sip. "Shall we go to rehab now?" She stands up with a big smile. I stand up too. But I'm a little wobbly from the revelation.

My mind starts forming a million questions. I take a long pull on the flask.

For the first time in my life I've spotted the needle in the needle stack.

"Mum I-I-I. This is so–"

My phone rings interrupting my thoughts. It's Deirdre, my editor. And she's got me on speakerphone.

"Oh, um, I've gotta take this."

"Deirdre, what's up?"

"What's up? My patience, that's what's up." Deirdre shouts down the phone. Have I missed a deadline? I'm all mixed up here. "Where's the manuscript, Hawkes? I'm looking at my desk where your manuscript should be and all I'm seeing is *War and Peace, The Brothers Karamazov,* and *Anna Karenina.*" She's got her ammunition locked and loaded, ready to be hurled at my head.

"No, I have another two weeks?" It's not really a statement and it's not really a question. It's a call to the governor hoping for a stay of execution.

"I've got it right here. David, manuscript delivery."

Mum grabs the keys off the park bench where we are sitting and gets into the driver's side of the car.

"No, you can't drive," I say.

She rolls down the window. "Then hang up the phone."

"Who the hell are you talking to?" Deirdre asks.

"Just my mother," I answer. "Mum, you've been ... you know." I mime the 'drinking' gesture forgetting that I still have the flask in my hand. I spill gin on my shirt. "Oh, Jesus."

"He's the only one who'll help you now," Deirdre says. I can hear her removing the dust jacket from the Russian novels. Less wind resistance, quicker projectiles.

"Deirdre, I'm not late. I'm sure."

But I'm not sure. I'm not sure of anything right now.

Mum turns the ignition. I half expect a car bomb to go off.

"Stop your bleating." Deirdre cuts through my wayward thought. "No one's putting a car bomb in your car."

Wait, did I just say all that stuff out loud? Did I say this out loud? Deirdre must have secret IRA powers from the 80s!

"I got the dates mixed up, it's David Hatton, who's got the deadline. That Protestant git," Deirdre says.

"You didn't get the dates mixed up, you've spilled chilli on your calendar, you dunderhead." It's Mick to the rescue! "I've told you not to diarise and eat," her secretary says. "The Hawkes manuscript is due next week."

"Where?"

"Right ther— wait, where is it?"

I can imagine them leaning over Deirdre's desk blotter calendar. I can also imagine ducks. Ducks are cool. Ducks can swim and fly! Like flying fish.

"Here, under the jam you spilled. Give me that," Mick says.

"My danish!" Deirdre shouts.

"David, this is Mick."

"Hi Mick." It's so nice to hear his voice. He's great. I wonder if Mick can fly and swim too.

"You're alright mate. You're due date isn't for–"

"Yeah I heard."

"I still want you to come in today. Status report on the mission," Deirdre barks.

"Can't we do it over the phone?"

"No. This is an unsecured line," Deirdre says. Is that a joke?

I can't tell. I decide to laugh loudly just in case.

I startle Mum. The car swerves. She looks over at me. Sorry, I mouth to her. "Ok, um … yeah …" I'm trying to think, but it's hard, Mum is retiring … from acting I'll finally get her away from all the bad shit.

"Well, Hawkes?"

"Sorry, no I'm not insane."

"No. When can you come in?"

"I've got a lunch date … with a person, not with food, I mean, we're eating food, the person I'm lunching with isn't lunch–"

"What time?"

"According to my watch it is …" I look at the tan line on my wrist, "around lunch time–"

"Three o'clock then," Deirdre decides.

"We can fit you in between the butter smudge and the split pea soup stain," Mick says.

"Don't you have work to do?" Deirdre snaps.

There's a brief pause.

Then: "What was that? You *don't* want any of the beef bourguignon I made?" More silence. Who knew you could disarm a paramilitary fighter with French cuisine? Napoleon said an 'army marches on its stomach', and the idea of burgundy braised beef can bring a soldier to their knees.

Mick again: "I'll be going now David, but we'll see you at three o'clock."

Deirdre picks up the receiver.

My mind is still muddled from Mum's revelation that Susan Wilde is retiring. It's getting muddledier. Is that a word, did I just invent a new word? Am I a word inventor now?

"Deirdre I'm a word inventorer! The new word I made up

is 'muddledier'. It means, um, something ..."

I take a celebratory swig of gin, toasting my new found skill.

"Have you been drinking, Hawkes?"

"No."

"You'd better not be. You should only be drinking to celebrate handing in your manuscript. Hemingway never drank before a deadline."

"I'm pretty sure that's not true."

"No it's not. But the point is it's called a deadline for a reason: if you don't meet it you're dead. Career-wise."

"Deirdre can I just say that there's a lot of ducks around here. Colourful ones. And they all have eyes. Every single one of them has two eyes. It's incredible."

"Hold on." I hear the intercom buzzing. "Yes, send him in."

"Deirdre I want to write for ducks. They are the most beautifully things God ... cremated. Their majestry knows no boundz. They fly on the wings of art. Wings-of-art. If you say it fast it sounds like wings of *fart*."

"Mm-hmm, great. Focus on the book, not waterfowl poetry. And be here at three sharp." The receiver slams down.

"Aye-aye captain." I salute, using my flask hand and spill gin in my eye. The sting is like a wasp and a jellyfish had a baby and poked my eye.

Through blurred sightlines I see leafy green surrounds. The light breaks through the clouds getting brighter and brighter until I have to close my eyes. I hear muffled voices. I feel like the car has stopped and I'm standing. Maybe walking. But I'm so tired. It must be from all the work. I try to keep my eyes open but the lights are so bright I have to close them.

Then I open my eyes.

The light is still blinding me, but it's not the light of the sun, it's a halogen bulb overhead. I'm damp, cold, and being cradled by someone in a baseball cap, their face in silhouette. What the hell? I squirm to get away. My breathing is shallow. Everything is a blur, probably because my glasses are gone.

"Just relax for a moment." A croaky voice says.

"I can't see."

"Your eyesight will return in time," the voice continues to croak.

"Who are you?"

The baseball cap comes off and hair falls onto my face and into my mouth. A throat clearing noise.

"Someone who loves you."

"Mum?!"

She embraces me. I gargle her hair.

"Where am I?" I say, blowing strands from my mouth. It's like angel hair pasta with a peroxide white sauce.

Mum doesn't answer, she just strokes my sandy blond hair, and hums an atonal series of notes.

Even without my glasses I can make out stucco walls, a solid door with huge reinforced hinges, and abstract art on the wall (although this could be my poor eyesight). There's two rows of track lighting along the ceiling, two freestanding dressers, two single beds, two finely crafted wooden bedside tables which nicely compliment the two touch lamps resting on them.

"Oh no. No, no, no!" I sit up in bed, locking my elbows.

"Shhh, David, not so loud. It's meditation time."

"This is that Mel Brooks Rehab!"

"'Gibson', darling, Mel Gibson."

"I don't care if it's the 'going to Mel in a handbasket' rehab. Why am I here?"

Mum laughs. "That's very funny, 'Mel in hand basket' that's the kind of joke Mel Brooks would do. You're so funny?"

"You're distracting me, you always compliment me when you're trying to distract me."

"You're right David," Mum sighs, She puts her hand on my leg and looks into my eyes. "But I suppose only someone so bright and gifted with naturally toned thighs like you could pick up on that."

There's a moment's pause while I try to get my bearings.

"I'm leaving."

I get out of the bed, looking for my glasses. It's harder to find your glasses when you don't have them on. For the first time I notice that I'm wearing a red, belted, Hugh Hefner-style, smoking jacket with my initials D.U.H. monogrammed on. Why did she give me the middle name Ulysses?

"Unfortunately that is not an option for you my dear."

I'm not really listening, "Mm-hmm, and why's that Mum?" I look inside the bedside drawer: empty.

"You are checked in here."

Another pause.

"You ... did you sign me into this place ...?" I'm simmering on a low boil.

"No, I did not sign you in here," she says, looking at her nails.

Thank God. I stick my head under the bead searching for my pants. Once I get my pants I'm out of here.

"You signed yourself in."

"What?!" I bang my head hard on the metallic frame. My skull feels like I've been sucker punched by the Tin Woodsman. "No I didn't."

"Granted you were a teensy bit on the tipsy side when you

did," she says, still examining her cuticles.

I don't remember that. In fact I don't remember anything after Dights Falls. Then it hits me, like a rhinoceros on a skateboard. "You drugged me!"

"Drugged is such an ugly word, David," Mum says as I crawl out from under the bed and sit down. "Why don't we just say I put a little something in your drink to help you sleep. You never minded when you were little."

"When I was ... wait, what?" A baby rhino hits my younger self. "Oh no, no, no. Magic Milk!? Not Magic Milk."

Magic Milk was what we called the warm milk she gave me before bed. But she would pretend to be a sorceress and enchant it so it became a sleeping potion.

Mum shrugs a half-hearted apology.

"So the 'spell' you put on it was–"

"Just the scientific name of the sleeping pills." Mum curls her finger and puts on a spooky wizard voice. "Chlora-form-otahal," she chants. She mimes a glass of milk in her palm, like Hamlet holding the skull of poor Yorick. He might have been a man on infinite jest, but I'm not in the mood.

"That's why I wet the bed when I was a kid." I point my finger at her. "Not because the cat licked my feet while I was— oh no ..." If I keep analysing the past I'm gonna ruin my perfectly unhappy childhood.

"The point is David, I did it so you could get a good night's sleep. I did that for you. "

"You did it for *you*."

"I did it for us. Just like I want you here now ... for *us*."

"I knew that gin tasted too smooth. Where did you even get–"

"The paramedics. Once again my adoring fans came to my

rescue. You know I've always depended–"

"On the kindness of strangers. Yes, thank you, 'Blanche.'" I sit down on the bed and put my head in my hands. I'm not in the mood for *Streetcar Named Desire*, my brain is hurting. It feels like Marlon Brando is screaming 'Stella!' at the top of his lungs, inside my brain.

Mum rubs my back. "David I need you in here … for emotional support. I'm in a time of transition. Entering an autumnal phase in my life. I've been acting professionally since I was 14. I owe everything to acting; to my craft. I wake up everyday knowing that my creativity, my emotional wellspring, will be on offer to entertain potentially thousands, nay, millions of people. Performing is the foundation which has given me everything: travel, a career, it even gave me you."

Being reminded of the circumstances of my birth makes my stomach do its Cirque du Soleil impression.

Mum tucks my hair behind my ear and cups my face, so I am looking at her. She kisses my forehead. I close my eyes. I feel my glasses slide onto the bridge of my nose.

My mother comes into focus.

"This is it David. I'm retiring from acting. I'm going to just be a normal mother, like all the rest of the boys' mums."

The strangest things about fantasies are that when they come true, it's never as satisfying as you imagined. The fantasy doesn't exist to be satisfied, it is by design an unquenchable thirst. It exists to get you to another day. It's function is to keep you functional. A safety valve; a protective mechanism.

"I don't need the adoring love of millions of fans, I just need your love."

"I believe you." Actually, I can't believe her. I have no clue what this whole field trip to rehab is all about but I don't care.

She's crossed the line for the last time. I'm getting out of here and I'm never talking to her again.

"That's why I need my favourite son–"

"*Only* son."

"Which reminds me, don't tell anyone that I'm your mother while you're here. The whole program is supposed to be anonymous."

"Don't worry, I don't want anyone knowing we're related."

The search for my pants continues. Inside the cupboard all I find is my mother's clothes. All hung nicely on wood hangers, or folded on shelves. There are a row of shoes at the base of the cupboard, but no pants. Between the skirts and dresses, no pants. Underneath blouses, no pants ... but there is a small hip flask. I knew she wasn't serious about getting sober. How many of these things does she have? I unfasten the belt on the thigh length robe she's put me in and I slip the flask into the tiny inside pocket behind the monogram. She can go without a drink in rehab.

I slam the wardrobe doors shut. The air blows the robe open revealing that I have ladies underwear on. I slam the wardrobe shut. How the hell did I wind up in rehab with ladies underwear on? I know why. I look at her.

She says: "David I need you in here with me."

"I'm not babysitting you in this rehab."

"Think of it as more of a holistic wellbeing centre for the facilitation, detoxification, and reintegration of the chemically dependent."

"It's a place for druggies and alkies–"

"Where you can also get a colonic," Mum adds.

"I don't want water up my ass, I want to know where my pants are. I'm leaving!" I throw up my arms in exasperation and the dressing gown comes open slightly.

I am about to tie the belt when just then the door opens. I'm startled by two big orderlies entering the room. They wear matching grey jackets with plaid underneath. The tall skinny one is bald with tufty side hair and eyebrows, the short, portly one has black curly hair and a big nose.

"What's all this then, it's meditation time?" one of the orderlies says.

"I'm glad you're here …" I look at his nametag. It reads 'Bill'. I look over at the other one, it says 'Scully'. "There's been a mistake."

"I'll say there has, sir. Half past two until three PM, is silent meditation time for all clients. But it seems like the silent part has fallen on deaf ears."

"I understand that, Bill," I say.

"I don't think you do, sir. You're still talking," he responds.

My impatience with this Muppet starts bringing out my inner Oscar the Grouch.

"Look, 'sir', I don't belong here, ok? I don't have a problem."

The other one, Scully, holds up the clipboard and taps to a place for Bill to read.

"Says here you gotta problem with crack, smack, and jack."

"Jack?"

"Daniels. You've got what we like to call: the trifecta of naughty habits; the unholy trinity of chemical dependency …"

Everyone waits for Bill to make a third rule of three analogy. We all lean in ever so slightly waiting for Bill to finish. But he leaves us unsatisfied.

"There's a perfectly reasonable explanation why I'm here!" I say.

"And what's that, sir?" Bill asks.

"My mother got me drunk, checked me in here, and then stole my pants, so I couldn't leave."

"Your trousers were soiled, not stolen, sir. During your induction you micturated in them."

"I what?"

"Did a wee-wee," says Mum.

"And where's your mother now?" Bill asks.

My lips tighten against my teeth. I feel like pointing at the woman on the bed, but I don't want anyone in here knowing our family drama. I don't even want to admit to myself that she is my mother. Sometimes I wish I was adopted. That would at least give me an out. But the only out I need right now is between these two goons.

Scully's watch beeps for the hour.

"That's 3 o'clock, meditation time's over," Bill says.

"Wait, 3pm? In the afternoon?! I've been out for five hours."

"Spot on, sir."

I grab a sheet off the other single bed and wrap it around my waist. Deirdre Slocumb is waiting, getting more angry by the nanosecond.

Fear grips me.

"I'm going to leave you now. I have an appointment with my editor."

I attempt a passage between Bill and Scully. They each take a step in, narrowing the path.

"Put the sheet back, sir," Bill says.

"Gentlemen, you appear to be two very large, but reasonable men—"

"Sir!" Bill's voice raises an octave.

"You don't understand, if I'm late."

Late— Katharine— I missed our lunch.

"No sir, *you* don't understand. We have two types of clients here. Compliant and defiant. Which do you want to be?"

"I don't belong here. I just want to get back to my life," I plead. It's 3:01, I can hear Deirdre running his fingers across the bookshelf picking out his literary projectile.

"That's reliant on you being a compliant client," Bill says.

Bill and I stare into each other's eyes. It dawns on me: there's no way out of this situation. I'm stuck here with Mum, wearing women's underwear, and this ridiculous monogrammed dressing gown that Mum somehow had made for me. Where did she even get the money for it? Where did she even get the money to pay for me? Ok, take a breath Hawkes. Think about this rationally.

"Ok, you win. I'll be a compliant cli—" I go to dart between the two behemoths. But they block me and I fall to the ground. The sheet splays out around me. I hear a metallic clunk.

The flask.

Scully picks it up, giving me a sceptical look.

"That's not mine!" I stammer.

"Then why are your initials etched on?" Bill asks.

Scully points the flask down towards me.

D.U.H.

It's so obvious.

I've been set up like a bowling pin.

"You don't understand. This isn't my robe. Those are my initials, but that's not my flask. It's hers. Tell them Susan!"

The orderlies look at Mum who shrugs her shoulders.

In that split second of distraction I scoot between Bill and Scully's legs. They turn to follow me but trip on the silk sheet and thud to the ground.

I'm in the corridor now. It's long, doors down both sides, with black and white chequered tiles. People are milling about in the hallway and I weave around them like I'm driving to the hoop.

"Stop him," I hear from behind me. People move out of my way.

Another orderly turns around. She looks like a former shot put champion that could thin paint with her eyes. Her black hair is permed and glistens in the harsh track lighting. I head fake left and spin around her. Hawkes is taking it to the imaginary bucket.

The Lady orderly clamps down on my robe. However the robe is unbelted so I burst out of it. Arms back, sailing forward, doing my best Leonardo DiCaprio impression from *Titanic*. I feel like the king of the world. That is until I remember I'm wearing ladies underwear.

I keep running.

I get to a set of swinging doors and go through them. I'm in a day room. I run past chairs, tables, and walls filled with picture frames that sport inspiring slogans like 'Achievement', 'Grateful', and 'Dare to Thrive'. I catch the blur of people setting up art supplies and I get the distinctive whiff of Elmer's glue as I dash by them.

Shouts echo behind me as I flip chairs to slow down my pursuers as I continue my harried escape.

To the right are windows. Natural light is coming in. Instinctively my direction shifts towards daylight and I find a door to the outside world.

I keep running, grass beneath my feet. There are planted trees and an old bishop's crook lamppost. Past those I see a stone wall a few feet high. Red brick, curved blackened concrete at the top. Easy to hop over. Even in ladies under garments.

As I'm running towards the wall it begins to grow in size. The closer I get the higher it gets. I don't get it?

I keep running towards it until I'm face to face with a 10 foot wall.

That's when it hits me.

From the side. Scully. To the ground I go with a rugby-style tackle. He must have come around the side of the building. The only problem is that he goes too high so I'm able to squirm out and keep scrambling to find my freedom.

As I run along the wall I look up and notice the ground is sloped down towards the base. It's what's known as a ha–ha wall. I can't find anything funny about it at the moment.

I spot an ornate cast iron gate and head towards it. The spikes on top look sharper than ninja swords. One false move and I'll puncture my boys on those spikes.

Bill and the Shot Put Lady orderly come from the other direction. With Scully behind me the only way is over.

Bill is holding the sheet from my room. He's like a Cockney bullfighter daring me to charge. "Think very carefully now, sir. What type of client d'you wanna be?

I start climbing. Scrotal puncture or not I have to go for it. Freedom is clearly visible on the other side. I climb higher.

That's when I feel it. A tugging sensation on my testicles.

It's the gusset of the underwear. Someone's grabbing my panties.

"Let me go!" I scream, "I'm a writer, I don't belong in rehab!"

The stitching gives way and rips. My bare bottom showing to all the world.

"You're a very defiant client," Bill says.

"You need to come back inside," Shot Put Lady adds.

Scully stays as silent as he has been the whole time and maintains his grip on my undergarments.

"I don't," I shout, as the underwear is torn from my waist.

"Yes you do, sir!" Bill shouts.

"I don't, I don't, I don't, I don't, I don't, I don't!" I continue shouting as the three of them pull me to the ground and wrap me up tightly in a sheet. I feel like a Cuban cigar, or a burrito, or a … I wait for a third Latino wrapping reference but none comes.

I'm left hanging like a broken piñata.

I am 'escorted' back towards the Italianate building which is now a rehab. I lift my slumped head and take in the creamy limewash walls, narrow windows, and turret levels which adorn the outside. It really is a beautiful building, this former 19th century asylum.

The orderlies drag me back inside.

"You don't understand I'm not supposed to be here," I say, as we pass other clients, going down corridors. "My girlfriend'll be wondering where I am. We were supposed to have lunch hours ago. She'll think I've been murdered. Or worse."

No answer.

We go deeper into the old building. Past offices, a back courtyard, and a kitchen.

"Ok. Seriously though. I have to go. I'm in trouble. My publisher is this mad Northern Irish woman who'll blow up my car if I'm late for this meeting with her."

No answer.

We get to a door with a sign that says, *Contemplation Room*. It's a padded cell. Obviously a hold over from this building's asylum days.

"You know what? I think I'm cured. I don't want to use drugs anymore. Or drink. In fact the whole idea makes me sick. So, I'll just check myself out. I checked myself in so I can check myself out right? Right?"

No answer.

They take me inside and put me into a straight jacket.

"Hey wait. How is this legal? Stop it. Do you hear me? Stop. Stop this right now!" They spin me around. I hear clinking metal. Buckles put in place. "Why do I get sense that you're not listening?"

I'm in it now. Both literally and figuratively.

I sit down.

Bill, Scully, and Shot Put Lady take deep breaths and look at each other. I notice her name tag for the first time: "Susan." My jailer's name is Susan. The symbolism is so thick and steamy I could choke.

"Cuppa tea time?" Susan suggests. The men nod their heads in agreement.

"Hey wait. You can't leave me in here. You can't hold me against my will. I'm a writer, I've got rights!"

"Shout all you want mate, the room is soundproof," Shot Put Susan says.

"Welcome to the Mel Gibson Rehabilitation Centre." Scully says, breaking his silence for the first time.

"You may take my life, but you'll never take my free—!"

The door slams.

"—dom."

I'm probably not the first person to quote *Braveheart* in this place. Not only am I trapped, I'm unoriginal.

The door opens. It's Susan.

The orderly.

"Back to tighten the straps on this thing you curly haired, fascist she-wolf."

She comes right at me.

"Please don't hit me!"

Brace for impact.

Susan the orderly leans down and picks up her keys, from beside me, then turns and leaves.

I flop backward against the wall, breathe out, and gather in my surroundings. That lasts about two seconds. Padded cells, the last unspoiled world for interior decorators. The blank walls, the angles, and the slightly tattered upholstery on the protective walls. It's got a touch of the Scandi shabby chic to it as Katharine would say. Katharine. How am I going to explain this to her?

I need to get a message out to Katharine. As a doctor she can sign me out as a patient under her care. She could pose as a podiatrist treating addicts with an experimental foot treatment. Or I could just try to reason with one of the doctors here. A medical professional will recognise I'm not addicted to anything. I don't have a problem. I don't belong here. And If I don't get out of here quickly I'm gonna lose my book deal, and my relationship.

I sit for a moment quietly. Then I start to formulate my plan.

Episode 16

My planning is going great. As great as can be expected for someone coming down off whatever drug cocktail Mum slipped me.

I hear the dead bolt on the door and keys jangling in the lock.

The orderlies come in and let me out of the straight jacket, give me some clothes, and lead me down the corridor to the mess hall. I guess my plan worked ... I'm out.

"Dinner time," Bill says. He hands me a tray and indicates towards the procession of addicts and alcoholics grabbing food from a serving table. I join the back of the queue and silently shuffle along. A compliant client.

There's slim pickings for the last person in line. The guy with amazing hair in front of me is loading his tray with the last and best of everything on offer. I grab some spinach salad and the last small piece of steak. The desserts and pastries have been picked through, but I spy the last chocolate pudding. My hand reaches for it but it's snatched up by the guy with great hair in front of me.

"Hey!" he says.

"Hey yourself!" I snap back.

Bill looks over at me. I look at him.

"I mean— you can have it," I say, not breaking eye contact with Bill.

"Hawkesy?"

I swivel my head. It's Jeremy. From Dienstag, DiSalvio & Fischer. My old law firm. He always did have fantastic hair.

"What are you doing here?" I ask.

"I can't lay off that, you know, 'white girl.'"

"You're in for sex addiction?"

"No. Not that I couldn't qualify." Jeremy winks at me, which comes off way less cool that he intends it. "It's that old Caucasian smelling salts … Peruvian baking soda." He sees I'm not getting it. "You know, booger sugar, Escobar's dandruff …"

"You're addicted to baking cakes with disgusting ingredients?"

Jeremy taps his right nostril.

"… Cocaine?"

"Yes," he says. "What are you in here for?"

Just then my mother struts in. Jeremy looks over at her.

"It's complicated," I sigh, grabbing a carrot cake and ushering Jeremy towards some empty seats.

"It always is my friend."

I sit with my back to Susan.

"Do I know her?" Jeremy says, eyeing my mother.

"You probably recognise a lot of people in here, it's a rehab for famous people after all."

"True …" he trails off.

Quick, distract him.

"Which begs the question why you're in here?"

"My dad donated a bunch of money to this place. They named the detox ward after us. I mean he didn't do it for the recognition, he did it to help people."

"Naturally."

"That's why I got in for free. I mean, obviously I can afford the 50."

"50 what? Grand?" hearing this makes both my ears and wallet bleed. That is if I knew where my wallet was.

"I know, right?" Jeremy bites into the steak he has on his plate. "They could totally get away with charging more," he says between chews.

"Yeah … totally."

Where the hell did my mother get 100 grand to put us both in here? Has she been lying to me this whole time about being broke?

"Your new career must be going really well," Jeremy says.

"Mmm, yeah … it is." I'm not really listening to him. My whole relationship with her is lies compounded on lies.

"You're a famous writer now, right?" Jeremy says digging into his mountain of mashed potato. "I mean, I don't really read 'books' per se, but I'm assuming people still read them. So you must be famous enough to get into here."

I shift focus from my Mother, the liar, who is getting a cup of tea, back to Jeremy.

"That's exactly right, Jez. Since I left the firm, I have become a famous writer. I'm writing book about a gruesome murder–"

"That's where I know her from!" Jeremy snaps his finger. "She's your mum."

The people near us turn to look at me and then her.

"No. That's not her," I say, lowering my voice.

"Yeah, she was at your going away drinks and sang a song."

My Mother cocks her ear to the side. The people around

me look back and forth between us. I'm sure she's loving the attention, but she also doesn't want to be outed as my mother. And I definitely don't want to be known as her son.

"Jeremy," I grab his forearm as he's spooning peach yoghurt into his mouth, "You were really, really high at that party. Weren't you?"

"Yeah."

"You were snorting lots of … white chocolate gunpowder, weren't you?"

That was a stupid euphemism for cocaine, but please God, let me be correct.

"Yeah. And I had been drinking."

"See."

"And not just wine."

"Spirits?"

"Absinthe."

"At work?" Even Jeremy can surprise me.

"I was entertaining some clients. At least I think they were clients."

"Long story short, you probably don't remember it that well."

"Yeah, my memory is a bit hazy. Especially after I dropped that ecstasy."

"See, there you go. You just misremembered. It's not her."

Jeremy pauses. "'Her' who?"

"My mother."

"Yeah, isn't that her over there?" Jeremy points her right out. "I met her at–"

"No!" I bark.

Scully looks over at me and frowns.

I lower my voice again. "I mean … no. It's not her.

Remember what we've just been talking about?"

"No sorry. They told me cocaine is bad for your short-term memory," Jeremy says, peeling his orange. "Or, maybe it was long-term memory. I can't recall."

"Just forget it." I sigh. "How is the wild world of probate law these days Jeremy?"

"I do remember that!" he says, pleased with himself. "Since you left it's been terrible. Just mountains upon mountains of paperwork."

"That's the job, Jez."

"I know. I just never realised it before you left. I think that's why I turned to drugs. Just to cope."

"You were doing drugs before."

"Different drugs," he says with a mouthful of orange. "We really need you back. I really need you back. You should totally come back. Will you come back? Just come back. Come *back*. Come back. *Come* back," he says stressing a different syllable each time.

I stare at him and bite my piece of carrot cake.

"Are you gonna come back?"

"Jeremy, no."

"Please?"

"Thanks, but no–"

"I'll give you more money," Jeremy interrupts.

"That's generous. But like you said I'm a famous writer now, so …" I shrug. I stare at Jeremy's leftovers; the carrot cake is nice but it's not a proper dinner.

We sit in silence for a second.

"I could give you a big raise. I have the power. They made old Jez-bone partner."

"What?" I almost choke on my delicious carrot cake.

"Yeah they promoted me after DiSalvio died."

"Frank's dead?"

"Or, no, he retired. Or, maybe it was Dienstag. Dienstag retired; or he died. I can't remember. Cocaine, man." Jeremy points at where his short term memory used to be.

My eyes blink like hazard lights. Which is more surreal: that one of my law mentors exists in some sort of Schrödinger Cat scenario where it's impossible to determine whether he's alive or dead, or that 'Jez-bone' made partner. Maybe the events are somehow quantumly entangled.

My musing on the physical laws of my law practice are interrupted by Bill making an announcement.

"Time for evening group. It's an all-in session so everyone is together in the Rockatansky Room," he says.

"Allow me," I take Jeremy's tray, as he goes off to the room named after a Mad Max character.

I grab a few big bites of his steak and potatoes as I drop off our plates. It's not very dignified but what can you do?

I walk down the hallway with Jeremy and the other patients. The walls are nondescript on the inside, but the floor has a lovely chequered pattern on it.

We come into a big room with chairs in a circle. It's a classic group therapy setting. I spot someone with a clean white shirt, round glasses, and a name tag that says, *Dr. Frederick, MD.* Finally a professional who will understand my situation. I go up and introduce myself.

"Uh hello, Dr. Frederick? I'm David Hawkes," I say, sticking out my hand.

"Ah yes, *the* David Hawkes," she says, shaking my hand, and staring at my face.

"You know my work?"

223

"Of course. You're the one responsible for the bit of excitement we had this afternoon," she chuckles.

"Yes, well … not my best work, I will say. That is yet to come."

"I'm glad to hear that, David. Really glad. A lot of people come here and they aren't quite ready to do the work," she points at her heart. "Work necessary to overcome their addictions."

"Addictions. Yes. I'm pleased you brought that up. You see the thing is…I don't actually have any. I'm not an addict."

"You're not?"

"No. In fact, I've never been addicted to anything. Unless you can be hooked on Choose Your Own Adventures books. I was obsessed with them as a child," I laugh.

Dr. Frederick laughs too. "Ah yes, those books were a bit of fun, weren't they."

"Yeah, they're great. I'm actually a writer myself" I say leaving an opening for her to ask about my book. She opts to go another route and stay silent. "Anyway, like I was saying, there's been a mistake, I'm not supposed to be here."

"Yes you are. Unless it's a second offence, clients only spend an hour in the contemplation room, you know, for a 'time out.'"

"Contemplation room, yes. I'm glad you mentioned that. I actually can't take any more time out to contemplate right now. I am super busy. I didn't mean to come here today, I was under the influence when I signed the forms."

"You were?" she asks. "That's serious."

"Yes. And I don't normally go around signing contracts while drunk."

"Glad to hear it."

"I am a very normal person. I have a house, a girlfriend, and a job. Well actually, I'm taking some time off."

"So you're unemployed?"

"You could say I'm freelancing right now. But my girlfriend is supporting us. Temporarily. But the point is, you're a doctor, you can see me, I'm not like ..." I motion with my head around to the seated addicts, "... *them*. I don't have a problem."

"You don't?"

"No. I was just with a woman, and she spiked my drink."

"A woman spiked your drink? Did you know her?"

"Not that well, apparently."

"So let me get this straight. You are an out of work man, whose girlfriend supports him, who was drinking with a strange woman this morning, and she spiked your drink, and then you signed into rehab."

"Yes! So you understand? Now I know how it *sounds*, but–"

"It sounds like adventure," Dr. Frederick says.

"Yes but I didn't *choose* it," I say. "Seriously though, can you sign me out of here?"

"Yes."

"Great, then I don't need to be here for the," I wave my hand at the group filling the seats. "what-have-you session."

"I will check you out...right after you've completed your treatment."

"No doctor, you're not understanding."

"Oh, I have a bit of an understanding."

"I respectfully disagree."

"Mr. Hawkes, do you believe in fate?" the doctor asks.

She doesn't wait for my response and keeps talking. Like it was destined that I wouldn't answer.

"Something has led you down this path. All the decisions you made have all led you here, tonight. So what I suggest is that you *choose your own adventure* right now, by taking a seat. How does that sound?"

"It sounds like—!" I start, raising my voice. But Bill and Scully glare at me and I sit down immediately. "—a great idea."

I fold my arms and fume. Tapping my toe. This isn't going to be my escape route.

"Hello everyone," the doctor raps her ballpoint repeatedly on her clipboard. "For those who don't know me, I'm Doctor Frederick. But you can just address me as 'Doctor', if you prefer. Now a bit of housekeeping before we start. Our head psychotherapist is still at a conference, but he'll be around in the next week, and you'll all be meeting with him one-on-one at some point. Now, as you can see, we have some new people here tonight. Can everyone please give them a hand."

Everyone claps except me. Scully looks over at me and mouths the words 'compliant client', and I clap too.

"Now we are going to go around," Dr. Frederick says, "and I want everyone to introduce themselves and say a bit about why we're here. And if it's your first time, feel free to share with us some of your story."

We start going around the circle. There are musicians, people from reality TV, a politician, and some well-known people from the business community. The whole sliding scale of fame is represented in this bunch. I am seated next to an ageing, leather clad, rocker-type with a beer gut. He's nodding in and out of consciousness and drooling on me. I keep having to push him off so I don't get drowned in spittle. On the other side is a Goth Girl with black hair and black lipstick who keeps smiling at me and brushing my knee with one hand.

She's vaping what smells like black cherry-scented gum. Heat begins to radiate from me as I stew in a rainforest of cherry scented mist and saliva. The reality that I might be here for a while sinks in.

Mum has taken the prompt of 'sharing your story' as licence to recount her drinking history while subtly dropping in career highlights. She may be retiring from acting but old habits die hard.

"I'm Susan Wilde. And I'm a former actor. I've been on soaps in four different countries, and I've been in a lot of TV movies. But I never did it for the fame. I mean it's embarrassing enough being at the Daytime Emmys when you are nominated for something. Who wants all that attention? But to be snorting cocaine with the Vice President of HBO and a Saudi prince in the toilet when they call out your category … Well, we all know what that's like. Right?"

Susan looks for acknowledgement, but the former soccer player and the meth addict from MasterChef on either side of her just stare forward into space. I can't look at her. Her voice, her everything, grates on me. Undeterred she resumes her oration.

"Alas, that was not my first time making a fool of myself in a professional environment because of drink and drugs. Once, early in my career, I was in this horror film. I had sipped a few chardonnays during lunch, and I accidentally exposed my breasts to an entire studio tour bus. I felt so exposed. I can recall I was just about to go in and perform a scene where the killer is chasing me with a cleaver while I am totally naked–"

"Thank you Susan," Dr. Frederick interrupts her, "Maybe we could let someone have a bit of a share. What do you reckon?"

"But Doctor, I was getting to the incident I had while playing a teacher in the movie *Substitute Lover*. Long story short chalk dust looks a lot like cocaine, and I–"

"Thank you, Susan!" Dr. Frederick cuts her off again, "Thank you for your …. experience, strength, and hope. But I'd kinda like to hear from someone else. David, do you have anything you want to say?"

I push the dribbling font of salvia off me and wave away the cherry vapour.

"Yes. I would like to say something."

"Glad to hear it," Dr. Frederick says.

"Can I be moved?"

The ageing rocker guy next to me starts snoring.

"Sure we can move you–"

"Great–"

"Back to the contemplation room. If you don't want to share."

"Ok, yeah, I've got something to share," I say, razor blades dripping from my tongue. "You ready? Here it is: I don't use drugs and I don't drink, and I want to go home right now. You can't hold me here against my will. I'm not an alcoholic."

"What about the hip flask the orderlies found on you?" Dr. Frederick asks.

"Someone planted that on me."

"Who?"

"Someone who has an agenda," I say, not looking at Mum, trying to keep my rage in. "I just need to get out of here, I need to finish my book. Otherwise, I'm screwed."

"I'm hearing a lot of obsession, paranoia, and denial, David. Does anyone in the group want to say something to David?"

The sleepy slobberer farts.

There are titters from around the circle.

The Goth Girl says, "Admitting you have a problem is the first step." As she exhales vape fumes.

"I don't have a problem!" I stand up, knocking over my chair and waking up the man next to me. "This is insane! I'm not like you people, I don't have a problem! I'm a writer! A writer, do you know what that is? Can anyone here even read? Anyone heard of Hemingway— bad example— I need to write."

I feel big hands clamp on my shoulders.

"No wait, wait! I'm sorry. I'll be a compliant client."

Bill and Scully pin my arms behind my back and carry me away. I watch as the rock and roll drooler lays down over my empty seat and resumes snoring.

"Who's next?" Dr. Frederick asks.

Mum's hand shoots up as I get dragged down the hall.

I'm back now in restraints as I spend the next few hours in the 'contemplation room' contemplating where I was and where I am now. What a nightmare. It wasn't that long ago that I was a probate lawyer. Writing wills, looking after estates, doing other probate lawyer stuff. Day in, day out. Monotonously working my way up the ladder until one day I could make partner, lose my hair, get an ill-fitting toupee, and then bore the life out of a junior colleague when he decided to leave. It was a soul sucking existence, but at least I was happy.

I never had to worry about things like which of my friends on the basketball team are cougar-lovers, or how flammable are my clothes, or will someone drug me and sign me into rehab?

I also didn't worry about my mother committing suicide. What if she had been successful in taking her own life? The thought of losing her destroys me inside, but having her in my life destroys my outsides. I always wish we could get back to being as happy as I was in that picture at Dights Falls.

But sadly, in my life, good memories are a lighthouse, there to warn me of danger ahead. They lure me in like a moth to a flame, then burn me. Over and over again until I'm charred like a cashmere sweater. The way she can draw me in like that, it makes me want to kill her.

I pull the emergency stop on my train of thought. Sure I've thought of killing my mother before but only in a joking way. This time is different. It's amazing how unrestricted your thinking becomes when you're in restraints. I'll never be free while she's alive. I'll never get my book published. I'll never become who I want to be with her holding me back. And she'll be free as well. No more worrying about her acting career. I'd be setting us both free. It's really the kindest thing I could do.

No. That's insane. As long as I don't see her for 24 hours I'll be alright. I just need a day for my rage to subside and I'll be ok. This contemplation room is exactly where I need to be right now. I just need a break from her and my killing rage will subside.

The door opens again. This time it's Susan…

Shot Put Susan, the orderly.

"What now? I'm trying to contemplate, like the room says."

From behind Susan steps Susan. Wilde. My mother.

"Hello darling," Mum says, stepping into the room.

She's wearing a white terry cloth robe, arms folded across her chest. "Thank you," she says. "Oh, and just a little non-fat milk, no sugar."

"Back in five," Shot Put Susan says, a big smile on her face, then she looks at me and the smile drops, hitting the floor with a clang.

The door closes.

We're alone in a soundproof room.

I lunge at her. But without the use of my arms my attempt at strangling her comes off more like a harbour seal being shot out of cannon. I flop to the ground and wriggle towards her. I'm not sure what I'm going to do once I get to her but the assault continues.

"David, if you want more exercise, there is a gym. With a trainer."

I am the inchworm of death inching closer.

"David, you're getting your nice white jacket all dirty."

I get close enough to bite her ankle.

She steps out of the way.

"You're mad at me. Aren't you?"

I burst out laughing, and roll onto my back.

"A mother can tell."

"You're not a mother, you're a lunatic." I can barely get this sentence out, I'm cackling so manically.

"I'm the crazy person?" Mum leans over, looking down on me. "Which one of us is in a straight jacket, darling?"

Damn, I hate it when she has a point.

"I'm only in it because of *you*." I snap. "The only reason I'm in any screwed up situation is because of you." Years of repressed emotions explode. "In another bravura performance you've taken the nicely ordered newspaper of my life, shredded it to bits, mixed it with glue and water, and stuck it together into some paper-mâché grotesquery." I can feel my face contorting and getting redder as I look up to her. "It's like, you couldn't be satisfied destroying your own life, you

231

had to destroy mine as an encore."

If my hands were freed I'd be doing a slow clap. Or putting them around her throat.

"So you can see that I did this for us."

I slump back down. Dead.

Mum continues, "David, I don't want to fight with you."

"Good, then just tell them to let me out of here."

"The contemplation room or the rehab?"

"Both!"

"You can't. When you sign yourself into the MGRC, you legally commit yourself to the full course of treatment for whatever package you choose. There's the *Lethal Weapon* package, the *Mad Max*, the *Passion of the Christ*–"

"And which package did I 'choose?'"

"You got the *Bird on a Wire* package."

"Which is…?"

"Three months."

"My deadline is in a week, Mum!"

"Just be glad you refrained from signing yourself up for the Year of Living Dangerously package. That one is six months."

This is bad. Bad, bad, bad. I can see my dreams slipping away from my grasp. All because of her.

"I'm on the What Women Want package. Which is similar to yours but with a feminine hygiene component."

"You don't get it. I am going to lose my publishing deal because of you. My editor is an Irish literary lunatic. She's known for destroying the lives of the writers who don't deliver on deadline. She'll kill the book, and then she'll kill me."

"Trust me, David I know the Irish. I was in that TV movie *Starvation* about the Great Potato Famine.

"Yes, I remember you were the only one in the cast who had to put *on* weight for the role."

I shift onto my belly and work my knees under me so I can heave myself upright. It's really hard without hands.

"The Irish are nothing if not a forgiving and understanding people. I will smooth things out with your editor and explain–"

"No! Don't do that."

"Let mama help," she says, going behind me and giving me a kiss on the cheek.

"You've done enough. I can't take anymore of your 'help.'"

Just then I feel the straps loosen on the jacket and my arms can move. She's freed me. I can move, I can breathe. I can put my hands around her throat.

Mum pulls a cigarette and lighter out of her robe with one hand. She can't light it because of the breeze coming from the vent. Instead of cupping her hand around the tobacco stick she goes to the corner to light up.

Her back is to me.

This is my moment. Alone in a soundproof room. I adjust my horn-rimmed glasses.

I hear the snap-snap of the flint. She's distracted.

"You'll have plenty of time to write," Mum says from the side of her mouth.

"I don't have my computer," I say.

It doesn't matter. I'm so creatively blocked even if I did have it I couldn't write. Unless I remove the blockage that is standing here before me.

"In between group therapy, art therapy, music therapy, dance therapy, one-on-one counselling, guided meditation, and 12 Step meetings."

This madness has to end.

"Oh, and colonics," she adds.

I don't want to do this, but it's the only way to be free from her. I raise my arms lurch towards her, white straps dangling like a Mummy.

Mum turns around and sees my outstretched arms ready to kill her.

She comes in close and hugs me.

"David, I love you. I just want to thank you for accompanying me into this facility. I know it wasn't an easy decision for you, but this is going to strengthen our bond. From now on I don't want there to be anything between us except love."

There is something between us. Is it love? It's rectangular, flat, and cold.

Mum pulls my laptop out of her robe, and puts it on my canvas covered hands.

"How did you …?"

"I have my ways," Susan Wilde flashes her trademark devilish grin. She sucks on her cigarette, allowing the smoke to waft gently from her lips, then sucks it in like she's inhaling the secret of the universe. "You see, David? Allow me to help you, and you can have exactly what you want." She strokes my face with her non-cigarette hand. Considerate.

"Anytime the muses speak to you …" she puts her hand on the Macintosh like she's swearing an oath. "Just ask, and I'll give it to you."

My murderous tendencies subside. But I'm still not ready to forgive her. For anything ever. Now she wants to emotionally ransom my computer, my writing, my future. The nerve. But then again, she wouldn't be Susan Wilde without that nerve.

"I'll hold on to it, thank you." I say pulling the computer. I don't want to be dependent on her for my creative juices to flow.

"David, they'll confiscate it and erase the memory. They take client privacy very seriously." She pulls the computer back.

"This has my only copy of the novel stored on it." I yank, but I can't get a grip with the canvas sleeves.

"Then I should have it. For safekeeping."

"Out of the question," I say

"I've got a secret hiding place. Don't you trust me, David?"

Before I can answer the bolt on the door slides.

"Quick!" Mum says. I let go of the computer and fold my hands in front of me. Mum stuffs the computer into her robe as the cigarette falls from her lips directly into the drain hole. She pulls a tiny bottle of Chanel #5 from her pocket and blasts a tiny spray. The mist gets in my eyes and stings me.

Shot Put Susan the orderly comes back in with a cup of tea.

"Thank you so much Susan," Mum says, taking the mug.

"I'm afraid you'll have to leave now ma'am. I'll get in trouble if anyone sees you in here with him."

"I completely understand. I've worked on sets with tattle tales, and let me tell you, it's the work that suffers most." Mum sips the tea. "Is that a hint of lavender I detect?"

"Yeah," Susan the orderly grins sheepishly.

"You are a doll." Mum touches Susan's shoulder, "Like I was saying, that sort of environment undermines trust." Mum leans in and stage whispers, "He slipped out of those restraints."

Shot Put Susan turns towards me. "Scully!"

Scully slips in past Mum and they both come towards me.

"Please, no."

Mum stands at the door and points to the computer beneath her robe, mouthing the words *Anytime*, as the orderlies grab me and refasten the restraints. She winks and slips out.

The orderlies finish tying me up and leave. I don't struggle this time. I'll play ball until I can find a way to get me and my computer out of here. No computer, no book. No book, no dream. No dream, no future.

Escape, by any means necessary. Even if it means faking like I have a problem. I have to create a person and then behave like they would behave. I am going to inhabit this character's skin, think like they think, act like they act. I have to become something I am not: a fictional person.

The only way out of here is to become the thing I hate most in this world: an actor.

Episode 17

It's morning now. I'm staring up at the ceiling of the contemplation room where I've spent the night. The mattress Scully brought in for me last night is completely made of memory foam with an internal heating source for maximum luxury. But being warm and cosy in an isolation room is cold comfort.

All night I've been preparing. Like an actor waiting in his trailer to be called to set.

The deadbolt on the door slides back and keys jangle in the lock.

Showtime.

"Breakfast time," Bill grunts at me.

As he takes off my straight jacket I breathe in deeply. I inhale oxygen as if for the first time, like I'm being born again.

Emerging from the contemplation room I walk down the hall taking deep breaths. I change up my steps so they reflect the new persona I'm adopting.

I head to the mess hall. Again, I am the last one to get there. A seat is open next to Jeremy and I sit down beside him. At least I have one friend here, even if he annoys me and reminds me of what I could be doing right now if I had only stuck with my old life and hadn't tried to become a writer.

I turn to the ageing, leather clad rocker with a beer gut sitting next to me. My new self should try to make some friends. Even if it is with the guy who was drooling on me yesterday.

"Dave," I say, assuming my new character. "Drug addict, Dave."

"Keith Curtis," he says in a London accent so thick it sounds more like *Keef Cur'its*.

I shake his calloused hand.

"This is Jeremy," I say.

The two men nod at each other. "We met before," Jeremy says.

"We were both at the same law firm. That's how we know each other," I say.

"I 'ate lawyers," Keith confesses without prompting. "Can't stand 'em."

"Oh ok." I say. "Well, I'm not anymore. I'm a writer now. Are you a reader?"

"Yeah, I read. Mainly for'choon cook'ies. You wrote any a 'fose?"

"Books. I mainly do books."

"He published one," Jeremy adds. "It had a really cool cover."

"Wha's it about then?" Keith asks.

"It's a detective story," I say.

"Who dunnit, then?"

"Done what?"

"The murda'?"

"Yeah, who did it, David?" Jeremy asks.

"That's a surprise. Do you want me to completely ruin it?"

"Don't split infinitives, lad, it's undignified," Keith grunts.

I can't believe this guy is lecturing me on syntax.

"Enough about me, what is it that you do?" I ask.

"Musician." Keith slurps his tea.

"Cool," Jeremy says. "What band?"

"The Whom."

"You mean The Who?" I say suspiciously.

"Yeah who?" Jeremy says. I can tell from the way he says it he doesn't know who The Who are.

"Not The Who. *The Whom*. We should 'ave been way more famous than them lot. Those arse'oles stole everything from us. Except proppa' English, of course."

"It's a shame people don't like their rock 'n roll rebellion with correct grammar."

"Too bloody righ', mate." Keith slurps his tea. "It doesn't mat'ta now. The band and I have par'edt ways for good."

"That sucks, they gave you the boot," Jeremy says.

"Yes." Keith drains his tea.

"For drinking?" I ask.

"Can't remember. I was in a blackout."

"That is the worst." Jeremy says. "I got fired in a blackout once. I showed up Monday morning like nothing had happened. It was so embarrassing because my dad owned the company." Jeremy pauses as if to think. "So they had to, like, give me my job back. So embarrassing for them."

Jeremy really has turned failing into a fine art. The way he lands his falls from grace so gracefully borders on ballet.

"Yeah, that job sucked. But now I'm a partner at my new firm, so silver lining. Speaking of which, where are you on coming back to work for us?"

Before I can answer, Shot Put Susan, the orderly, comes in with a clipboard and an announcement.

"Ok clients listen up. We are going to be breaking up into

groups. A Group will be doing art therapy."

"It should be 'Group A', so there ain't confusion between the indefinite article 'a' and the modifier of "A" as it relates to the group participa'in' in said art 'ferapy," Keith interjects.

Shot Put Susan glowers at him.

I give Keith a thumbs up to let him know he's right. I might as well try making friends.

"And B Group will be doing group therapy in the studio. Does anyone not know which group they are in?"

My hand goes up.

"It's alphabetical by last name. A–M, for A. N–Z for B."

Thank god, I'm not with Mum.

"You're in A Group," Susan the orderly orders. "Both of you."

I look to see whose hand is up. And it is, who else, but my mother, Susan Wilde. She must be checked in here under another name. Her real name? I don't know if her original name is even her legal name anymore.

"Excuse me. Can I change?" I start, shaking my raised hand. Bill and Scully stare at me. *Be a compliant client.* I put my hand down.

The orderlies nod in unison.

Everyone gets up, puts their dishes in the washing up tubs, and divides into their allocated groups.

"Hey, so … tell me who did it?" Jeremy whispers.

"Did what?"

"The murder in your book?"

I shake my head. Jeremy told me he'd read it.

"No spoilers."

"Fine. I'll just wait for it to become a movie," Jeremy says, and toddles off to do group therapy.

Drug addicts and alcoholics of varying degrees of fame, fortune, and notoriety go off in different directions. I am now one of them. I have to act like them, be like them, think as they do. What is it like being addicted to something? To be fixated and obsessed by something no matter how great the personal cost?

What sort of state of mind would that throw you into? It would make you want to kill …

And that's it! The jigsaw pieces begin fitting together. That's what I need to finish my new book. That's the missing ingredient: sacrifice. My detective is looking for someone who killed out of hate but he needs to be looking for someone who killed out of love. A misguided love, but a love nonetheless.

My mind is a bag of microwave popcorn. Little kernels of sodium-rich thought explode against each through the force of tiny targeted microwaves rays, causing a chain reaction of expansion to the very limits of the brain bag. These calorific nuggets cascade through my … ok I've reached the limits of this metaphor.

All I know is that the creative blockage that has been with me for days is finally gone!

I arrive in the art room consumed with the high of inspiration. I sit at a table that looks like a Jackson Pollock painting. Various art supplies sit at the centre of the table alongside reams of thick white paper. I dip my hand into the pile of drawing tools and come out with a big purple crayon. I begin scribbling out notes on a piece of paper, allowing the creative juices to flow onto the page. The agonising days of frustration and blockages are destroyed as the plot for my book spills out onto thick construction paper.

The art teacher introduces herself and the task at hand. I don't hear a word she says. The other rehab artists pick up materials and start drawing out their feelings. I keep writing. Nothing can stop me now.

I'm deep in the flow when the art teacher stops me by putting a hand on my shoulder. She's soft spoken and wears a black shirt, black skirt, black framed glasses, and has a black scrunchy to keep her hair in a tight bun.

"I'm glad you're so enthusiastic, um ..." the art teacher says.

"Dave. Drug addict, Dave." I say, James Bond-style. "What's your name?"

"Karylyna," she says, pointing to the whiteboard at the front that has her name spelled on it. Despite the spelling she pronounces it 'Carolina', and in North and South.

"Did you hear the instructions I gave to everyone?" she asks, compassion dripping from her voice.

"Sorry, I must have forgotten already. My short term memory is shot because of drugs. I did lots of drugs. And alcohol too. I drank alcohol ... alcoholically, like an alcoholic. I'm just writing something down so I don't forget it later."

"And I want to take this moment, Dave, to honour you. For being so vulnerable and speaking your truth about your substance abuse and *your* journey with short term memory loss. It's something you should be proud of."

"Don't end a sen'ence wiff a preposition," Keith says, not raising his eyes from his finger painting.

Karylyna ignores him. "What I'd like you to do now, Dave, is to channel those words into images, and draw me a picture of your rock bottom. Can you do that for me?"

I nod in agreement and take another piece of paper from the stack. My purple crayon begins to draw a magical world of depraved depression. It's my bottom. Junkies, meth-heads, and drunks, oh my. It goes from madness to obsession to … Karylyna walks away … I lift up my purple world of pretend pain and continue plotting my novel.

The other people at my table don't take much interest in what I'm doing. They are too absorbed in their own colourful bottoms.

The rehab art teacher continues to weave amongst the rehab artists. "There's no right or wrong here," Karylyna says. "Whatever you feel, just let it out on the page. Use any combination of paint, marker, pencils. Really explore your pain through colour. Any colour you like." She compliments everyone on what a wonderful job they're all doing.

Mum and I basically ignore each other. From art therapy we go to group therapy. I don't share, but Mum takes the opportunity to again make the session all about her. I'm sure some of the stories she's telling are actually plotlines from one of the soap operas she used to be on. But I'm not sure. I want to call her out, shout that she's a liar, that she booked me in her against my will. But I don't. It won't change anything and it'll just make me feel more crazy. For the sake of my mental health I bottle up my rage. But then I realise that I should actually channel it into my characters.

During lunch, or as it's called 'nutrition therapy', I'm able to scribble down some more notes using a napkin and a pen that I steal from one of the kitchen staff. Then to music therapy, fitness therapy, cognitive behavioural therapy, and finally massage therapy. In stolen moments here and there I'm able to jot down more story notes.

This pattern goes on for a few days. In between meditation therapy, neurofeedback therapy, and dialectical therapy, I write my novel bit by bit on scraps of paper. All while playing the part of 'Drug Addict Dave', who now has a fully fleshed out back story. I'm embodying this other persona. It feels weird but it also feels good. It seems like the only way I can truly be myself is to be someone else. I'm discovering who I am through being someone else.

I haven't spoken to Susan Wilde in days but when I've got enough story material together I make my approach.

After dinner I sidle up to Susan as everyone is filing out of the mess hall.

"I want the you-know-what," I say under my breath.

"Pardon me, sir?" she says, not making eye contact with me.

"You know, what you've got ... *under the robe*."

"I'm sure I don't know what you're talking about."

"I haven't had it in ages. I just need a little bit of time on it. Don't tease me with it then take it away."

"Truly, young man, I am flattered. But I am not into breast feeding kink."

"What are you talking about, Mu—" I catch myself, "Ma'am, um, Madam." That was close. I put my hand on her shoulder. "Plus you're way too old to—"

"How dare you!" She grabs my hand, then slaps me across the face.

An orderly comes over, "Is there a problem here?"

I'm so startled I can't say anything. She hasn't hit me in years.

"This young man was getting fresh."

"No I—"

"He wanted to breastfeed!" Mum says, making a scene.

"Is that true?" the orderly asks.

W.W.D.A.D.D.

What Would Drug Addict Dave Do?

"… Yes. Yes it is. I'm sorry. I'm breast obsessed. It's part of my addiction."

"There's an appropriate time to deal with that," the orderly says. "Family therapy."

That statement hangs in the air like a yo-yo spinning at the end of its string.

"In the meantime do you want to make a formal complaint, Susan?" the orderly asks her.

"No, he didn't mean any harm. He's obviously had a troubled childhood," Mum says. "Haven't you?"

"No. Not really," Drug Addict Dave answers. *He* had great parents.

"Yes, it's obvious he's got lots of issues relating to poor parenting."

"But I don't blame them," I say. "They did the best they could."

"Well it wasn't good enough. They could have done more, been there for you."

It's like she's trying to apologise in the most roundabout way and in the most inappropriate manner. But as my father used to say: when it comes to family, son, never expect the truth.

The orderly just stares at us. There is a weird moment of tense silence, which Susan Wilde finally breaks.

"No hard feelings," she says, "Shake on it."

She looks directly into my eyes and does the double-handed handshake. I feel a note slip into my hand. I smile broadly, and bow slightly, the way Mum always taught me. Courtesy is the best misdirection, she taught me. The polite rarely look guilty. I shrug my shoulders and slide the note into my pocket.

That's the final lesson; never look into your hand right away.

Mum and the orderly move on. I carry on to my room and wait until the door is closed to unfold the perfectly folded piece of paper. In graceful looping cursive it reads: *Mop closet. 10pm. Sharp. Destroy after reading.*

I swallow hard. Mainly from the paper going down my throat.

At the stroke of ten I'm at the mop closet. My pockets are bulging with my notes as if my trousers had the mumps.

I sweat a little. Nine o'clock is after room curfew and if they catch me I'll be back in the contemplation room.

Waiting. Mum is nowhere in sight. I can hear the sound of footsteps down the long hallway. It's the slow steady rhythm of a security guard, each step punctuated by the jingle of keys hanging from a belt loop. The steps get closer. I'm totally exposed where I am, the mop closet is directly in the middle of the hallways with equal distance between corners of the building. The steps jangle louder.

I can see my future in the padded room becoming more clear.

Stepping backwards I feel a hand on my shoulder.

This is it. Back to isolation.

Episode 18

I go to scream but a hand covers my mouth as I'm pulled backwards into the mop closet.

"You're late." I hear in a perfect staged whisper.

A lamp flicks on. Perfectly illuminated, in film noir style, is the face of my mother, Susan Wilde.

"So are you." I shoot back in my whisper.

"I was expecting the secret knock, David?"

"The what?"

"Three long and two short. It was on the backside of the note."

"I must not have digested that bit."

"Absolutely fine my darling. I am just so thankful you came at all." She kisses me on the cheek. I pull back slightly. I'm not ready to forgive her for stranding me in rehab.

"Where's my computer?"

Mum shines the lamp over to the back of the mop closet. A shelf has been cleared out and a folding chair placed in front of it. On the shelf is my laptop. It's a perfect little workstation. How did she set all this up? There's even a mug of tea steaming beside the computer.

I sniff the air. "Lemongrass?"

"With honey. For my honey."

I look sideways at her.

"There's no catch," she says, translating the expression on my face. "An artist must have the best possible space to get the creative juices flowing."

"In rehab?"

"Art thrives on limitations, David."

Damn. She's not wrong. I hate it when she's not wrong.

She guides me to the chair and sits me down. The fragrance of the lemongrass wafts up my sinuses. I taste the tea.

"Is that a hint of lavender I detect?"

Susan grins. Nods.

"Now when the muse speaks to you, my love, you can work here. Provided the inspiration comes between 10pm and 2am. Oh, and not on Sundays. Or Saturdays. But any other time you want to answer the call of creativity … just give me five hours notice and all this shall be provided for you instantly."

"What if someone comes in?" I ask.

Mum moves the lamp over to the desk, lighting her face from below.

"Don't fret. Mama has taken care of everything. Only the day custodian has keys to this closet. Shift change is at 2am, so you have a 30 minute window. Knock on my door and this will all disappear like *Brigadoon*."

I wish she would disappear like that stupid Scottish town. I'm not sure why she drops this analogy to the Broadway musical, about a village that only appears once every hundred years and then disappears into the mist. But she's got me over a barrel, or a *bah–rrrel* as the Scots would say. If I try to smuggle my computer out to my room Bill or Scully will find it for sure. They've already tossed my room twice looking for contraband. This is probably the only way I am going to be able to reach my deadline. I need her devious ways more than ever now.

"Mum did you really mean what you said after dinner in the hall, about my childho–"

"Shhh." Her index finger pins my lips shut so tight that I can smell the adhesive on her press-on nail.

Footsteps fall directly outside the door then pause. Keys jangle like a broken wind chime.

We both hold our breath, eyes darting. Her French tip nail is tickling my nose hairs. I can feel a sneeze welling up. Mum sees this and covers my mouth with her other hand.

Then the footfalls move away from us.

Mum breathes out, removes her finger and I sneeze. The footsteps stop again. Then move on.

Mum whispers, "The patrols come by at quarter to and quarter past the hour. So don't type too loudly when they're coming past. Remember, when you finish transcribing your prose, come to my door and do the secret knock."

"Can you just hold on a sec."

"Three long and two short." She opens the door bathing her in moonlight from the hall windows. For the first time I notice she's in a floor-length white silk nightgown.

"Mum, wait."

"David, your mother needs her beauty sleep." She says doing a hand gesture down her body. "Do you think these good looks are purely the result of good genetics?"

"I certainly don't."

Susan Wilde closes the door silently and glides away. Her feet make no sound as she disappears like Brigadoon into the mist.

I sigh, looking around my surroundings. The broom closet

of a rehab isn't exactly the sanctuary of literary inspiration I imagined for myself working in. But if I can finish my novel by the time I get out of here then, even if Deirdre fires me I'll still have my book done.

The dank surroundings of rehab turn out to be a hovel of creativity. I go to it, turning my scribbles on scraps into something resembling a book. The smell of lemongrass and cleaning products create a potent aroma of self-expression. As I weave my story I come to the realisation that some of the great writers in history have produced great works while confined: Gandhi, Oscar Wilde, the Marquis de Sade. I'm not saying I'm in a similar league with them, just that we have something in common. Our bodies are imprisoned but not our imaginations.

At 2am I leave the computer and go to Mum's room. I do the secret knock. I don't want to lose the only copy of my book, but I really don't have any other choice but to trust Mum. I crawl into bed and get a few hours sleep before breakfast.

* * *

The next day I am feeling tired; but the good kind of tired. The kind of tiredness that comes from a job well done, instead of the normal nervous exhaustion I am accustomed to feeling recently. The feeling of being able to unburden myself both creatively and emotionally is like having an emotional colostomy bag attached to my soul. I get to write at night, get fed well during the day. I get to express myself through my art, through group, and through my new self as Dave. Rehab is becoming the most inspiring place I have ever been.

I'm finding freedom in the character of Drug Addict Dave.

I can do and say almost anything as him, as long as it's in character. The need to be David Hawkes, the lawyer, the writer, the boyfriend, the son, is slipping away. Who needs that guy? He was annoying. He had lots of problems.

As my father used to say: "Son, just be yourself. And if you can't, then be someone else."

Everyone in rehab loves Drug Addict Dave. Karylyna compliments his clay sculpture of his "inner child's pain". Shot Put Susan compliments his behaviour as a compliant client who follows all the rules during the day. Dr. Frederick, the group therapy counsellor, compliments Dave's emotional vulnerability as he shares about some of the painful experiences that he's had when I was a hopeless smack addict who drank a bottle of Jack Daniels a day. This feels like the role I was born to play. A recovering junkie by day who moonlights as detective novelist by night channelling his painful experiences as addict into emotional truths about society through the lens of crime. I'm freer as Dave than I ever was as David.

And there's only one person in the world who I have to thank for that. My mother, Susan Wilde. Well, she's not "Dave's" mother, which is a huge relief. Miss Susan Wilde is just another drug addict/alcoholic in rehab with me. Nothing more, nothing less. She is just another person to Dave. I don't have to worry about her behaviour because she's not my mother anymore.

The hours stretch to days, to weeks. I think. I am beginning to lose track of time. Partly it's from sleep deprivation. Partly because time flies when you're having fun. I really don't even know what day it is now.

It must be morning though because I'm in group therapy and the sun is out. Dr. Frederick is leading a discussion about 'what happens when we use' with the Goth Girl, Keith, Jez, and a few others. "Leading" is a strong word though. Susan is in the middle of performing a monologue for the group.

"I just thought black outs and vodka went to together, like bangers and mash–"

"Thank you, Susan!" Dr. Frederick cuts her off, "I feel like it's time to hear from another person. We haven't heard from you in a while, David?"

"It's Dave," I remind her.

"My apologies. Dave. Would you like to share?"

"I don't know ..." I say.

"C'mon, mate. Share wif us." Keith shouts.

Everyone else pipes up encouraging me to share.

"Speak your truth, Hawkesy," Jeremy says.

"Ok, ok. Yeah, I would like to share actually. Thank you, Dr. Frederick, for encouraging me. And thank you Susan. For your honesty. It's given me the strength to share something with you all. Something I've never said to anyone. I've been here at the MGCRC for a little while now and it's given me the time to really confront the demons inside me. And if it wasn't for all the love and support I received from you all I wouldn't have the strength to say this right now. I have a problem. And it's staring me in the face right now." I look across the circle. "It's so obvious who is really to blame here. Me. I'm an addict. I thought I would find love in all those chemicals but all I found was a soul sickening loneliness that chewed my insides up."

Everyone in the circle claps for me.

"Go on," Dr. Frederick says.

"And ... I really debased myself," I did things that I swore I would never do to get the hit I needed. I would even go so far as to say that I prostituted myself to get what I needed from the person who had it." I choke up with tears.

"It's a safe space, Dave," Dr. F says, "Let it out."

I signal that I don't want to keep talking, the emotion is clogging my throat.

"I'm a whore!" I wail. "I'm a whore. I would do anything to get a hit of that sweet material." I break down in tears and fall to the ground.

Everyone gets up and picks me up and hugs me. There's a chorus of, *we're here for you* and *I know your pain.* They pat me on the back, give me Kleenex, and put me back in a chair. I notice a guy with a staff pass hanging around in the back of the room. Just observing. I wonder what he's doing but then Dr. Frederick interrupts again.

"I think we can all appreciate what a big breakthrough Dave has made today. Does anyone want to say anything to Dave?"

"I think Dave is really brave for sharing that," Keith says.

"Dave, you're my new hero," says Jeremy.

"You're amazing, Dave." The Goth Girl says.

They all embrace me in a way I never knew I needed.

"Anyone else?" Dr. Frederick asks.

"I just want everyone to know that, I also … am a whore," Susan says. She falls to the ground sobbing as well. It's very awkward. It's quite clear she's just trying to copy me.

"Ok, Nobody touch her, just give her the dignity of her own experience," Dr. Frederick says, "Now, who else wants to share?"

Someone pipes up and the group therapy continues. I am not really listening as I compose myself, and dab my tears with a tissue. The story is fake but affection is real. I just have to pull up the painful places of myself and bring them to my story. That's how I make it believable for these people. And for myself.

After group therapy I go to dance therapy with Gustav, the dance instructor. I dance out the pain over the time I shot heroin in my eye. Then I go to art therapy with Karylyna and I make a sculpture of a knight saving a damsel. At the unveiling in front of everyone I name it: I Saved The Heroine But She Turned Out To Be Addictive. Everyone claps. After art therapy we do animal therapy with Yvonne, where we have to act like an animal and demonstrate how our diseases manifested. Mine is the Gopher of Denial, who occasionally pops his head up but prefers to hide in his burrow of shame. Dave's world is becoming more and more real.

Afterward animal therapy I am surrounded with Keith, Jeremy, and the Goth Girl. Susan approaches us.

"Dave. I really liked your ferret," Susan says to me.

"It was a gofa'," Keith corrects.

"Originally I thought of doing a prairie dog," I say. "But I felt like that was too much in my comfort zone. I find more truth when I strip away comfort."

"Next time you could do a naked mole rat," the Goth Girl says suggestively. "If you really wanted to get out of your comfort zone."

"That's a good idea," I say. I'm not sure if we're flirting or not, but I go with it.

"How did you like my Swan of Salvation?" Susan asks.

"It was so good, Susan. Powerful yet, understated. Nuanced, yet moving. You gave it your all. I really thought you were, what's the word ... committed."

Susan leans in and looks around at everyone else. Waiting.

"What did you guys think?" I prompt.

"Very committed." Keith says.

"Extremely committed." Jeremy adds.

"I thought of someone who should be committed when I watched you," the Goth Girl says. The Goth Girl cradles my arm.

"You are all too kind. I must confess though. I have retired from the acting world. But it is nice to exercise those muscles again."

"Yes, exercise. That's also what I thought when I watched you," the Goth Girl says.

Susan stares so hard at the Goth Girl I think she might burn a hole through the layer of black eye shadow.

Then Susan laughs. So does the Goth Girl. "You have a wicked sense of humour."

"It goes with hair."

Everyone else laughs.

"Yes, and your soul," Susan says under her breath.

"Look guys, I need to talk to Susan for a second. I'll catch up with you in … in … what's next?"

"It's colonic therapy," Jeremy says.

"Just start without me."

"It won' be the same wifout you, mate," Keith says.

"Oh, I'm sure you'll have a blast."

Everyone laughs as they walk away. As they walk I hear their voices as they fade out.

Keith: "He's so funny."

Goth Girl: "I love a man with a good sense of humour."

Jeremy: "Yeah, he must get it from his dad."

I face Susan.

"I'll be needing you-know-what tonight?" I tell her.

Susan nods.

"Is that all you want to say to me?" She eyes me.

"You really were good in that Swan thing you improvised. Don't listen to those guys."

"As you know David, even during my acting days I didn't care about the opinions of people like that. They're cultural Phoenicians."

I think she means Philistines, but I don't care about correcting her.

"I just want to make sure you are … ok."

"I'm great. Thanks for asking Miss Wilde."

"It's Ms. Wilde, David, and I–"

"Dave, it's Dave."

"Yes, 'Dave', I want to thank you too."

"For what?"

"You who helped me to realise my acting career was over."

"Was it something I said in group therapy Ms. Wilde?"

"No it was before that. You helped me to realise I could no longer carry on the way I was. I was trying desperately to maintain some fantasy. When I came back to Melbourne to revitalise my career, I thought the mountain I was facing was a new challenge, but it turns out it was the hill that I was over. The quicker I accepted my fate as a failure, the quicker I could move on. Move on to focus on my family."

"That sounds like a real breakthrough." I say, looking into her eyes as she finishes her soliloquy. "I am just glad both of us are getting the help we need," I say, not breaking character.

"David, you're not an addict," she says, trying to be real. "You can drop the performance."

But being in character is my new reality.

"It's Dave. And I used to think so too. But I am. I feel it. Being here has taught me a few things. These people have loved me back to life. It's all thanks to you."

"Fine then. Shall we go on to the next activity then, Dave?" Susan says.

"Oh um. You know what, we've probably missed our spots by now."

"I'm sure they can squeeze us in,"

"Actually," I say. "I'm enjoying this."

We sit down in the little seating area in front of the stage and chat. Not as mother and son but as two addicts connecting. She and I have spent so much time in theatres together. Whether it was London, New York, Melbourne, or on a cruise ship somewhere in the Pacific, she would rehearse while I read a book or did school work. We would be together, but alone. Now for the first time we are in a 'theatre' connecting with each other. She, as herself, and me as Drug Addict Dave.

Later we go to dinner and she sits with my group of friends. She is her typical charming yet self-obsessed self. She makes gaffs, faux pas, and brings most subjects back to herself. But I keep committing to my role and feel zero embarrassment by her behaviour. Acting, that is what our relationship has needed, nay *craved,* all these years. I look over at her and realise what a blessing it is to have her in my life. In this make believe way.

After dinner we go our separate ways. I get up at midnight and go to my broom closet of inspiration and begin the night's work. Opening the door I see my computer and a warm cup of tea. The tea brews as does my creativity, and after a marathon session at the computer I go to Susan's room and do the secret knock. Her hand reaches out and takes the laptop. I flop into my bed exhausted and content. Therapy, connection, meals provided, and a workspace where I can toil uninterrupted by the chaos of life.

This is absolutely heaven.

Episode 19

Bliss. That's the only way I can describe my surroundings. Familial love is in the air. It's a sunny day and today is family day at the Mel Gibson Celebrity Rehab Centre. Loved ones come from far and near to visit their beloved addicts and alcoholics. There are circular tables set up around the day room for families to mingle. I sit at an empty table awaiting the woman who I love most in the world.

And then, there she appears. Lithe, gorgeous, hair flowing and in all white. My girlfriend, Katharine Nichols.

I adjust my horn-rimmed glasses.

She dodges in between the table and chairs of my new best friends: Keith, Jeremy, and the Goth Girl, and arrives at my table.

We embrace.

"Oh David, thank god you're ok," Katharine says.

"Why wouldn't I be?" I say.

"Um, because you disappeared, with no explanation and left a typed note that said 'going on holiday to spend some quality time with mum.' Who, by the way, has also disappeared."

"Did I? A lot of that day is a blur." In fact a lot of my time pre-MGCRC is becoming a blur.

"The only reason I found you was because you listed me as

259

your personal physician. They called me after you ended up in the isolation room for the second time in a day."

"It's the contemplation room, Katharine," I correct.

"They wanted my medical opinion on whether it would be safe to give you shock therapy. I covered, even though it's unethical, and told them it wouldn't because you could lose some of your memory and not be able to write."

"That was the old David. I don't go in there anymore," I reach across the table and take her hand.

"Well that's good. Cause they said, the only reason you didn't get electro shock is because the head psychiatrist guy wasn't here to sign off on it. But one more incident and you could be ... you know. *ZZZZzzztttt.*"

I love it when Katharine tries to do sound effects. Her embarrassing failures are so endearing.

"Again, that's old David. New Dave doesn't get in trouble."

"Well that 'old David' also listed me as his wife."

"Did I? Look, that must have been the drugs."

Katharine pulls her hand away.

"It's why I'm here, for family day."

"And I'm so grateful you are here. Have you done something different with your hair?"

"I washed it ..."

"It looks fantastic."

I look deeply into her eyes, smiling. I try to reach for her hand again.

"Are you ok, David? You're smiling vacantly like someone in a cult."

I consider the question. "I am ... amazing," I say. "And it's Dave now."

"Dave ...?" She strings the word out like it's one she's never heard before.

"But enough about me. How are you? I want to hear all about you."

"All about me? Hmmm, well let's see. In the past few weeks, I've been worried sick about my boyfriend who vanished without a trace with his mother. And then I find, to my surprise, that he's checked into rehab. All the while I'm fielding calls from his basketball team wondering why he isn't at games, and from his editor wondering why he's missing deadlines."

"Oh yeah, Deirdre," I say remembering my paramilitary editor. "How's she?"

"She's irate."

"Would you say she's I.R.-Ate?" I laugh. Katharine doesn't laugh.

"What is going on here?" Katharine looks around the room as if she's suddenly realised that she's on a hidden camera show. "Have you lost your mind?"

"No. I've gained my sanity. I feel alive inside here."

"Don't make this a joke. Deirdre's threatening to sue you if you don't hand in the manuscript on time. Maybe I can turn in what you have so far. Where is your laptop, it's not at the house?"

"I don't know," I lie.

"Don't you care about your book deal? David, this is what you've been working towards all your life."

"Yeah and where did it get me? It was a totally miserable existence," I say, trying to keep my pre-rehab memories from bubbling up within the cauldron of my mind.

"Your life with me was miserable?" Katharine's breath becomes slower. More deliberate.

"Not 'miserable' miserable. Mildly miserable. I don't know. Here, everything is so simple. I just do what people tell me. I say what they want me to say. Go where they want me to go. I emote when they want me to emote. They feed me well. And I have a special place where I can go when I need time to regroup and get my creative energy up."

"You're basically describing the life of an actor," Katharine says. I sense that she is irritated by her own revelation. "You hate acting, remember."

I give my memory cauldron a stir with my wooden spoon and no unpleasant associations about acting arise.

"Nope ... and I'm not acting, Katharine. This is me now. This is Dave." I say looking around at all my beautiful addict and alcoholic friends. "I'm not that anxious, fear-ridden person anymore. Now I just accept who I really am and I boldly go–"

Keith gives me the stink eye as he hears me splitting infinitives.

"I mean, *I go boldly* into the future." I say, as Keith and I share a wink. I lean back in my chair and sense the sunlight from the big bay windows.

"Look, I'm gonna try to sign you out of here as your doctor." Katharine says, looking around to find someone in authority.

As Katharine looks around the room. I follow her gaze as she spots Dr. Frederick going around to the different tables. Also I spot the man who was hanging in the background at group therapy the other day. He's doing the same thing today. Observing from a distance.

"David!" Katharine snaps, closing off the path of my wandering mind.

"Yeah?" I say. I notice the observing man drift over to

Susan's table.

"I'm trying to get you out of here?" Katharine says with a strident edge to her voice.

"You mean, leave the centre?"

"Yes, leave the centre! Come home. With me. Resume our life together," she says.

I hesitate.

"I'm starting to sense you don't want to come home with me?"

I hesitate again.

"David …?" She strings the word out like it's one she's never heard before.

"Why would I leave?"

"For starters you're in a rehab and you don't even have a drug problem!"

Other people look over.

"It's Dave. And keep your voice down. This is family day."

"Yes, and I am your family." Katharine says in a harsh whisper. "Your mother has pissed off to God-knows-where again. Abandoning you; abandoning us. You disappear and then are mysteriously in this 'celebrity' rehab centre. You haven't even explained to me how you ended up here."

"It's complicated," I stammer. "I can't explain it, but I'm happier here."

"What could possibly make you happier in here, than outside with me?" Katharine demands to know.

Just then the actress known as Susan Wilde struts in wearing a long flowing white gown.

Katharine watches. Her silent fuming is so palpable I feel like I'm getting a steam burn from across the table.

Susan strides past the other tables and sits with a man whose back is to us. She kisses him on the mouth, but I can't get a glimpse of his face.

"Katharine … Katharine …" I try to draw Katharine's gaze back into mine. But she's staring at Susan like a bull ready to charge. "Katharine, it's not what you think."

"You know what— David, Dave, or whoever you are— I don't care. I've sat by while this whole sick thing with your mother played out. And I was supportive. I thought that if we let her into our lives, it would help you sort out all of your childhood stuff. But all it did was bring out the worst in you, and in me. And, you know what, I'm done with it."

"And how are we going here?" Dr. Frederick says approaching our table.

"Going. Yes, we are going," says Katharine, matter of factly. "Actually, it's just me. *I'm* going."

"So soon?" Dr. Frederick says. "We were going to start doing trust falls in a little bit."

"Unfortunately I can't spend another minute here. Dave seems happy though. I think he'd like to be here forever," Katharine says.

"Well he is kind of our star client at the moment." Dr. Frederick touches my shoulder.

"That's wonderful, as his doctor, I'm so pleased about that. In fact feel free to give him shock therapy or colonics or whatever you do here," Katharine says smiling like an assassin. "I just want him to get better."

"She's not really my doctor," I say.

"He's so funny," Katharine says. "I'm Dr. Nichols," she says, presenting her APA card.

"I'm Dr. Frederick. And I'm sorry you can't stay. Maybe we can discuss a bit of a treatment plan for Dave over the phone.

For when he comes home."

"Well unfortunately I'm not going to be attending to him anymore." Katharine says, staring right at me.

"That's a shame," Dr. Frederick says.

"Yes, this is really more of an exit interview. I'm going to leave him in your capable hands."

"Katharine, Dr. Frederick's right. I need you still." I plead, grabbing her arm as she gets up.

"You don't," Katharine says, detaching herself from me. "You need someone with a more matronly instinct."

"I agree. There is something maternal from his life that is a bit lacking," Dr. Frederick says.

I look over to the "something maternal" sitting across the room. I still can't see the face of the man she's talking to. Who is he?

Katharine pushes in her chair and starts to leave. "Goodbye David."

"I'll just walk her to the door," I say to Dr. Frederick, getting up quickly and knocking my chair over. I pick it back up and mouth "sorry" to everyone as I try to catch up to Katharine who is reaching the door.

"Don't try and do another runner, Dave," Dr. Frederick laughs. But Bill and Scully still watch me like cats at a mousehole.

"Wait? You had an escape attempt?" Katharine turns and says under her breath. "Actually, I don't want to know." She keeps walking.

"It wasn't my fault." I say grabbing her arm.

She wheels around and asks, "Whose was it then?"

I break eye contact and stammer instead of answering.

Katharine shakes her head and continues her march to the

door.

"I get it. You're happier in here with her. "

"No, Katharine, I'm not in here because of her— well, it is because of her— but it's not what you think."

"Don't you dare tell me what I think. After you pulled your little Houdini-act I did actually have time to think. And I thought, it is so peaceful here. And then I thought: I have put up with you, and your mother, and all your craziness for long enough. You want to be locked in here with her, then that's fine. I have wasted five years of my life on you and I'm not going to waste another second. I'm not going to keep renting when I can buy. I'm not going to wait for your novel to come out so we can start the next phase of our life together. I'm not going to keep living this temporary existence."

Katharine bangs on the door, indicating she wants out. Out of the Centre. Out of our relationship. Out of my life. For good.

The door opens. I go to say something but I can't.

"I'm done wasting time," she says, getting choked up.

Katharine puts something in my hand, and closes my fingers around it.

"Goodbye, David."

Now's my chance: I can bolt through the door and possibly to freedom.

What Would Drug Addict Dave Do?

The door closes with a clang. And I hear the bolt click in. Through the glass I watch as she disappears.

I feel the metal object in my hand. It's my TAG Heuer Monaco watch. The same worn by Steve McQueen in the film *Le Mans*. The one my father gave to me when he missed my birthday one year. Katharine had a new battery put in it, put leather conditioner on the band, and replaced the glass on the faceplate. The second hand ticks along.

It's 11:33am.

I look over the watch and realise it's the second time it's been given to me as a present from someone who won't be around much.

I rub the new faceplate on my old watch feeling the cold metal and glass.

A hand touches my shoulder. "David?"

"What!" I bark, jostled from my melancholy. "Alan?"

It's Alan Dinsdale, my boss from the old law firm. He's taken aback by my snapping at him and his toupee moves ever so slightly off-centre.

"It is you, David. What are you doing here?" he says. "Do you have a drinking problem?"

"Yes, I mean, no. I mean, kind of. I don't know anymore," I stammer out. "I mean, yes. I do have a problem."

"Was that Katharine I saw just now?"

"Yes," I say, breathing hard.

"Is she coming back in?" Alan says, looking through the glass in the door.

"No, I think … not."

"Say 'hi' to her for me," Alan says. "You picked a good one when you married her."

"We aren't married yet, Alan."

"Really? Well, you still have time." Alan slaps me gently on the back.

Do I? I look down at my watch. I've got my timepiece back, but I've run out of time with the person who delivered it to me.

"What are you doing here, Alan?" I say.

267

"Visiting Jeremy." Alan points over to a table where I see Jeremy; along with his mother, father, and his older brother sitting together. They're all wearing golfing clothes, ready to hit the links right after their stopover in rehab.

We walk over to a more secluded corner of the dayroom.

"You know he's got a terrible problem with the drink," Alan says to me, as if it's some sort of secret. "It got so bad it was starting to affect his work."

"'Starting' to?"

"Yes. In fact," Alan clears his throat. "It got worse after you left. The quality of his work just fell off a cliff."

"You don't say." Alan doesn't pick up on my sarcasm.

"No matter. How are you?"

"I'm doing ok."

"You know a lot of lawyers pick up the drink after they leave their practice. Is that what happened with you?"

I open my mouth to answer but Alan is already ploughing forward into a monologue.

"All that free time on your hands? It's not healthy. Lawyers need structure. If we don't have it we go to pieces. You know, like someone finding out they've been left out of the inheritance at the reading of a will. I remember a former colleague of mine. Brilliant legal mind. Knew the tax code inside and out. The way he could organise the trust funds for deceased estate was like watching Mozart compose a symphony. I mean this guy ..."

Alan drones on for a full four minutes about how great an estate lawyer this guy was. Finally I cut in.

"So what happened to him?" I say.

"He retired."

"And he drank himself to death?"

"No, he's living in Armidale. But all he does is play bingo at the local hall. That game has no structure. It's just random balls spit out of a cage. I suppose the little card where you cross out the bingo numbers is structured but each card is different. The numbers aren't in order like in a good estate tax filing…"

Alan keeps going on. Despite the fact that his stories wander like the Israelites in the desert there is a strange comfort in them, and in him.

Finally I cut him off.

"I heard that Frank DiSalvio died, or retired. Jeremy was hazy on the details."

"Frank's not dead, and he didn't retire."

"That's good."

"He had a stroke though. Totally incapacitated him."

"How come nobody told me?"

"I suppose no one thought of it," Alan wonders out loud. "We had to reassign a lot of his clients to Jeremy. And then that didn't work out because of the drinking, and the cocaine, and marijuana. So we had to send him to rehab and scramble to keep up with his workload. It's the type of stuff you could do in your sleep, but you were gone. I guess it all kind of got lost in the mix. Sorry."

"I'll have to drop by his house after I get out of here."

"Just drop by the office," Alan says.

"He's still coming into the office?" I say. I can't believe this.

"Of course he's coming in. He needs the structure. I mean he goes out for his physical therapy and what have you, but he's there, every morning at nine like clockwork. Otherwise he'd just end up at the bingo hall. By the way, what are your plans after you get out of here?"

"I honestly don't know," I say. This is the truth. I have actively tried to suppress the idea of leaving this comfortable, comforting place. I never want to leave here. This fake reality is my safe space. The fact that I won't have Katharine living with me anymore makes the outside world seem even less appealing.

"Why don't you come back to Dienstag, DiSalvio & Fischer," Alans suggests.

For a moment I entertain the notion of becoming a probate lawyer again with all the will writing, estate planning, and the–

"Structure," Alan interrupts my thought, but also completes it. "You'll need structure when you get out of here. You and Jeremy can support each other. I can hire you back, same job, same salary, same secretary. It'll be as if you never left."

I could essentially erase the last six months. Aside from Katharine breaking up with me.

"Where would I sit? You've probably given my office away," I say, trying not to sound too interested.

"You can share with Frank DiSalvio. He's really quiet."

"I don't know."

"Look, David, it's fine. You don't have to say yes right now. An old mentor of mine told me before making any big career decision, wait 48 hours. Otherwise you'll regret it."

"You're very generous Alan. But I'm not going to accept."

"Just take 48 hours. This old law mentor of mine, he didn't follow his own advice and made a big career mistake."

"Where did he end up? A traffic court judge?"

"Worse." Alan slaps me on the shoulder and shakes his head. "A bingo hall in Armidale." He treats this man's fate with the solemnity usually reserved for those fallen in World Wars.

Lest we forget.

"Forty-eight hours," Alan says and walks off to the table where Jeremy and his family are. His mother and father stand up, adjust their matching golf visors, and get up to leave. Alan joins them, adjusts his toupee, and gets ready to leave too.

I look over to where Susan is sitting to see if I can identify the mystery man who came in to see her. However Dr. Frederick is standing in my sightline making an announcement: "Ok everyone. Time to say goodbye to your loved ones. Family members, if you could kindly make your way out now. And clients, we will be having a bit of afternoon tea right now in the cafeteria. And then after that we'll just be doing just a brief debrief session on 'How my drinking and using affected my family, and why might they be a bit sad about it.'"

As families get up I try to see the face of the man who came to visit my mother. But there is no one sitting at her table now. I look through the crowd to see if I can recognise anyone. But I can't.

I should just let it go. Who cares who she invites in here as her 'family'.

… But I can't.

During afternoon tea I sidle up next to Ms. Wilde who's standing with Keith and the Goth Girl.

"Hello Susan."

"Hello Dave."

"Did you have a pleasant time … at family day?"

"I did."

"I couldn't help but notice that you had a visit from a family member as well."

"No, sadly; no one from my family came to share my company today."

271

"So who were you talking to?" I ask.

"Oh, no one," Susan says, in an offhand way. "Just the head psychiatrist here."

"You weren't talking to Dr. Frederick," I say.

"She's *not* the head psychiatrist."

"Who was it then?"

"One of the people I was talking to."

"People? So there was more than one? Who was the other person?"

"Dave!" Keith breaks in on the game of verbal cat-and-mouse. "She ain't a witness on the stand. And you ain't a lawyer."

"Yeah, why do you care anyways?" The Goth Girl says.

"Anyway," Keith corrects.

"We were discussing a private family matter. And I would prefer to not divulge his identity, Dave." Susan says.

"Whose identity? The man who came to visit you or the head psychiatrist?" I ask.

"Both."

I give up on this game. I could feel myself breaking character and going back into David Hawkes. But that's not me anymore. I'm not a lawyer. I'm not her son. I'm not in a relationship with Katharine anymore. I'm not a lot of things.

"Who was that striking woman who came to visit you today, Dave?" Susan asks, changing the subject and keeping up the charade that we aren't related. The Goth Girl looks interested in the answer.

"My girlfriend."

"Oh ..." says the Goth Girl, suddenly looking less interested.

"My ex-girlfriend."

"Oh?" says the Goth Girl, suddenly looking re-interested.

"Yeah she, um, she broke up with me."

"That is so depressing," the Goth Girl says. The way she says depressing seems to make her happy.

"Bring it in mate," Keith says, as everyone comes in for a group hug. I feel a hand grabbing my crotch from behind. This time I'm pretty sure it's not my mother's.

"I also received some rather distressing news," Susan says, ready to launch into a story.

"You should probably talk to the head shrink about that," the Goth Girls says as she and Keith walk me off to lunch, leaving Susan behind. At lunch everyone tries to comfort me but it's no use. Katharine's gone. She's not coming back. The rest of the day is a haze.

Later that day I find myself walking the Goth Girl around the grounds.

"You must be just totally destroyed emotionally," she says, suppressing a smile.

"I had it coming. She was right. My life is a temporary existence," I say.

"All our lives are a temporary existence, that is what makes them so painful. That's why we have to squeeze every ounce of pitiful joy we can grab from life. If we didn't have pain we'd have nothing to live for. That's why we create, otherwise we'd all just be podiatrists. "

The Goth Girl looks at me and pulls my head down to kiss her. I hesitate for a moment and kiss her back. I can't get Katharine out of my mind. Maybe that's the problem. I need to get her out of my mind.

"Bad things are good for you. That's why we did drugs," the Goth Girl tells me.

We keep walking. She leads me inside and to her room.

273

"Hey look, I don't want to get in any more trouble."

"You're not going to get in trouble, my roommate's gone. They took her to get a colonic yesterday and she never came back."

Is she still on the machine?

"Or maybe it was electroshock treatment. I can't remember."

"Well, it's easy to conflate the two," I say.

"I'll tell you what you can conflate." The Goth Girl pulls me inside her room and starts kissing me. Then stops.

"You know I wrote a song about you today? It's called 'Horny and Pathetic.'"

"I'm flattered."

"You should be."

The Goth Girl starts kissing me again. She starts taking off our clothes. This feels so wrong, but Drug Addict Dave can't say no.

She starts pinching my nipples.

"Do you like that?"

"More than you'll ever know," I say.

"I bet your ex-girlfriend never pinched 'em that way. That bitch."

We start kissing again.

Down to our underwear now we get into her bed. The Goth Girl's torso is tattooed with names that are crossed out: Ryan, Trey, Wayne, Alexis, Dad."

"Who are these people?"

"People who used to like screwing me."

"Dad?"

"That screwing was purely financial."

"That's good."

She gives me a face.

"I mean not good, financially speaking," I say.

"The ink is a living reminder of sorrow," she says, almost gleefully. "If you can't name your pain then how do you know you're through to the other side? What's the name of your pain?"

"Oh, I don't know," I lie.

"It doesn't have to be the name of your ex, it could be anything or anyone," the Goth Girls says, then starts biting my nipples.

I look deep inside me and realise something in that moment.

"Hey, you know what? I realised that I don't even know your name." I say.

"Excuse me?" she says with a mouthful of areola. "You were going to fuck me without even knowing my name? What do you think I am, some groupie on the European leg of a tour?" She spits out a hair.

"I'm sorry," I say.

"Do you have any idea how hurtful that is?" She seems almost happy as she says this. "My name is in the name of my band."

"You're a musician? That's so cool. I like music."

"Fuck you, asshole." She pushes me out of bed. "Get out of here."

I get dressed quickly

"You won't tell anyone about this?"

"I won't get a tattoo if that's what you're thinking. Dick."

"It's Dave."

She looks up at me with heavily mascaraed eyes.

"Oh, right … I'm a dick," I say, zipping up my pants.

I check the hallway before I leave her room. As I head

around the corner Keith and Jeremy come up to me in the hall.

"Nice lipstick." Keith says.

I wipe my mouth and see black smudges on the back of my hand.

"Hey were you just with–"

I cut Jeremy off. "No. I was just eating some uh, charcoal, from the art room."

"Bullshit. What was she like?" Jeremy asks.

"I didn't get that far, she kicked me out."

"What did you say to her?" Keith asks.

"She got mad that I didn't know her band," I say.

"You've never heard of Susie and the Motherfuckers?" Keith says.

I shake my head.

"Is she Susie?"

They both nod their heads.

What is it with me and people named Susan? It's like vinegar and baking soda. Harmless apart but messy together.

"Look guys, just don't say anything, ok?"

They both nod their heads. I wander down the hall and to my room.

That night in the janitor's closet I finish my book. The victory is an empty and hollow one. I've finished but for what? I feel depressed and not happy-depressed, like Susie.

I've sacrificed a lot to finish this project. But at what cost.

Episode 20

The next morning Jeremy, Keith, Susan, and I sit at breakfast. Susie, aka the Goth Girl, comes and sits with us.

"Morning everyone," she mumbles.

There's a chorus of good mornings from everyone but me.

Keith and Jeremy's eyes dart back and forth between me and the black haired woman sitting with us.

Nobody says anything. I'm wondering who is going to break the silence between us. It's not who I expected.

"What is going on here?" Susan Wilde finally blurts out. "There is a distinct tension here. I used to be an actor and I know when there is tension in a scene."

"There's nothing," I say.

"Someone's not saying something."

"We've said nothing, Susan," I say.

"Yes but even saying nothing, says something," she replies.

"How could nothing say something if there's nothing to say?"

"Because there's saying nothing because there is nothing to say, and then saying nothing because something has to be said, but isn't being said. Do you see what I'm saying?"

"I see. You've certainly taught us something about saying nothing," I say. The laughter this elicits successfully ends this wacky conversation. Everyone goes back to their eggs, bacon, and toast.

"Ok! Who had sex with who?" Susan demands. The orderlies look over at us.

"It's who had sex with whom," Keith corrects.

No one says anything. We look among ourselves and keep quiet.

"Fine. Don't tell me. Leave me out!" Susan Wilde gets up and leaves with dramatic flourish.

"Nosy old bitch," Susie mutters. Keith and Jeremy chuckle.

"She'd 'ave to be; wif a nose job like the one she's 'ad," Keith says.

"Hey she's—" I nearly say, *mother*. "—probably just bored."

My desire to defend Susan is still strong. In a single parent family you really do have to rely on each other in ways more traditional families don't. Because despite all the advances in society, someone raising a child alone is still seen as being deficient. And my mother may be deficient in many areas but that doesn't mean that I didn't love her. When it's just the two of you, you often have to come to each other's defence because there is no one else who will.

Jeremy and Susie keep giggling.

"I could swear I've seen her someplace," Jeremy wonders.

I jump in: "Probably on TV."

"She's a soap opera 'actress," Keith says.

"If you could call that acting," Goth Susie adds.

"Yeah I've seen Muppets who are better actors than some of those drama school rejects," Keith interjects.

"Imagine pretending to be someone else day in and day out," I say.

"Let's get some more coffee Jez-bone" Keith says, grabbing

Jeremy and going. I start to protest but they're already gone, leaving me and Goth Susie alone.

"Hey look I'm sorry about last night," I say.

"It's ok, I overreacted," Goth Susie says.

"You didn't tell anyone, did you?"

"Not a soul. Hey, try some of these baked eggs, they're amazing."

I open my mouth to tell her I had some already, but she uses the opportunity to spoon baked eggs into my mouth. I bite down on something hard. I think it's a big piece of shell but it's circular. I pull out a small ring.

Susie whispers. "It's from my left breast. Maybe later you can put it back in…"

I see Scully eyeing me and I quickly pocket the nipple ring.

As we get up and get ready to head off to group therapy, I see Susan Wilde standing near Bill and Scully whispering in their ear. She's got a look in her eye. The same one she used to get right before she keyed someone's car after losing an acting award to them. As we all start filing down the hall I hear Bill say: "Not you."

"What?"

"You're not going to group," Bill and Scully start leading me down the hall.

"But I didn't do anything," I protest.

"It doesn't matter. You're going to see … Ted."

Everyone looks over at me.

"Who? I mean, whom? I mean, what?"

There's nervous looks and whispers among the patients as I am frogmarched between them.

"You've got a meeting with Ted," Scully repeats tonelessly.

This must be the doctor who administers colonics and

enemas.

I am escorted past massage rooms, past the yoga studio, past the janitor's closet, to a room way deep in the bowels of the building. The sign on the door only reads "TED". Why is it capitalised? Technical Enema Delivery?

I bite my lip, steel my nerves, and pray that they have warm water.

"Really guys, I don't need an enema or a colonic or whatever. I'm regular, like the mail."

Technical Electroshock Device.

The door swings open and I'm escorted in.

I'm in a whitewashed room with a daybed, a wooden door to the side, and a scary looking machine built into the wall. The electronic contraption looks like it's left over from a World War II garage sale. It has switches, a metre, knobs with words like *volts* and *intensity*. Two conductors, like old telephone receivers, hang on either side.

They're going to turn my brain into smashed avocado on toast.

"No wait, you can't do this." The orderlies sit me down on the day bed.

"How is this even legal? I'm not crazy. You don't have the right to give me—"

Suddenly the wooden door creaks open and warm light breaks in.

"Thank you, doctor," a woman says, shaking an unseen hand behind the door. She has white bandages around her head and an unsteady gait. Obviously her brain's been mashed and sprinkled with black pepper and rock salt.

"Thank you, 'TED.'" A disembodied voice corrects her.

Bill helps the woman walk out of the door.

There's a brief moment. I contemplate my fate. Should I run? It didn't end well last time. I hear a click-ticking sound. Is that time running out on me?

"Come in, David," the voice beckons.

The click-ticking hangs in the air.

Scully gets me up and walks me towards the door.

The click-ticking sound gets louder.

My eyes dart around looking for an escape route.

The click-ticking, methodical, relentless.

I'm at the threshold, I hold my breath.

The click-ticking echoes around me.

I'm pushed through the frame and arrive in what appears to be a consulting room from the 1930s. Luscious red velvet furniture, a mahogany desk, and a built-in bookcase that runs the entire back wall of the room. Several cast iron busts of unknown old white men look inwards towards the desk. There's an antique grandfather clock in the corner. But it's not working. It's motionless.

"That'll be all, thanks guys," a well-tanned man says in an American accent. He wears a Hawaiian shirt, khakis shorts, and has metal rimmed glasses and a flat top hair cut. He's as out of place in this room as a Klan member in a synagogue. He flips closed a manila envelope, smiles, and sticks out his hand. "I'm Ted," he says.

I shake his hand.

He maintains his eye contact and smiles as he withdraws his hand and squirts some Dettol on it. I realise he was motioning for me to sit down.

"Sorry," I say, sitting down. I also realise the click-ticking is coming from a Newton's Cradle right next to the pump bottle of hand sanitizer on his desk.

"Quite alright, dude," Ted says, sitting down. "It's good to finally meet the illustrious David Hawkes."

"Thanks?" I say.

"I'm a big fan."

"Of what? Buying clothes at Kmart?"

He laughs. "Ya know, that's the sarcastic wit I'd expect from the guy who wrote *The Blonde Wore Black*."

"You've read my book?"

Ted moves to the far side of the bookshelf, sandals snapping against his heels in perfect time with the Newton's Cradle. He pulls a dog-eared paperback from the shelf and tosses it to me.

"Great stuff, are you working on a sequel?"

"Yes. So please don't give me electroshock treatment," I stammer. "I'll lose my short term, um, whaddya call it." I start hyperventilating. The click-ticking continues.

"David, David ... Dave ... Can I call you Dave?"

"That's what everyone calls me."

"Can you do me a favour?"

I nod.

"Relax."

He stops the Newton's Cradle.

The room goes totally silent.

"Electroshock therapy isn't what I do."

"But what about that woman who came out of here with the bandages on her head?"

"She was in a drunk driving accident."

"Oh thank god." Relief in my voice.

Ted looks at me.

"I mean, um— so what's that machine in the waiting room then?"

"It's a defibrillator. We're required by law to have several around. I just went with the vintage casing to match with my décor."

"Man. I feel like a jerk." I roll my eyes at myself.

"That's actually what I do," Ted says.

"You're a jerk?"

He laughs again. "No *feelings*. That's my game. I'm the head psychotherapist here. You may have seen me talking to people at family day. But I'm more than just a psychotherapist."

Here it comes.

"Drug and alcohol therapy isn't just about getting off the pills and potions."

"It isn't?"

"No. It's about relationships. It's about becoming intimate. Not just with yourself, but with others. "

"Ok, doctor ..." I glance at his name plate but it just says TED, PhD. "... Doctor Ted?"

"I had it legally changed so I'm just Ted; like Plato, Aristotle, or Bono. But don't worry, dude, even though I'm a mononym, I still keep it profesh."

"That's reassuring."

"Dave, do you often have trouble accepting forms of intimacy?"

"Me? No."

"So if I told you to think of me less as a psycho-therapist and more as your psycho-friend, you'd be comfortable."

"Not when you put it that way."

"What I'm getting at, Dave, is ..." Ted looks around, finding the words, "It's about *relationships*. And you can't have a real relationship when you're being a fake."

"I don't know what you're talking about."

"Dave, you're not addicted to drugs. No one calls drugs 'sweet material'. Your 'Gopher of Denial' sculpture in art therapy was way too self-aware. Everything about you calls attention to the fact that you are a drug addict. It's all an act isn't it?"

This is my chance. Finally a sane person.

"Yes. It's a whole character I made up. Drug Addict Dave. I go by David. I always have. I'm not a 'Dave.'"

"No, you're totally not a Dave ... Dave," Ted says smiling.

"You don't know how good it feels to *not* get this monkey off my back," I joke.

"What are you addicted to? Why are you here?"

"It's all been a big misunderstanding, my mother signed me up for this place. It's her fault I'm in here."

"Mother, hmmmm?"

"Yeah, she's the sick one, she's the alcoholic. She's the one who totally fucked my life up and drives me insane. She's the reason I'm here."

"If your mother were here right now what would you say to her?"

"Nothing."

I adjust my horn-rimmed glasses.

"Why not?" Ted asks, rubbing his goatee.

As my father used to say, when all else fails, tell the truth.

"Because there's nothing to say," I say.

And when that fails, keep lying.

"Well, you're finally away from her. Do you feel better?" Ted asks.

"I guess."

"I'm sure she's probably worried about you. You probably got her attention by just disappearing, is that what you wanted?"

"No, I don't need her attention. She's the one who needs me. I don't need her. She'd be dead without me. I had to put fire extinguishers in every room of every house we lived in. I could have been a firefighter with the amount of experience I've had putting out blazes."

"Why didn't you?"

"I don't know, I'd rather be creative, I guess. Fighting fires is just, saving people's lives … or whatever."

We sit in silence for a few moments. I can feel myself breathing, hear Ted breathing. I notice, on one of his shelves, a little Buddha. Amoghasiddhi, he who will not be turned from the intention of his aim. The same little Buddha I have on my desk at home.

Ted finally speaks. "I am going to propose something to you David: you've never truly cut off your mother because it fuels your creativity."

I look up at him.

"You don't want to be free from your mother because if you didn't have her you wouldn't have the thing that drives you to create. You need her just as much as you claim she needs you."

"I don't need her."

"I think you need to ask yourself: do you really want to be a successful writer or do you just want to get your mother's attention?"

This statement hits me with the force of Icarus, wings melted, slamming into the ocean from the sky. I pass the silhouette of my father as I plummet.

"If you want to be successful then this is the price you pay." Ted strokes his goatee.

285

"But I've got a normal life, I used to be a probate lawyer, I had a stable girlfriend. I'm not a classic tortured artist," I say.

"No. You're just tortured. If you want to be an artist you need to accept your mother and all her shenanigans as the price of admission," Ted says.

My chest feels like a water balloon filled with searing hot liquid hate. What if he's right? I feel my insides sloshing around spreading hot liquid to all corners of my body.

"Do you understand what I'm saying to you?" Ted continues.

I nod my head.

"That was a pretty big breakthrough you just had." Ted reaches over and puts up his hand for a high-five. I slap it with a clammy hand.

"That's what I call a Ted talk, Am I right?"

"You're right Ted. You're totally right."

"It's all part of the service we provide here at the MGCRC. I totally cured you in, like, under an hour. That's gotta be some kind of record."

"So can I go home then?" I ask.

"No. You're one sick ticket and you need some serious help with your mommy issues. In fact I am going to recommend that we extend your stay to the *Braveheart* package. You'll be staying with us for at least a year."

"What?" I say standing up. "You can't do that!"

"We can. It's what you agreed to when you signed yourself in. Your release is conditional upon doctor's approval. And when I spoke to your personal physician yesterday, she said she would be fine if we kept you."

"Wait, you mean, Katharine? She wouldn't do that."

The devastation that my girlfriend would do something

like this stabs me like a scorpion tail. I've broken something between us that I might not ever be able to repair. It begins to dawn on me that this whole Drug Addict Dave performance might have backfired on me.

Ted pulls a sheet of paper from his desk drawer, and looks over the signature.

"Um, yes, Dr. Nichols," Ted says. "She was quite adamant that we keep you. In fact she signed the committal form without reading it."

Before I can protest more, Ted pulls out another sheet of paper and slides it over.

"Speaking of signing things, can you give me a John Hancock on this?"

I have a quick lawyer look over it. It's a release form, signing over my story rights to become a psychiatric case study for publication under Ted's supervision.

"We're just scratching the surface on your case, Dave, but I figure there's at least a few articles here, if not an entire book."

"I'm not a subject, I'm an author. And I've got a deadline that I'm missing by being in here!" I shout. "My editor is probably wondering where I am right now."

"Wait. So you sabotaged yourself by checking yourself in here?" Ted starts taking notes.

I tear up the release form and throw bits at him.

Ted pulls out another sheet of paper and slides it over.

"Easily a book," he says, more to himself than to me, as he scribbles more notes.

Ted pushes a buzzer on the table. "It's ok to feel confused David/Dave. You've got a sort of distorted duality going on. Electro shock will help with that."

"I thought you said that one in the waiting room was fake?"

Bill and Scully enter this office of Antique Hell and surround me.

"Yeah, but the one in the basement is real," Ted says, sweeping the confetti into the wastebasket. "I'll show you tomorrow."

Oh shit.

"In the meantime, you need to go back to group therapy," Ted continues. "Dr. Frederick is running a session on getting in touch with your truth."

The orderlies grab me and start pulling me out of the office.

"Be gentle with him!" Ted orders the orderlies as I'm dragged out of earshot. "He's going to be with us for a while and I don't want him hurt."

Episode 21

Bill, Scully, and I arrive in the day room while group therapy is in session. The cast of characters sits around in a circle, cups of coffee and tea, listening as Dr. Frederick presides. It's hot in the room. Hotter than I would like, and the sun beams in through the big windows illuminating the steam emanating from everyone's warm drinks. The thought of staying in this place another year sets me to boil like a witch's cauldron. I feel like some bony-fingered, wart-nosed crone is boiling newt eyes, salamander testicles and snake scales inside me and I'm ready to bubble over.

And there she is, the object of my disaffection, Susan Wilde. She's in the middle of a speech as I am placed in an empty chair near Jeremy. Keith sits nearby, and Goth Susie directly across from me. They all look as bored as the rest of the addicts. As always Susan Wilde expressively recounts her story.

"It was perfection in a bottle. Everything about him, our courtship, the wedding. Grayson was a perfect gentleman. When we met he had just finished his surgical residency at St. Stephen Hospital and was moving on to private practice. He was going to specialise in brain surgery; for babies, and those with really tiny heads whose brains were starved of oxygen. He was rich, handsome, and, even though it felt like we had all the time in the world, it was a whirlwind romance that look us from Europe, to Dubai, to Goa, to–"

"Thank you Susan, I–" Dr. Frederick interrupts.

"Hold on, I'm just getting to the good part. It was so romantic we got matching tattoos in Sanskrit and rode camels on the beach. But then, our dream honeymoon turned into a nightmare when the Indian resort got hit by Cyclone Jacinta and we were hurled from our beach-front bungalow into the sea. For eight agonising hours I clung to a palm tree until I was finally rescued. They found Grayson that night buried in the mud. Physically he was fine but he'd inhaled so much mud that it had cut off the air supply to his brain, and he was brain dead. Grayson needed a surgery so specific that he was the only one in the world with the expertise to perform it. So I unplugged the machine."

Susan starts to cry.

I start slow-clapping the performance.

"Thank you for your honesty, Susan," Dr. Frederick says. "That must have been a harrowing experience."

"So harrowing," she says. "It's why I had to go back to work to support myself."

"So Dave," Dr. Frederick says, "Susan was just sharing with us a bit of a story for the past half-hour, from her life. The topic is getting in touch with our truth."

I look at my mother, the reason I am going to be stuck in this place for God knows how long. My breath gets more constricted and nasal. I can't take it anymore.

"Truth? I guess the truth hurts sometimes, huh?" I say.

"Yes, Dave. Truth." Susan says, dabbing her eyes with the monogrammed handkerchief. "It can hurt, or set you free."

"I know truth is rarely pure and never simple," Keith adds.

"It's also stranger than fiction, which is what you're spouting." My accusation hangs awkwardly like an unrequited high-five, "*Fik–shun*." I enunciate both syllables.

"Dave, please, this is a safe space," Dr. Frederick admonishes.

"For what? Lies? That epic love tale was from a plotline on *Destiny's Hope*."

"Wait, you just made that all up?" Goth Susie interjects.

"Of course not," Susan says. "The writers did."

Everyone groans.

"And while I must admit that my character did go through that particular ordeal on television, it doesn't mean that I didn't genuinely feel those feelings myself through the character." Mum's attempt to defend herself only makes it worse

"Where does the truth start and the lies end?" I say.

"It begins with me," she snaps.

"Of course it does, it always begins and ends with you! This is what it's been like my entire life."

I cross my arms and shake my head.

"Do you two know each other from outside of the Centre?" Dr. Frederick asks.

"I swear I've seen you before," Jeremy says. "And not just on TV."

With a sweeping smile and a lilt in her voice, my mother says, "Think carefully about what you are going to say next, Dave."

"I don't have the benefit of someone else scripting my lines for me," I fire back.

"Dr. Frederick," Susan puts on her compassionate voice. "Dave is obviously suffering some kind of 'episode', probably from a lack of oxygen to the brain. He might need to be in isolation."

"Maybe we should take a bit of a break–" Dr. Frederick starts.

"You're the one who needs to be in isolation. Mother!"

Everyone gasps.

"Yeah that's right, she's my mum."

"He's delusional. He's probably an obsessed fan."

"If only I was a fan. Then I'd happily put up with all your drama."

"That drama put clothes on your back and food in your belly young man."

Everyone gasps again.

"Fine. I admit it. He is my son. But not my favourite son–"

"I'm your only son–"

"True. But, my only son, my so-called 'drama' is responsible for putting you through school, university, and providing a home for you young man. And for entertaining audiences all over the world."

"It also convinced me it was a good idea to smuggle drugs all over the world because, 'no immigration officer is going to cavity search a minor, David.'"

Everyone in the circle murmurs with interest.

"Well I was right. And I have always provided for and protected you."

"You've protected your career! And I fought a losing battle trying to make you think I was as special as the audience. Trying to write was just my way of getting your attention. But love and attention aren't the same thing."

Susan starts to cry. But I'm not falling for the theatrics this time.

"David, if I hurt you I'm sorry. I worked hard because it's always been just the two of us."

"Because you never told me who my father was," I blurt. "That is right everyone, she never told me. She just kept making up these elaborate stories about who he was and where he was. And how he really loved me but couldn't come to my birthday this year because he was away on business. Like this watch," I hold up my Steve McQueen TAG Heuer. "She told me it was a gift to say sorry because he couldn't make my birthday. After a while I figured out that he was a fiction. So I had to make up a dad. I made up life lessons he taught me. I made up everything. I had to live in this fantasy world because you would never tell me the truth."

I stand up.

"Everything I've been trying to do is to get your attention. But I don't even love myself enough to tell you to fuck off."

I knock over my chair and storm off. I head down the hallway and into my room, laying down on the bed. Hours pass. People come to see me: Goth Susie, Keith, Dr. Frederick. They all come to ask if I'm ok. I don't want to talk to any of them. I just want to go back to my old life. Before I ever started writing, before I ever quit my law job. Back to Alan boring me to death with his stories. Back with Katharine. Back to vacations in New Caledonia. Back to before I ever tried to make a career of writing, before I ever let my mother back into my life.

But there's no going back. And now I'm stuck in this gilded prison of a rehab with its pretentious shrinks, Neo-Renaissance architecture, and a basement with an electroshock machine that's going to turn my brain into guacamole tomorrow.

I've got a novel, but I've lost my life.

That evening after skipping dinner I lay in bed staring a hole in the ceiling. Another knock on the door comes.

"Go away," I call out.

The door opens. It's Jeremy.

"Leave me alone. I don't need cheering up."

"Oh, I'm not gonna try to cheer you up, bro."

"Good." I'm probably going to be here another year, I need to pace myself on being cheered up.

"I'm just here to say goodbye."

I roll towards the wall. Jeremy, never one to take a hint, sits down on the bed and says, "Here." He hands me a note.

"I don't want anything from her."

"It's not from your mum, it's from Alan."

Rolling back over I take the note and open it. All it says is *48 Hours*. With a circle around it.

That's when it hits me like a golf ball to the skull. I grab Jeremy by the shirt sleeves, but he mistakes this gesture and starts giving me a hug.

"I'll miss you too, mate."

"No Jeremy," I say, wriggling out of the hug. "Tell Alan I want my job back."

"Awesome!" Jeremy says.

"Yeah. I am ready to go back to work."

"Great. When will you get out of here?"

I adjust my horn-rimmed glasses.

"It could be a year." I say, defeated. "Whatever document I signed when I came in here apparently gives them the right to hold me until the doctors say I can leave. But I have no idea how binding it is because I was drugged when I signed it."

"We could always file a motion to say that you were *non*

compos mentis at the time of the signing therefore rendering your intake conditions invalid. We could follow that up with a writ of *habeas corpus* forcing them to produce you, provided you signed a general non-enduring power of attorney, making us provisionally responsible for your medical care."

"How do you know all this stuff?" I ask.

"Jez-bone is a lawyer after all, motherfucka'. Who knows if it'll work, but it's worth a shot."

Jeremy minus cocaine and absinthe is actually switched on, legally speaking. The lack of heavy narcotics has really limbered up his mind. If this is what sober Jeremy is like I might not have a job when I come out.

"When are you going to see Alan?"

"I'll see him at work on Monday," Jeremy says. "Some mates of mine are picking me up and we are going to go out for a drink at the Casino to celebrate my new sobriety."

"Just remember to tell Alan that I'll take my old job back.

"I can remember that. I'm only going to have one beer. When did that ever get me in trouble?"

Jeremy laughs.

I laugh.

But it's the laughter where I'm trying to keep from crying.

Jeremy's *one beer* with mates is going to turn into a weekend bender. He'll never remember this conversation.

"See you soon mate," I say.

Jeremy leaves and so does my hope of ever getting my job, or any semblance of my old life back. Katharine will move on. Work will move on. Life will move on. But not me. I'm stuck in the Mel Gibson Celebrity Rehab Centre, the guinea pig of some surfer dude head shrinker with an aesthetic decor borrowed from *Antique Roadshow*. I stare at the ceiling until the orderlies turn off the lights.

Mum will move on too. If nothing else I'm finally free of her.

I'm locked up, but free.

I begin drifting off into sleep when I hear the creak of the door and a voice say.

"David, my darling, are you awake?"

I can't believe it.

"I've got the key to your freedom?"

Episode 22

"David … David …?"

I stay silent.

She keeps creeping into the room.

"David, this is your mother, Susan Wilde."

"I know who it is, Mum."

"Shhh, David." She puts her finger to my lips. I can smell her recently applied nail polish as her finger nearly goes up my nostril. She's crawling on all fours, wearing an all-black cat suit. "It's dark, I just wanted to make sure you knew it was me."

"Leave me alone."

I roll away from her.

"David I'm trying to apologise to you." She pokes me repeatedly until I turn back to face her.

"No more 'sorries', Mum. It's over. Ted was right, if the price of creativity is you in my life then I'll let go of my dreams."

"*Ted* is a pompous ass who is not fit to psychoanalyse a pork chop let alone *my* son. The man is more concerned with his picture on the dust jacket than the contents of any book. He's talentless and fame-hungry. Trust me, I know the type. And he is way out of line trying to keep you in here for a year."

How does she know all this?

"But you're right David, I was a terrible mother."

"I'm done playing this game," I say, rolling away from her again. Hopefully if I ignore her she'll move on.

"I know how I hurt you. But you don't know the power of acting."

Strangely I do now.

"Auditioning, callbacks, the screen tests, rehearsals, each step of the journey people are saying 'I want you' you have that 'it factor' inside you. Then the performance, the applause. That feeling of being special in the eyes of another is all I have yearned for since I was a little girl. You cannot imagine what it's like to be raised by parents who ignored you because they were too busy at work."

I stare at the wall darkly. I think back to my childhood. The constant moving, the step-fathers and boyfriends, the drugs, and the lies. Then I think about my life before Mum came back. So what if I was dying slowly at least it was predictable.

Mum carries on. I forgot, ignoring her is like catnip. "David I hurt you in ways that I can never truly comprehend. I can never take back the pain I caused, but I want to make it up to you. And I shall start by telling you the truth."

"Ok, then who was that guy I saw you with on Family Day?" I catch myself. "Oh, god, I don't care. Leave me alone."

"He's my new agent. And he's lined something up for me on the outside."

"I knew it, you're not retiring from acting," I hiss at her. "Go away!"

"That's the idea David. I'm leaving tonight. But I need your help."

I hear keys jingle.

I look at her through the darkness. The sound of freedom.

But freedom with my mother isn't freedom at all.

Mum jingles the keys one more time.

"Come on. Shift change is in a few minutes."

"Forget it."

I turn away from her.

"David, it is impossible for me to get out of here alone. I need you."

"You don't need me Mum, you never needed me. I was just a method acting exercise to you."

In the darkness you can practically hear the pause that comes next.

Finally she says, "I understand. And once we are out of here I can leave you alone. I promise that I will stay out of your life, forever."

There's no crocodile tears. No emphatic pleading. Nothing. I don't budge.

"Before I do go, David, just know one thing."

"What? That you 'love me'?" the sarcasm oozes out of me like thick tree sap.

"No. They are going to give you electroshock treatment tomorrow. Ted told me. After we had sex. That's how I got his keys. He's incredibly unprofessional to have sex with a patient. I should know. I played a few psychologists on TV. But if you do not come with me now they will scramble your brain like eggs."

I say nothing.

"You should have this. Not that you'll be able to do anything with it once you get brain zapped."

She gets up and puts something on the bed. Something rectangular. It's my laptop. With my novel.

Mum glides silently towards the door.

This is the choice. I could have my memory erased by the electroshock machine. Or I could erase my memory by getting out of here, getting my job back, getting Katharine back, getting my book deal back, and never seeing my mother again. It would be like the last few months never happened. It won't be easy, I'll have to eat crow and go back to the law. Katharine will take some convincing. But telling her that we never have to see my mother again, that might give me an ace in the hole. And Deirdre. Well, Deirdre isn't that unreasonable. She would understand being drugged by your mother and then locked in rehab against your will. She'd probably only throw a medium size book at me. *The Trial* by Franz Kafka, perhaps.

"Wait."

I get up and join her.

"You promise to leave me and Katharine alone for the rest of our lives?"

"Scout's honour."

It's not legally binding but this will have to do. I nod my head, and she understands what I mean. That's what 37 years together will do for you. We are totally fluent in silent communication.

"Put these on."

Mum hands me some slippers.

"Why can't I wear my own shoes?"

"The silk won't make any noise when you're walking."

She does have a point. Normally I hate it when she has a point. But not this time.

"Hold it under your top," Mum indicates towards the laptop. "David, once we get out in the hallway we have to be totally silent."

Mum opens the door a crack, grabs my hand and looks down at my watch. The light from the hallway illuminates the dial.

"Wait. Before we go I want you to tell me who my father is."

"Now?"

"Yes, now."

"Not, *now*. We have to go!" she hisses.

"Tell me, or I won't help you."

But it's too late. Susan Wilde dodges around me and into the main passage. We exit my room and creep down the hallway, the slippers muffle our footfalls in the echoing concrete. We move slowly through the corridors. The sound of an orderly's feet comes from around the corner. We stop before we turn a corner. We hear a key turning in a lock and a door click shut. We both nod our heads and carry on.

Mum uses a key to get through a doorway and we enter another long hallway. There's a mop bucket and mop, but no janitor. We both look at each other but hear nothing, and decide to carry on.

"Before we take another step I want you to tell me who my father is."

"Quiet David."

"If you don't tell me right now, I am going to scream at the top of my lungs and get us caught. They'll extend your stay here and you won't get to do whatever job it is you've lined up on the outside."

"David, if we get caught, we both might get electroshock."

"Spill."

I stop, plant my feet, and fold my arms in front of me.

Susan Wilde, stares at me right in the eye, nodding her head slowly. The look she gives me is halfway between pure animal vengeance and grudging admiration. Her breath is deep, regular, like she's breathing back the smoke she would normally blow up my ass.

"Fine." She composes herself, turns to face me and holds my arms. "Your father's name is … Ron."

"Ron who?"

"No. *Run!*"

That's when I hear Bill shout: "Hey!"

Susan and I bolt. The orderlies chase us down the hall. We run through the dividing door to the group therapy room, but it's locked. Bill and Scully shout something unintelligible. Mum can't find the right key to go in the lock.

"Quick David do something," she screams as she fumbles with the lock.

My fingers grip the laptop tight. The laptop with my only copy of the novel on it. Bill and Scully are gaining. It's the only thing I can throw at them to slow their progression towards us. It's the only thing that will buy us precious seconds. If I throw it then I'll have nothing for Deirdre. I'll have no book. No dream to follow.

I chuck the laptop like a rectangular discus at Bill and Scully. It folds open in mid-air as Bill blocks the projectile with his hand. It falls, smashes into two pieces. Scully steps on one half it and trips over it, knocking over the mop bucket and spilling grimy soapy water all over the hard drive. Bill then slips on the water and falls too.

I'm free. I hear the click of an unlocked door.

Susan and I run across the group therapy room as Bill and Scully struggle to their feet. I run to the door which feeds into the lobby and the main entrance, but Susan runs to the side door.

"I don't have the key for that door."

"Are you kidding?" I say. But she's gone before I can finish my sentence.

Susan runs to the side door that opens to the courtyard and dashes out. I follow close behind. Outside now. Grass beneath my feet. There's planted trees and an old bishop's crook lamppost. That's when it hits me. We're outside on the lawn with the ha–ha wall.

"This way," Susan shouts, as we run towards the ornate cast iron gate. I stare up at the gate that took my underwear last time. The spikes on top look sharper than ninja swords. This time with jeans on I'm a lot more willing to risk climbing over. My jeans tear as I put a leg over. As I fall over the spikes on the other side my pants get ripped to shreds. Then I hear the creak and the gate slam. Mum is there holding up what looks like a key in the dim light.

"I was trying to tell you. I had the key for this padlock, but not the front. Come on, our chariot awaits," she says.

I stumble in the dirt getting fresh soil on my torn T-shirt as I follow Mum. I spy the front entrance and see a taxi. Mum points towards the idling vehicle but begins to slow down to a trot as she looks around in disbelief.

"Where are all the cameras?" she says, stopping completely.

"The what?" I pull her arm towards the waiting cab.

"There were supposed to be paparazzi here to capture my escape."

"This was some sort of publicity stunt?"

"I can't believe he lied to me! I'm calling him," she pulls out a cell phone. How long has she had that? "You can never trust agents."

I feel like I'm going to shake with an anger so violent that it will register on the Richter scale.

"Hey stop!" I hear as Bill and Scully come out of the main entrance.

"Come on David," Mum says, but I run in another direction. I hear a door slam and hear the taxi pulling out. Shouts of "Stop!" and "Come back!" continue as I tear off across Yarra Boulevard and through Bellbird Park. If I continue on this side of the river they might catch me. The sounds of twigs snapping underfoot and flashlights beams signal the pursuit is still on. I get to the muddy banks of the Yarra and start swimming across. It's disgusting but it's the only way to freedom.

After running across the Yarra Bend golf course I have to swim the river again. I get to a final crossing and dash across a bridge right next to Dights Falls. Where this whole rehab journey began. But this time the only thing I'm drinking is the murky water I've got in my mouth from the river.

I head across town trying to stay in the darkness of public parks and away from anyone. It's possible the cops are going to be called on account of my escape so I travel up through Edinburgh Gardens, Princes Park, and Royal Park on my way back to Brunswick. Fortunately the vigorous walking and warm night air dry my clothes as I hurry. Unfortunately my feet are now bare because I lost my slippers in the river.

Finally I get to my place and bang on the door. I try it a few more times but eventually realise Katharine isn't home. She must be staying with her sister or something and I don't have my keys. I look through the front window and notice that a lot of the furniture is gone too. Did Katharine move out?

I'm left feeling as empty and fragile as an abandoned wasp nest. I sneak around to the side of the house and look in the windows but all the blinds have been pulled down. I lie down in the bushes and cry myself to sleep. My home isn't my home, my girlfriend isn't my girlfriend, and my book is gone forever. I drift off into a dismal sleep.

In the morning I wake up to birds chirping overheard. Rolling out of the bushes I compose myself as much as one who slept a night in the bushes can. I head out onto the street and begin walking. The pain in my feet against the concrete is unpleasant but I soldier on. I'm like the buddha, Amoghasiddhi, he who will not be turned from the intention of his aim.

I arrive at the podiatry clinic a little after nine AM. The receptionist is taken aback as much by my presence as by my appearance. I say 'hello' and head back to Katharine's consulting room.

"Dr. Nichols can't see you right now."

I don't bother to respond.

"David Stop!"

I march down the hallway. This is the second time in 24 hours that someone has tried to stop me from going down a hallway towards a door. I couldn't be stopped the first time.

"Wait!" I hear.

I barge through the door with the nameplate *Dr. Katharine Nichols DPodM.*

"Katharine! I need to talk to you."

The room is totally empty. No furniture. The receptionist catches up to me.

"Where is she?"

"That's what I was trying to tell you," the receptionist says. "She's not here anymore."

Has Katharine totally pulled up stakes and left? The

crushing feeling in my chest feels like compression bandage from hell has been put around my heart and squeezed. She wasn't kidding around when she said that she was moving on. It's really over. She's gone. I'll never see her again.

That's when I hear, "David?"

Katharine appears, silhouetted by the light coming from another consult room.

"That's what I was trying to say," the receptionist says. "Dr. Nichols isn't *here* in her normal room because she's switched to the larger office."

Tears form in my eyes.

Katharine is taken aback as I brush past her into the consultation room. She looks professional, wearing her freshly dry cleaned white coat, hair pulled back in a ponytail. It's just now I realise how filthy dirty I am and how messed up my feet are from walking barefoot. And how much I stink from the smell of the river.

"I'm so sorry for what I did to you," I carry on."

Katharine just stares at me.

"Mr. Weir, you remember my boyfriend David. David … Mr. Weir."

I notice a portly, balding man, sitting in the examination chair. Socks and shoes off. His toenails are clean and clear this time.

I adjust my horn-rimmed glasses.

"Pleasure to re-meet you … um, again."

"Same here, mate."

There's an awkward pause.

"Seems like that fungicide cleared everything up, Mr. Weir," I say.

"Yes. So, let's follow up in about three months," Katharine

says. "You can book at reception."

"Thank you, Doctor." Mr. Weir puts on his shoes and socks. There is complete silence as I stare at the ground and Katharine stares at me staring at the ground. He goes to leave.

"Nice to see you," I say.

"Same here, mate." Mr. Weirs slams the door shut.

"What the hell, David?"

"Katharine, I'm sorry."

"I'm not playing this game anymore David–"

"There's no game. This is real." I take her hand. "You were right. This whole thing with my mother is sick. Letting her back into my life, our lives. All it did was bring out the worst in me, in us. The one thing I figured out in that stupid rehab was that wanting my mother to think I was special was alienating me from you, from my life, my job, everything. It kept me searching for the life I could have as opposed to the one I had right in front of me. But I'm gonna get my old job back, I'm giving up on writing fiction. I don't need to be creative and I don't care if my mother thinks I'm special. I don't care what she thinks of me. The only woman's opinion I care about is yours."

I get down on my knee.

Katharine's jaw drops. Her breathing quickens.

I take her hand.

"Katharine Gertrude Nichols, will you marry me?"

I pull out a ring. It's the nipple ring I had in my pocket that the Goth Susie gave me.

Katharine hesitates. Her pregnant pause is so long she nearly brings it to full term.

Then she says: "If you think I am going to marry you after all the craziness you put me through … then you don't know me at all …"

My head sinks.

"But, if we got married, then you'd get a chance to know me that well."

I look up at her smiling face. I stand up and kiss her.

"I'll marry you on one condition though," she says.

"Never speak to my mother again? I'm already ahead of you," I say, kissing her.

She pushes me back

"Now, take a shower," she laughs. "You smell like a swamp donkey."

We both laugh and kiss as I slip the ring on her finger.

"Where did you get this?" she says, holding out her hand.

"I'll tell you after my shower."

We go out to the foyer and Katharine tells the receptionist to cancel her appointments for the day.

"Don't you want to announce our engagement?" I whisper to Katharine.

"Let's hold off until you don't look like a hobo."

"Fair play."

We go out to the car and Katharine rolls down the windows all the way.

At home on my way to the bathroom I look into mum's room and notices that it's been totally cleared out. No Louis Vuitton, no creams, no pills, or bottles.

"Katharine," I call. "Did Mum come and pick up her stuff?"

"No?" Katharine says joining me.

We both stare around the empty room. The lady vanishes. As easily as she entered stage left, she exits stage right. Susan Wilde, my mother, has disappeared without a trace.

"Should we try calling her?"

"No. Let's close this particular chapter."

Episode 23

After I shower, shave, and put on a suit. I feel like a new man. I call and make two appointments for the afternoon. One easy, one hard. Seeing Alan and the folks at the law firm will be a piece of cake. Seeing my Belfast-born editor Deirdre, and telling her there's no book will be a piece of lead pipe. Hopefully without explosives in it.

Katharine and I share some brunch. The kitchen is in a warm wash of morning light. Sunshine warms me from without and the coffee warms me from within. Katharine's smile is a mix of relief and gratitude. I look back at her thrilled to be eating in a quiet room, with the woman I love most in the world.

"I'm just so glad this is over," she says.

"I just want to put it all behind us."

"Did you at least get any insight into your relationship with her?" Katharine asks. "Was there any therapy?"

"If you could call it that. There was this nut of a doctor named Ted."

"Ted what?"

"Just 'Ted'. Anyways he basically said that my writing, and the need to be a successful writer, was just a way to get mum's attention? Like trying to prove I'm special."

"I've always thought you were special. I wouldn't be with you if I didn't," Katharine says, taking my hand. "I don't care if you never write another word. I love you for who you are, not what you'll achieve."

I stare down at my honey toast. "Thanks." Why does unconditional love feel so uncomfortable? It's going to take some practice. I relax my shoulders and look back up at my future wife.

"I'm sorry for all the stuff that you had to go through. It'll be different from now on. I'm not going to see my mother anymore. I made a deal with her, and she's promised to stay away from now on."

Katharine nods slowly.

"Probably for the best," Katharine says. "Just so you know, I don't blame you for what your mother did. I do blame you for bringing her into this house but not for what she did."

Katharine laughs. I laugh. We laugh together. The first time as an engaged couple. God, I am becoming one of the people I hate. But I love it.

"Speaking of houses," I say, trying to be nonchalant. "After I get my job back at the law firm I was thinking we could go to the bank. And start looking into buying property."

Katharine looks at me with eyes of disbelief.

"I want us to move into our new home as husband and wife," I say. "I know it's old-fashioned, and you're not really into that traditional gender role stuff, but—"

Katharine grabs the lapels on my suit, pulls me towards her, and kisses me, smothering the end of my sentence.

"I can make an exception this one time," Katharine says, cradling my face and looking directly into my eyes.

Katharine and I go to Dienstag, DiSalvio & Fischer first.

We park and go up the historic Lombard Building, with its Queen Anne Revival façade, and ride the hydraulic elevator to the fourth floor. Alan and Jeremy meet me at reception.

"Good to see you back, and lovely to see you, Katharine," Alan, my former, and future boss says.

We exchange pleasantries and go back to Alan's office.

"Now this is just a memorandum of understanding, it's not the full offer …" Alan trails off as he goes looking in a desk drawer for the piece of paper.

"I'm just glad to have old Dave-o back working directly under me." Jeremy slaps me on the back a little too hard. "I promise I won't ride him too hard." Then Jeremy whispers so that Alan can't hear. "Not as hard as you probably rode him when he got back from rehab."

Katharine looks at him with one of her icy stares that puts a frost on Jeremy so cold you can practically see his breath as he steps back.

I take hold of Katharine's hand and breath deeply.

Alan finds the memo and resurfaces. "I'll have Rebecca draw up the full paperwork in the next few days and you can have your lawyer look at it," Alan chuckles at his own joke. "You can start next week if you want," Alan says.

"Or sooner," Jeremy pipes in.

"I might actually take a week," I say.

"Totally fine. It's hard transitioning out of a facility. It took Frank DiSalvio awhile, he's still not totally back to normal," Alan says.

"Isn't that because of the stroke?"

"Sometimes the best thing is to just get stuck back into work," Jeremy says. "I'm back already and I've got heaps of work, you know, piling up, that needs to get done."

"We've actually got some celebrating to do." I say, holding up Katharine's left hand to show them the engagement ring. "I was thinking we'd take a little trip up the Great Ocean Road to celebrate."

"Is that right Mr. Hawkes?" Katharine says with a smile.

"There's a seafood place in Lorne that I heard does a great lobster thermidor," I say to Katharine, patting her hand.

I stand up and give a little stretch and shake Alan's hand across the desk.

"You'll be hearing from me," I say, as Katharine and I leave my new/old place of work.

From the law firm, Katharine and I drive to the converted brick factory in Collingwood that serves as the headquarters of Hepburn Publishing. We slowly creep up the car lined street looking for a parking place.

"Just drop me here," I say.

"You don't want me there for moral support?" Katharine asks.

I stare with steely-eyed determination into the distance.

"No, I've got to face this alone."

"You sure? I can wait."

"Just go home and have a look at some places we can stay along the Surf Coast. I'll just get a taxi home," I say, as I kiss Katharine goodbye and get out of the car.

I climb the stairs and say 'hi' to Michael Ruggles, aka Mick, aka the receptionist.

"She's expecting you," he says flatly. Normally he's got a smile, a warm welcome, and some baked goods for me. Not today. Perhaps he knows what's happening, that I'm basically going to my own literary execution and he doesn't want to waste a good Cornish pasty or a lamington on me.

313

Mick leads me to an empty conference room and shuts the door behind me, locking it.

"What's up Mick?"

"She's in the secret office," he says, as he goes over to a bookshelf in the corner and slides it aside. Mick motions for me to follow. We go through a hole in the wall into another room which appears to be a storage space. Mick goes to another bookshelf, sliding it and moving us onto a different room. We keep going through rooms until we reach what has to be the end of the building.

Mick slides the bookshelf aside and reveals a small dingy office. The walls are a yellowing brown, and there's a smallish window. All I can see is an old wooden desk, a bottle of Bushmills Original Irish Whiskey, and a high back leather chair along with two guest chairs. A cigar lays smouldering in a crystal ashtray. The leather chair swivels around and reveals none other than my editor, Deirdre Slocum.

"Come in. And shut the door quick."

I hesitate at the precipice. Fear grips me. Deirdre's hand is under the desk and smoke appears from beneath the desk. Does she have a flaming copy of *The Iceman Cometh* ready to throw at me?

I adjust my horn-rimmed glasses and step through to the small room. It's time to face the music.

"A cigar? For my favourite client," Deirdre opens a box with Cohibas inside. I half expect her to clamp the lid when my fingers get near.

"Is that why you're back here? To smoke?" I ask.

"It's the only place I can smoke and read, the rest of the place has too much paper. Could go up like a tinderbox. Plus it's illegal, but when did that ever stop me."

Deirdre winks at me.

"Cigars aren't in order. There's nothing to celebrate today, Deirdre. My manuscript won't be ready. Ever."

Deirdre takes a deep breath and considers this statement.

"Fine," she says.

"In fact it probably won't be ready anytime soon."

"Ok," she says shrugging.

"What I'm trying to say, Deirdre, is that I'm quitting. I'm never going to finish the book. It's a long story but the book is, I mean, it's not, um," I keep stumbling over words. Deirdre is just sitting there looking at me smiling. "What I mean is … the book is gone."

Deirdre looks at me with beaming encouraging eyes. She raises a cigar from beneath the desk and takes a puff.

"It's completely down the–"

A flushing toilet interrupts me.

Then a door opens to my right. And out steps, none other than, my mother, Susan Wilde.

"I don't know what it is about Irish whiskey, David, but it goes straight through me. You remember when I was doing that Eugene O'Neill play off-off-Broadway, and I was drinking all that Jameson to get into character."

Susan sits, picks up the lone cigar in the ashtray, and takes a puff.

"O'Neill was American," Deirdre corrects.

"Maybe it was a Beckett play then. I was very drunk at the time."

If ever there was a time when 'flabbergasted' was the right word to describe my emotional state, it is now. What is she even doing here? How did she know I'd come here? What about our deal to never see each other again?

315

"You were saying ... something about your book?" Deirdre prompts me. But I'm too dumbfounded to get any words out.

"Oh, his book. It's fantastic," Susan says, "Best book I've read in years."

"I thought you were gone?" I finally get out.

"Hardly. Not when there's so much work to do, David," Mum says, giving me her 1,000 watt smile.

"Yeah for both of you." Deirdre says.

"Deirdre, there is no novel. The only copy was on a computer that's been smashed and drenched in mop water. The dream is over. I'm going back to my law practice, I'm giving up writing."

Deirdre and Susan just look at each other and break into laughter.

"You're not quitting the writing game," Deirdre says.

"The hell I'm not," I say, finally standing up to Deirdre. I'm getting angry now. They can't bully me anymore. "I'll pay back my advance but I'm not going to completely rewrite the book from scratch."

"You mean this one?" Susan produces a USB from her purse and puffs on her cigar. She flips it over to Deirdre without looking. Deirdre catches it with one hand while keeping her eyes on me. Mum backed up my book. I can't believe it. My mother, Susan Wilde, actually thought ahead and made a copy. Something even I was too dumb to do.

"David, we'll publish your detective novel. And you can even pay back your advance, if you want. In fact you can pay it back with the bucket loads of money that's coming to you."

"How do you know it's going to sell, you haven't read it," I say.

"I meant with the money for the book that I've spent the

morning pre-selling into 15 different territories?" Deirdre says.

"My memoir," Susan says. She pronounces the word, *mem–wah*, as if she's a French intellectual. Or just French.

Deirdre produces a glass from a desk drawer and pours a few fingers of whiskey. She pushes the glass across the old oak desk.

"You see David, this has all been orchestrated with my new agent. Leaving New York, 'retiring' from acting, the rehab, the escape. You see, darling, this has all been part of a carefully crafted plan."

"Publishing a tell-all memoir. One which will be read by all the people who have watched her in soap operas and TV movies over the years; and who are the exact target market for juicy tell-alls, filled with sex, drugs, and showbiz gossip."

"It is all part of my grand comeback, David. The book, followed by a one-woman show, to promote the book. Followed by … well, who knows what the future holds."

"I know what it holds for me." I say, taking the whiskey bottle by the neck, and downing half of it in one emphatic chug. "I'm going back to the law, marrying Katharine, and we're buying a house." I look at Mum, "A house that you won't have the address for." I go to the bookshelf and try to slide it open but I can't. "Let me know how it all works out for you. Or better yet, don't."

I'm pushing the bookshelf but it won't budge. Once again, I'm trapped with my mother.

"David, you misunderstand me. I need you."

Where have I heard this before?

"For what?"

"Writing my memoir."

"I'm not helping you."

My breathing becomes more laboured.

"Listen David," Deirdre starts, "co-writing a guaranteed best seller like this is your ticket to the big time. She's acted in more soaps in more countries than anyone else. I even pre-sold this in Latin America because of her time on that telenovela, *Amantes Ridículos*."

"David, I am making things. But one thing I am not is an author, a bard, like yourself. I am merely the keeper of my secrets. They lie inside me bursting to come out, but I need your talents, your genius, to weave my tales into literary gold. David … consider this. For this memoir and my comeback to be successful I would have to divulge everything to my co-author."

I stop trying to get the bookshelf to budge and look over at her. I breathe in deeply. The sticky smell of cigar smoke invades my nostrils. The haze hangs thick in the air.

"Everything …?" I say.

"Ev … ree … thing …" her lips articulate every syllable. "You will help me 'father' this literary baby."

It's a disgusting analogy but that's when it hits me. Like an asteroid from the stratosphere. I would have her captive. She'd have to tell the truth. This memoir is her ticket back to the spotlight and it's my ticket to real answers. Doing this means we can both get what we want. She gets a chance at reviving her acting and I can write something that has a real chance of being successful. And I might find out who my real dad is.

Deirdre breaks the silence. "We want the book to have a very confessional tone."

"Agreed," Mum says, puffing on her cigar.

I sit down and pour myself another drink. Deirdre reaches under the desk and produces another cigar. She clips the tip with a cutter.

"The only way I would agree to a project like this would be to have full autonomy."

I sip at my whiskey. "I get to decide what goes in and what stays out."

"Naturally," Deirdre hands over the cigar and a Zippo lighter.

"You're in control of this process, David," Mum says.

I look at the cigar and lighter in my hand, sparking the flint a few times. Finally igniting the flame.

"Ok, I'll do it."

I light my cigar.

Deirdre smacks the desk and pours a drink for herself. She goes to pour one for mum but I put my hand over her glass.

"I need her sober."

Deirdre laughs, I laugh. Mum doesn't laugh.

"Seriously though." I shake my head. "No booze for her."

"Come now, David," Mum says. "Let us all be civilised, and seal this deal with a teeny-tiny drink."

"I thought you said I was in control of this process?" I stare directly into her eyes.

Susan stiffens a bit, takes a manicured finger and slowly taps ash into the ashtray. Then she says, "Perhaps my son—"

"Favourite son," I cut in, giving her a little smirk.

"Exactly. Perhaps my *favourite* son is right," she says through pursed lips. "It is *not* necessary to seal this deal with a drink."

"Glad we all agree on something," I say, as my smirk turns into a smile.

"But we do need to seal this deal," Deirdre says, grabbing

some papers from her desk. It takes about 30 minutes, but by the time we get up to leave we've inked a deal for me to co-author my mother's memoir. "Mick will cut you a cheque for your advance," she says, as she opens the bookcase and ushers us along the secret passage back to reception.

At the front desk Mick makes out a check for 75 grand. He also gives me some chocolate chip peanut butter cookies he whipped up last night.

"And Michael dear, may I have my advance in cash?" Susan asks. "I spoke to my accountant and he said it was better for my liquidity."

"I'm sorry, I didn't realise the advance was to be in two cheques." Mick reaches his hand out for the check. "I can redo it."

"Don't put yourself out Mick." I say blowing on the ink. "Mum taught me the value of sharing from a young age."

"But David—"

"Come along Mum. Lots of work to do." I guide my mother out the door, and down the stairs to the streets of Collingwood.

Downstairs it's a sunny day and we both breathe in the caffeinated air from the myriad coffee roasteries around us. I can hear the squawk of a cockatoo flying overhead. It's a great day.

I adjust my horn-rimmed glasses.

"So Mum, there's only one question I have before we start."

"Yes."

"Who's my father?"

"I'll tell you when the time is right."

"And when, pray tell, will that be?"

"When you give me my half of the advance."

"Touché," I say, slipping the cheque into my wallet. "Have your agent call me. I'll transfer the funds to him."

"David, I need to pay my bill at the Intercontinental."

"Is that where all your stuff is?"

"Yes. I needed a night alone after the ordeal at the Centre."

"Fine. I'll pay for last night. But you can't stay there."

"But that is *always* where I stay when I'm in Melbourne."

"You're staying with me and Katharine. We need to be close in order to make this book happen."

"Will Katharine be ok with that arrangement? I'm not sure if you picked up on this, David, but I have felt some tension coming from Katharine towards me in the past. I am not sure if she should be staying at the house with us."

"Well, get used to it because we're getting married."

I start walking. Mum follows behind.

"Pardon me?!"

"I proposed this morning."

"David, that is wonderful news. A spring wedding would be perfect for me. I have just the dress picked out, only a few thousand dollars mind you, so I might need some of that advance money."

"I'm thinking I'll get married when I feel like it. And I'm also thinking you get your stuff and bring it home. I'll tell Katharine, that you're coming back."

"Do you want me to be there for moral support?"

"No, I've got to face her alone," I say, with steely-eyed determination.

I get Mum into a taxi and then I call and make two appointments. One easy, one hard. Telling Alan and the folks at the law firm will be a cakewalk. Telling Katharine there's a new book that I'm writing with my mother, Susan Wilde, will be a plank walk. Hopefully with no circling, hungry sharks in the waters below.

After delivering the bad news to Alan and the firm I go to the bank and deposit the check. I speak to my banker and he tells me that with this sum and Katharine's income we can easily qualify for a mortgage.

When I get home Katharine is sitting on the couch reading with a cup of peppermint tea. I come in whistling and give her a kiss so passionate it would make Romeo look like a schoolboy lover. Which, in fact he was, but whatever.

"You're in a good mood. Did it go well with Deirdre?"

"It went better than you can imagine."

"That's good.

"Well she understands business. And that's why she's contracted me to write a new book. One that's going to sell so well that she gave me a 75 thousand dollar advance."

"That's amazing. That could go towards a wedding and a house down payment."

"Already ahead of you, babe," I say. "I went to the bank on my way home." Now I brace myself for what's coming next. I take a deep breath and speak. "There is a one, slight, teeny-tiny catch though. I'm not going back to Dienstag, DiSalvio & Fischer."

"Excuse me?"

"Well, two catches, I don't get to keep all that money for the book."

"Wait. So what is this book you've sold?'

"Excellent question. I've got good news and bad news. The good news is that this book is going to help me understand the thing that's been blocking me all these years. It's going to help me work through a lot of my issues, and it might even give me insight into her and myself. Plus it is pretty much a guaranteed best seller."

Katharine stares at me, but not with her death stare. With wonder, amazement, and most of all hope.

"So what's the bad news?"

In that exact instant, the doorbell rings.

And I've started my new life.

The End

... But David and Susan will return in *Celebrity Mum 2: Mother's Day*... stay tuned.

Acknowledgments

I would like to acknowledge all the people who helped out with this book. First and foremost, David Swann who worked with me while this idea was a sitcom. Our time together chatting about ideas, and our mothers, was invaluable. He always pushed me to go deeper and make the pathos and humour real, as opposed to always going for a cheap joke. He succeeded … sort of.

I would also like to thank Melissa Cranenburgh who read an early draft and gave me great feedback. My proofreader Julie Faulkner, thank you for being my final set of eyes on the manuscript and catching any little gaps in story logic or character inconsistencies.

A huge thank you my wife, Merrilee McCoy, who has stood by me on the epic 11 year journey to seeing this project through to completion. She has been my rock, my inspiration, and my best friend in the world. She encouraged me to finish this manuscript during our time in Covid lockdown. So I did, because she's my wife and I always do what she says; so for two weeks I sat at the computer for 6 hours a day and typed. If I didn't have her support I don't know where I would be.

Finally I would like to thank my family. I am so grateful for your support over the years. I'm trying to think if there is anyone else I should thank … nothing comes to mind … oh, wait, I would like to thank my mother, Dee Samuels. The best lawyer a boy could have representing him as his mom. How could I forget to thank her!

About the Author

Josh Samuels was raised in Marin County California, where his mind was warped by the joint influences of Jam Bands, Beat Poets, the 49ers, modal jazz, redwood trees, and the Pacific Ocean. Oh, and a heavy dose of Marxism (Groucho, not Karl). He was so obsessed with marsupials that he moved to New Zealand. Finding none there he moved to Australia. He writes a lot of stuff, some of which is good, and some which his wife tells him is good so she can placate his desperate need for approval (and also so she can get back to reading her John Mayer subreddit). One of his formative life experiences was working in a video store called Video Kamron which specialised in foreign and independent cinema. For those who don't remember, a video store was like a much less convenient version of Netflix where you had to talk to human beings in order to access movies and pay extra money if you didn't do a thing called "rewind." It was medieval. Anyways, I think this bio is now over, it has sort of gone off the rails. I told you his mind was warped.

You can connect with me on:
🌏 https://www.joshsamuels.com.au